Praise for Denise Hunter

"Can romance be any more complicated than a bride who doesn't remember running away from her groom? Denise Hunter's take on a woman's attempt to find her way back to happily ever after again is sweetly endearing. Readers will keep turning pages, wanting to know how true love ever went so wrong . . . and if *The Goodbye Bride* gets her chance to say 'I do.'"

—BETH K. VOGT, 2015 RITA FINALIST AND
AUTHOR OF *CRAZY LITTLE THING CALLED LOVE*

"I've been a long-time fan of Denise Hunter's, and *The Goodbye Bride* has everything I've come to love about her romances: a plucky heroine with lots of backstory, a yummy hero, and a terrific setting. Her fine attention to detail and the emotional punch of the story made me want to reread it immediately. Highly recommended!"

—COLLEEN COBLE, *USA TODAY* BESTSELLING AUTHOR
OF *MERMAID MOON* AND THE HOPE BEACH SERIES

"Denise Hunter has done it once again, placing herself solidly on my must-read list! *The Goodbye Bride* is a tender, thoughtful look at the role memories play in a romance. The clever plot kept me up way past my bedtime—and happy to be so!"

—DEBORAH RANEY, AWARD-WINNING AUTHOR
OF THE CHICORY INN NOVELS

"*The Goodbye Bride* is one heart-stopping, page-turning romance that will leave the pickiest romance reader delighted and asking for just a few more pages."

—CARA C. PUTMAN, AWARD-WINNING AUTHOR OF
WHERE TREETOPS GLISTEN AND *SHADOWED BY GRACE*

"[*Married 'til Monday*] . . . leaves one knowing that love is worth fighting for."

—*RT BOOK REVIEWS*, 4-STAR REVIEW

"Hunter is a master romance storyteller. *Falling Like Snowflakes* is charming and fun with a twist of mystery and intrigue. A story that's sure to endure as a classic reader favorite."

—RACHEL HAUCK, AUTHOR OF *THE WEDDING DRESS* AND THE ROYAL WEDDING SERIES

"A handful of authors dominate my must-read list, and Denise Hunter is right at the top. *Falling Like Snowflakes* is a taut romantic thriller that will warm you to the core."

—JULIE LESSMAN, AWARD-WINNING AUTHOR OF THE DAUGHTERS OF BOSTON, WINDS OF CHANGE, AND HEART OF SAN FRANCISCO SERIES

"A beautiful story—poignant and heartwarming, filled with delightful characters and intense emotion. Chapel Springs is a place anyone would love to call home."

—RAEANNE THAYNE, *NEW YORK TIMES* BESTSELLING AUTHOR ON *THE WISHING SEASON*

". . . skillfully combines elements of romance, family stories, and kitchen disasters. Fans of Colleen Coble and Robin Lee Hatcher will enjoy this winter-themed novel."

—*LIBRARY JOURNAL* ON *THE WISHING SEASON*

"This is an emotional tale of overcoming the fear of loss to love again and God's love, made manifest through people, healing all wounds. The heroine's doubts, fears, and eventual acceptance of the gift God has given her are told in a sympathetic and heartwarming way. The hero's steadfastness is poignantly presented as well."

—*ROMANTIC TIMES*, 4 STARS ON *DANCING WITH FIREFLIES*

"Romance lovers will . . . fall for this gentleman who places his beloved's needs before his own as faith guides him."

—*BOOKLIST* ON *DANCING WITH FIREFLIES*

"Hunter's latest Chapel Springs Romance is a lovely story of lost and found, with a heroine struggling to accept that trusting God doesn't make life perfect—without loss or sorrow—but can bring great joy. The hero's love for her and willingness to lose her to save her is quite moving."

—*Romantic Times*, 4 stars on *Barefoot Summer*

"Jane Austen fans will appreciate the subtle yet delightful Austen vibe that flavors this contemporary cowboy romance—and not just because *Pride & Prejudice* is protagonist Annie's favorite book. *The Trouble with Cowboys* is a fast, fun, and touching read with the added draw of a first kiss that is sure to make my Top 5 Fictional Kisses of 2012. So saddle up, ladies: We have a winner!"

—USAToday.com

Just a Kiss

Just a Kiss

A SUMMER HARBOR NOVEL

DENISE HUNTER

THOMAS NELSON
Since 1798

Published in Nashville, Tennessee, by Thomas Nelson. Thomas Nelson is a registered trademark of HarperCollins Christian Publishing, Inc.

Thomas Nelson, Inc., titles may be purchased in bulk for educational, business, fund-raising, or sales promotional use. For information, please e-mail SpecialMarkets@ThomasNelson.com.

Publisher's Note: This novel is a work of fiction. Names, characters, places, and incidents are either products of the author's imagination or used fictitiously. All characters are fictional, and any similarity to people living or dead is purely coincidental.

Library of Congress Cataloging-in-Publication Data

Names: Hunter, Denise, 1968- author.
Title: Just a kiss / Denise Hunter.
Description: Nashville, Tennessee: Thomas Nelson, [2016] | Series: A Summer Harbor novel
Identifiers: LCCN 2016013633 | ISBN 9780718023751 (softcover)
Subjects: LCSH: Disabled veterans--Care--Fiction. | Man-woman relationships--Fiction. | Amputees--Fiction. | GSAFD: Christian fiction. | Love stories.
Classification: LCC PS3608.U5925 J87 2016 | DDC 813/.6--dc23 LC record available at https://lccn.loc.gov/2016013633

Printed in the United States of America

16 17 18 19 20 RRD 5 4 3 2 1

Author's Note

Dear friend,

I can hardly believe we're at the last book of the Summer Harbor series! Even if you haven't been along for the whole journey, I think you'll enjoy *Just a Kiss*. It's written to stand alone, so you won't feel lost at all.

If you've been following the series, I hope you're eager to find out what happens next. I've been planning Riley and Paige's story since the very beginning of the series, and I can't wait to share it with you. And let's not forget Aunt Trudy and Sheriff Colton! They've been waiting a long time for their happily-ever-after. Will they find it? I'm not telling! You'll have to read and see.

Lastly, friend, I want to say thank you. Thank you for reading my stories. Thank you for telling others about them. And thank you for all the kind notes you send. You make it all worthwhile. I'm ever grateful for your encouragement and support and so honored that you choose to spend a few of your precious hours with me.

Blessings!

Denise

Chapter 1

*P*aige Warren checked her watch, then peeked around Miss Trudy's silver head for the dozenth time. Riley's plane had landed, and the steady stream of passengers moving toward Bangor Airport's baggage claim had begun to dwindle.

Beau and Zac Callahan, Riley's black-haired brothers, stood just alike a few feet away, muscular arms crossed, broad stances, faces set as they scanned the unfamiliar faces.

"Shouldn't he be here by now?" Paige fiddled with the ring hanging from her necklace.

"Stop your worrying," Miss Trudy said. "He'll be out soon."

Stop her worrying? She'd done nothing but worry since the midnight call three weeks ago. Beau's words had sent her heart into palpitations, and it hadn't stopped racing since.

Miss Trudy grabbed Paige's hand, stilling it. Only then did she realize she'd been frantically zinging the ring on her necklace back and forth.

"You're about to drive me up the wall with your fidgeting."

"I can't help it. I won't feel okay until I see *he's* okay."

"He's coming home," Miss Trudy said. "It's going to be fine."

"Yeah, but—"

"Don't borrow trouble. Beau said he was in good spirits, and we should thank the good Lord he's coming home at all."

"I know. I know you're right."

Who would've thought when Riley left for Afghanistan fifteen months ago he'd be coming home in June? And like this? There'd been so many decisions and arrangements to make since the phone call, and Paige had taken on the lion's share. It had soothed her to be doing *something*.

Riley was a strong man—always had been—but she couldn't imagine anyone taking this in stride. There were big adjustments ahead, but she was determined to be there for her best friend every step of the way, just as he'd been there for her through every difficulty she'd faced since she was fourteen—especially the death of her father. Riley had spent many nights just listening as she tried to untangle the knots of unresolved anger.

"Where is he?" Beau wandered back over. In his shadow was Zac, towering over them all.

"Y'all are starting to make *me* nervous with all your fidgeting and pacing," Miss Trudy said.

Beau slipped his arm over his aunt's shoulders. "Everyone's out. He should be here."

"Maybe he didn't make the flight," Paige said. The thought made her stomach sink like an anchor. The past few weeks of waiting had been torture for all of them. Beau had wanted to fly to Germany to be with his brother, but Riley insisted he stay.

"He'll be here." Zac ran a hand over his tightly trimmed beard. He looked almost out of place without Lucy at his side. The two had been joined at the hip since their fall wedding.

Between Zac and Lucy's recent nuptials and Beau and Eden's

engagement, Paige was feeling a little fifth-wheelish lately. It'd be good to have her Riley back home. Nothing had felt quite right since he'd left. She had girlfriends, sure. But no one who knew and understood her like Riley.

It might be touch-and-go for a while, she reminded herself. She couldn't expect the old Riley to come strutting around the corner. She'd done some research and, despite what Beau said about his brother's spirits, she expected some fallout. It was time for her to be the strong one.

❧

Riley Callahan gave the attractive brunette his most charming smile as she pushed an empty wheelchair down the Jetway toward him. She was tall, slender, about his age, and heck, the sight of any female was a treat these days. She reached the bottom of the Jetway where he waited in the onboard wheelchair.

"Mr. Callahan? I'm here to assist you." Her professional tone matched her bland expression.

His lips drooped at her flat-eyed smile.

Reality check, idiot. Girls don't dig guys in wheelchairs.

A month ago her response would've been different. She might've even flirted with him. Maybe tried to slip him her number. All that was different now. People saw the chair first and then him. And the *him* they saw was the same *him* he saw in the mirror.

She wheeled the chair beside him and set the brakes. "Need some help?"

"I got it." Taking a deep breath, he made the awkward transition to the chair, his arm muscles tightening under his weight. He gritted his teeth against the pain as his body finally settled in place.

During the transfer his duffel fell, landing right beside his dignity. The bag he retrieved; the other was gone for good.

"You comfortable, sir?"

"Fine. Thanks."

He'd slept two hours last night, his leg was aching like a son of a gun, and he was stuffed into a wheelchair like an invalid. Not to mention a woman was tending to him. Everything about that seemed backward.

She released the brakes on his chair and set it in motion, pushing it up the Jetway.

At least he was off the plane. The trip to the lavatory in the onboard wheelchair had been humiliating. In between, people thanked him for his service, for his sacrifice. He'd wanted to crawl under the seats.

As they reached the gate, the cool whoosh of air-conditioning brushed his skin. Good old US of A. He was home. Back in Maine. His family was waiting just down the way. His brothers. His aunt. Paige. For months he'd ached to see them—especially Paige.

But not like this.

His chest tightened, his breathing was as labored as if he'd just run a marathon. Ha. Wouldn't be doing that anytime soon. He'd be lucky to reach hobbling status, and not even that without months of painful therapy. His eyes dropped to his legs.

Leg.

The trouser leg on his right side drooped into the hollow space where his knee used to be. Now the leg ended in a grotesque stump that alternately ached and itched. The past three weeks had been a nightmare. The surgery, the painful recovery. The nightmares. His emotions teetered on edge, dark thoughts pushing him deeper into the shadows.

Just coming home was an act of courage. He didn't want them to see him like this. Didn't want Paige to see him like this. Who knew when he left that he'd return half a man?

He tightened his fingers on the metal armrests, swallowing against the hard lump in his throat. A sweat broke out on his back and forehead. The bleak thoughts threatened to take him under, and he fought them with everything he had.

Improvise. Adapt. Overcome.

The words had been beaten into him for fifteen months. Had gotten him through some pretty bad stuff. But they did little to help him now.

Come on, man. Buck up. You can't let them see you like this.

His brothers had spent all this time worrying over him, all because he'd been stupid enough to enlist on the heels of their dad's death. On the heels of—

No. He couldn't think about that now. Suffice it to say he'd left for all the wrong reasons. But that was his own doing. His family had already been through enough.

The wheelchair bumped over something, jostling his leg. He winced, his hand moving over the left pocket of his trousers where he kept her picture. His heart thudded at the realization that he was about to see her, and not her image on Skype. It seemed like an eternity since he'd looked into her sea-blue eyes. Since he'd heard the feminine lilt of her voice or breathed in her sweet, flowery smell.

If things had gone differently, he'd be anticipating their reunion. He'd be strutting toward her on his own two legs, anxious to tell her the truth as he'd planned. But one IED had changed everything. Now his only plan revolved around figuring out how to put some space between them without hurting her feelings.

Chapter 2

"Is that your family?" the woman pushing Riley's chair asked.

His eyes darted toward the baggage claim entrance where his family clustered. He set his shoulders back, lifting his hand. Made his lips widen to a full-fledged smile, made sure his eyes crinkled at the corners like they were supposed to.

Beau waved back, his other arm curling tightly around Aunt Trudy. Zac grinned, a tall shadow behind them. Riley's eyes slid to Paige, and his breath left his body.

Man, she was even more beautiful than he remembered. Her silky hair was blonder and longer, and he'd forgotten the way her subtle curves softened her athletic build. The sight of her tanned legs stirred up thoughts he had no business thinking.

She cupped her hand around her mouth, her eyes tearing up as he rolled closer.

When he was still a car's length away, she leaped forward, falling onto her knees. Her arms came around his neck, and the soft weight of her melted into him.

He held her close, his eyes falling shut. In an instant it was just the two of them. Old times. Kindred spirits. Callahan and Warren. Man, he'd missed her. He pulled in a deep breath of her. Flowers. Sunshine. Home. He buried his nose in her hair and soaked her in, remembering every night he'd lain in his rack staring at her picture, longing for a moment just like this.

His throat emitted a choking sound, and he disguised it with a hearty laugh. Forced energy into his voice. "Hey, now. What's all this, Warren? You're not crying, are you? You know you go straight to the ugly cry."

Paige leaned back, swatting his shoulder as she surreptitiously wiped her eyes. "I missed you, you big lug. Are you in pain? Can I get your meds for you?"

Great, more fussing. "Naw, took some on the plane. I'm good. Wicked awesome."

Beau reached in, edging out Paige. He grasped Riley's hand in a bro-grip. "Good to have you home, brother. You had us awful worried there."

"Good to be home. Man, is it ever."

Zac ruffled his hand over Riley's high and tight haircut. "Can't even tousle your hair anymore. What fun is that?"

"Hey, Zac." Riley smiled up at him. "Good to see your ugly mug. Gotta say, though, you're practically a giant from down here."

"All the more reason to get you back on your feet."

"Hello . . . ?" Aunt Trudy said from the back. "I know I'm just the lowly aunt, but do I get a turn?"

Riley aimed a smile her way, reaching out. "Get over here, Aunt Trudy."

She slipped between Paige and Beau and embraced him. She smelled like lemons and starch. Her narrow shoulders and thin arms felt frail, but her size was misleading. She could stop an army with a mere look.

"Lord have mercy, you're wider than the chair. Did your muscles grow muscles?"

"Something like that," he said as she pulled away.

"How was your flight?" Beau asked. "Get any rest?"

Riley glanced at Paige as she dabbed at the corners of her eyes again. "Little bit." He shot Aunt Trudy a look. "What I could really do with is one of your big ol' roasts. Sooner the better."

"Lucky for you, I've got one in the Crock-Pot at Paige's house."

"And corn bread, mashed potatoes, plus Paige's pecan pie," Zac added.

Riley palmed his stomach. "Oh, man, you're killing me. Between the MREs, the hospital food, and the airline chow, it's hard to say which was worse."

"Did you check any bags?" Aunt Trudy asked, moving behind his chair and releasing the brakes.

"Just my chair. I gotta give this one back." He clapped his hands once. "All right. Let's get this show on the road. I can't wait to get home, eat some good chow, and sleep in my own bed." He rented a room at the back of the Roadhouse, Zac's restaurant. It wasn't much, but it was his.

Zac and Beau froze, trading glances. Paige shifted, and Aunt Trudy started rooting through her purse for something.

A cloud of unease bloomed in his gut. "What? What am I missing?"

"Um . . ." Zac didn't quite meet his eyes. "Your old room isn't exactly there anymore. I expanded the kitchen over the winter. Lucy and I were planning to let you have our guest room upstairs when you came home, but . . ." His eyes bounced off Riley's leg.

Yeah. Not on one leg. Sure, he might be able to manage on his crutches, but moving was painful and cumbersome, and the last thing he needed was a nasty fall to set him back even further.

His stomach deflated like a week-old party balloon. So much for the privacy of his room. "Guess I'm staying at the farmhouse then. That'll work just fine."

Their aunt had broken her leg a while back, and they'd made the formal dining room into a bedroom. He tried not to let the thought of being fussed over 24/7 bleed into his expression.

"Um, yeah . . ." Zac rubbed the back of his neck. "The farmhouse is kind of under construction at the moment." He gave Riley a look that made all kinds of red flags wave.

"We just started renovating," Beau said. "Aunt Trudy's wedding gift to Eden and me. The whole downstairs is a wreck at the moment."

"It won't be finished for a month at least," Aunt Trudy said.

"No worries, though." Paige patted his shoulder. "I told them from the beginning I wanted you at my place. I've got that nice master suite on the main floor. It's perfect. The old doorframes are nice and wide, and your brothers have already built a ramp and put in handicap bars . . ."

Everything faded as his thoughts spun. He was staying with Paige? His eyes flew to Zac, who was sending him some kind of telepathic apology, then back to Paige, whose words died off— probably at the look on his face.

Her eyes clouded with confusion. "Is—is that not okay? You want to stay someplace else?" A flicker of hurt flashed in the blue depths, but she shut it down quickly, covering with a smile he'd known her too long to buy.

Darn it. He was trapped. He forced a smile, crinkle lines and all. "Yeah. I mean no. That's great. Wicked awesome. But I can't take your room. I'll sleep on the couch or something."

She straightened. "You will not. I've already moved my stuff upstairs. It's a done deal."

His eyes flickered off Zac before returning to Paige. He held the smile, not an easy feat with his jaw knotted as tight as a dock line on a cleat. "You're a pal, Warren. Hey, why don't you guys go get the car, and Zac can help me with the chair. We'll meet you out front in a few."

Moving behind him, Zac edged Aunt Trudy aside. "Sooner we get home, sooner we get a taste of that roast."

"That's what I'm thinking," Riley said.

The others headed toward the exit, and Zac set the chair in motion. Riley rubbed his mouth with the tips of his trembling fingers, trying to calm the rising storm. How was he going to spend the next however many weeks cooped up with Paige?

But what choice did he have? Wasn't like he had a pile of cash in the bank for his own place. And even if he did, he was nowhere near ready for total independence—much as he'd like to deny it.

Just the thought of her fussing over him, helping him with clothes and all the other things he still needed help with . . .

God, are You trying to kill me here? Can't I have just a little dignity? Would that be too much to ask?

So much for his plans to put space between them. He'd be trapped in the six hundred square feet of the bungalow's main floor. With Paige.

This was all Zac's fault. He squeezed the metal armrests until his hands ached. He worked to get himself under control as he watched his family exit the building. Then he turned to Zac.

"What the heck were you thinking? I'm staying with Paige? Do you have any idea what you've done?"

"Whoa, now." Zac stopped in front of the moving baggage carousel. "First of all, it was a group decision, so it's not like—"

"But *you're* the only one who knows. I thought you had my six, man."

"It's not like there were so many other options, Riley."

"*Any* option is better than this!"

"All right, calm down. I get it, this isn't what you were expecting." Zac set the brakes. "But maybe you could look at it as an opportunity, you know?"

"An opportunity for what? To have Paige help me with my gory dressings, help me get in the shower, take care of me like a flipping invalid? Is that the kind of opportunity you had in mind? Because I'm pretty sure my pride's already in the toilet, but maybe if we try a little harder, it can sink even lower."

A curtain of guilt closed over Zac's face. He grabbed the folded wheelchair from the moving carousel and set it up. "You've been through a lot, I get it. But she's your friend, and she wants to help. Shoot, actually being able to help feels a lot better than having you hurting thousands of miles away and not being able to do a thing. Maybe this could bring the two of you closer together. Maybe this is your chance."

Riley gave a humorless laugh. "Yeah, just what she always wanted. A cripple."

Something flickered in Zac's eyes. "You're the same person you've always been, Riley."

Not even close. Not on the outside, and sure as heck not on the inside. He pressed his lips tight before it came spilling out.

Nothing would ever be the same. Paige deserved the best, and that sure wasn't him.

Zac's gray eyes narrowed as he studied Riley. "What happened to the big smile, bro?"

Riley clenched his jaw, turning to watch the belt as it squeaked its way around an endless circle. "Move the chair over here."

"Why am I getting the feeling you're not half as 'wicked awesome' as you claim to be?"

Riley took a long second to compose himself. "I'm fine. I just—I was planning to put some space between me and Paige. Now I'm stuck." He gave Zac a flinty look. "If I try and get out of it, it's going to hurt her feelings. Or worse, she'll know something's up."

The suspicion on Zac's face cleared as he moved the chair and set the brakes. "Wouldn't be the worst thing in the world."

"Not happening."

He was just going to have to suck it up. Work his butt off with exercises and therapy until he could get his prosthesis and manage on his own. Because the sooner he was independent, the sooner he could get out of Paige's life—out of Summer Harbor—for good.

Chapter 3

*P*aige turned off the TV and crept toward Riley's wheelchair. After a loud, celebratory supper the family had cleared out pretty quickly. Maybe they'd sensed Riley's exhaustion, despite his valiant attempt at lively conversation.

The topics had centered around life here in Summer Harbor: Zac's restaurant, the brothers' quickly evolving love lives, the family Christmas tree farm. Paige had glossed over the recent financial difficulties at the shelter. He didn't need to worry about Perfect Paws or her livelihood. He needed to focus on his recovery.

She stopped beside his chair, squatting down, taking in his handsome face, not quite relaxed, even in sleep. Twin furrows crouched between his brows, and his lips remained together. He'd changed in the fifteen months he'd been gone. She'd noticed the evolution on Skype, but it was more obvious in real life.

The planes of his face were more angled, his jaw more square. Harder. She supposed war had a way of changing a man, inside and out. His dark lashes fanned across his skin, the only thing even remotely soft or boyish about him.

She'd known him so long. Knew him so well. Maybe that was

why she wasn't quite buying the jubilant act. He'd avoided talking about everything he'd been through the past several weeks. His injury had been the elephant in the room tonight.

Her cat, Dasher, slinked by, rubbing against her, her gray tail swishing, her nose twitching toward Riley.

"It's good to have him back home, isn't it, baby?"

She studied Riley's forearms; they looked hard as steel, leading down to strong, calloused hands and thick fingers. She'd always liked his hands. Manly hands. Lobstering had always kept him in good shape. He was happiest when he was out on the water, the wind in his hair, the waves rolling beneath the boat's hull. That's why she'd been so surprised when he'd enlisted.

Surprised and dismayed. And yes, she admitted to herself, angry. He'd dropped it on her like a hot brick, after the fact. He was leaving her, and she'd felt abandoned—an all-too-familiar feeling.

But now wasn't the time to dwell on that. He was back, and he needed her.

"Riley."

The furrows deepened. His head rolled to the side.

She hated to wake him, but there was no other way to get him into bed, and his dressing needed to be changed. She'd already turned down his covers and made sure the path to his bed was clear. There was a glass of water on his nightstand beside his bottle of pills, and the crutches she'd picked up for him were within reach of his bed.

She set her hand on his arm, her fingers brushing lightly over the dark hairs. "Riley, it's time for—"

He startled.

The next second she was flying backward, airborne. She hit the wood floor, sliding. Her elbows flew back. Her head smacked the wall, and the heavy ring she wore on a chain thunked her in the chin.

She blinked, orienting herself, assessing. Burning elbows. Thudding head. Aching rump. Ouch.

"Paige!" Horror etched itself on Riley's face. He unset his brakes and wheeled toward her.

"I'm fine. I'm fine." She sat up, moving carefully to her knees, a little dizzy from the whack to the head. She fixed a smile to her face as he wheeled to a stop beside her. "Man, Callahan. You got stronger over there."

"I'm so sorry. I didn't mean to hurt you."

She gave a huff of laughter. "I'm fine. Come on, I'm tougher than that." She brushed the hair back from her face.

His eyes narrowed on her forearm. "You're bleeding."

She gave her arm a quick check. "Just a scratch. Little Band-Aid and it's all good. Let's get you—"

"You hit your head too."

"Really?" She gave him a saucy grin. "It all happened so fast, I was thinking you had a new superpower. Like that *Twilight* guy."

He pounded his fist on the chair's arm. "Dang it! Stop making jokes. It isn't funny. This isn't going to work."

Her lips fell as a weight settled in her midsection. "Don't be silly. It was my fault. You're just back from war—I knew better. I've done a lot of reading, and this kind of thing is common. I'll be more careful next time."

"You shouldn't have to be 'careful' in your own home, and you shouldn't have to take care of me." His fingers tightened on the chair grips.

Releasing a breath, she set her knees down, put her hand over his. So many things swimming around in those green eyes.

Regret, frustration, anger. There were probably a dozen other emotions that hadn't even come to the surface yet. Maybe they were negative emotions, but at least they were authentic. She preferred them to the fake jovial thing he'd had going on since he got off the plane.

"Listen here, Callahan. I'm going to be here for you whether you want me to or not. That's what friends do. That's what you'd do for me, and you know it. Now, we're going to get you into bed, and you're going to get a good night's rest because tomorrow's your first appointment with your physical therapist. From what I've read, he's going to be the new villain in your life."

He clamped his lips closed, and his nostrils flared. Some emotion passed through his eyes before he turned away, his jaw as hard as the boulders at Lighthouse Pointe.

"It's going to be okay. We're going to get through this." She gave his hand one last squeeze. *Please, God. Let it be okay.*

Chapter 4

The cacophony started the moment Paige entered the kennel area. High-pitched barking, tails thumping, paws prancing. A hint of disinfectant hung in the air, mixed with the lingering smell of dog chow. She tugged the leash, coaxing along the male boxer, who was less than eager to return to his kennel.

"Hey, guys! Who's happy today, huh? Are we all fed and raring to go? Oh, we're so feisty, yes we are!"

She gave attention to the animals as she passed, exclaiming over each one before finally stopping at the last kennel to let the boxer inside. Before closing the door she knelt to scratch behind his ears. Her heart squeezed at the forlorn look in his eyes.

"It's okay, baby. We'll find you a home."

The boxer was brown with a white muzzle and flews. He had floppy ears and the wrinkled forehead so characteristic of the breed. They'd found him on Bristol Road four weeks ago, dehydrated and starving. His weight was coming up, his nose was bright and shiny, but the hollow look in his eyes remained. She'd been calling him Bishop from the get-go. She didn't name all her animals, but the name had flashed into her brain the instant she'd laid eyes on him. Sometimes that happened.

Something about the sad look in his eyes reminded her of Riley. She wished she could bring the dog home. She had a feeling the animal would be good for him. But she was renting her house, and the owner allowed only one pet. Probably a good thing, or Paige would've had a menagerie by now.

The past three days Riley's demeanor had been cheerful enough—if stubborn. He wanted to do everything himself. She knew it was important to his pride and his recovery. But watching him struggle for ten minutes on a thirty-second task was painful.

She worried about him, home alone during the day. But the family was making regular stops, and he had plenty of food, that was for sure. Every single woman within a twenty-mile radius had brought over a casserole or pie. Still, she'd checked in by phone a lot the past few days. He didn't seem to mind, and it put her mind at ease.

Speaking of which . . . She checked her watch. It had been a couple hours. She closed Bishop's kennel and left the clamor for the relative quiet of her office as she tapped her phone.

He answered on the third ring.

"Hey there!" she said. "What are you up to?"

"Same thing I was up to an hour ago." She heard the smirk in his voice.

"Well, I had a few minutes and just thought I'd—"

"Paige. I'm fine. You don't have to call me every hour."

"I'm not! I was just calling to, uh, to see if you wanted takeout from the Roadhouse tonight."

"No, you just wanted to make sure I hadn't strangled myself in the drapery cords or something."

"Don't be silly. I don't even have drapes."

"Paige."

Okay, fine, she was hovering. But what if something happened while she was gone? What if he fell and couldn't get back up?

"I'm sorry. I don't mean to smother, but I worry about you. I wish I could afford to take some time off."

"And do what? Sit here and watch me do my exercises? I can take care of myself. I'm getting around fine, and I keep my cell phone on me. If I need anything I'll call."

Her gut clenched at the thought of letting loose. But she was probably going to drive him crazy if she didn't. "Promise?"

"Cross my heart."

The bell over the front door tinkled. Lauren was out to lunch, so Paige wrapped up the phone call, making a mental note to stop at the Roadhouse on the way home.

Margaret LeFebvre was waiting behind the counter as Paige entered the lobby.

She looked as fresh as usual. Her smart fashion and elegant figure put Paige in mind of Diane Keaton. Margaret owned the Primrose Inn and served as chairperson of the shelter's board.

Despite the woman's friendly smile, Paige's stomach twisted. "Margaret. This is unexpected. How are you?"

Margaret removed her glasses, letting them dangle from the metal chain around her neck. "Oh, I'm fine, dear. Business is quite good, and my daughter just had her baby."

"Congratulations! That's four grandchildren now, isn't it?"

"Yes, indeed. This one's my first granddaughter though." She extended her phone, showing a photo of the sleeping baby. She forwarded through a dozen more photos.

"Oh, she's just precious."

"Sofia Grace, for my mother. She would've been so pleased."

"What a beautiful name. You must be thrilled."

"I am. I only wish they lived closer, but I'll be making a trip to meet her soon. Only for a couple days, though. The inn is like a short leash sometimes, but I do love it." She tilted her head. "While I was in town I heard the Callahan boy is back."

"He is. It's so good to have him home."

"He's had a rough time of it."

"He sure has. But we've got him hooked up with a good physical therapist, and he'll be back on his feet in no time. He's at my place for now."

"I'd heard that. Well, just be careful. Traumas like that can really affect a person. One of my friend's sons came back from Iraq a completely different man. Sullen and angry and violent. He got into trouble with the law and ended up serving prison time. Such a shame."

Paige's spine lengthened even as the memory of being shoved across the room flashed in her mind. That was different. Riley had been asleep and unaware of what he was doing.

"Riley would never do anything like that. He's strong and independent. He'll come out of this the better for it."

"I'm sure you're right, dear." Margaret dropped her phone into her bag. "Do you have a few minutes to talk?"

Paige's chest felt weighted with a cement block. "Of course. Lauren should be back from lunch any minute. Come on back." She led the way to her office.

The room was small and basic with brown paneling and an old oak desk. Paige kept her space clean, and if it smelled like dog, she'd long ago lost the ability to tell. Her only adornments were her monster fern in the corner and a desk photo she'd taken with the Callahans several years ago on the Fourth of July. She'd jumped onto Riley's back just before the camera's click, and the candid shot captured his surprise.

"Have a seat." Paige gestured toward the only other chair in the room. "Can I get you some coffee? Water?"

"No, thank you. I just had lunch at Frumpy Joe's. My stomach hasn't quite recovered." Margaret shifted on the chair, making her straw handbag crackle.

Paige laced her hands on her desk, pushing back the anxiety that wormed in her gut. "I can tell something's wrong, so why don't we just get it out on the table?"

Margaret gave her a look that could only be described as pitying. "This is difficult. I know how much Perfect Paws means to you, and how hard you've worked. I'm afraid I've come bearing bad news."

Paige braced herself, her heart thundering in her chest. The shelter had been running on a shoestring budget for a while. She imagined all the possibilities. Maybe they'd lost another sponsor. Or were going to have to start charging for their free services. She balked at the thought. There were so many who couldn't afford vaccinations and spaying, and those things were critical.

"Just tell me what it is. I can take it."

Margaret gave a strained smile. "I'm afraid we have to close the shelter."

The sucker punch drove the breath from Paige's body. "What? No!"

"I understand this is upsetting—"

"We can't close, Margaret. The community needs us. The animals need us. Even right now there are—"

Margaret leaned across the desk and placed a hand over Paige's fist. "I know, dear, I know. Settle down. Take a deep breath."

Paige tried, but her lungs seemed to have shrunk in the last ten seconds. At this very moment she had twelve dogs and nine cats that needed care. What would happen to them? To all the animals they saved and found homes for every year? Not to mention the wounded wildlife that she maybe sort of rescued—off the record.

"You know funding has been drying up the past couple years. Some of our benefactors have moved from the area, and others have had setbacks. It's a tough economy."

"But we've found new funding."

"Not enough. Not with the free vaccinations and the free spay and neuter clinics we did last year."

"Those things are important. And they pay off in the long run because—"

Margaret held up her hand. "I know all the benefits. The problem is that they cost a lot of money. The vet fees, the medications, the vaccinations . . . Those services drain our funds, and now we're in an untenable position."

Paige blew out a breath. Priorities. She had to think. "All right. I know I've been a little stubborn about this in the past, but we'll just have to start charging for those services. I don't like it, but it's better than nothing."

Margaret shook her head slowly. "I'm sorry, dear, but it's too late for—"

"I'll find a grant. *Grants.* I'll make it work somehow."

"You know how long it takes for grants to come through, if they ever do. We don't have time for that. The board doesn't see any reasonable alternative."

"A fundraiser then! Remember the lobster dinner benefit we

did a few years ago? I can throw that together pretty fast, and the town will come through, you'll see."

"Paige . . ."

"The community needs this shelter, Margaret! You know it does." The image of Bishop's sad eyes surfaced in her mind, and her throat closed up tight. "Animals will die without it, dozens of them, needlessly."

Something in the woman's pale blue eyes softened.

"Just give me three months. I'll find new sponsors, do fund-raisers, get grants, whatever I need to do. Just don't let them do this."

"You've already got your hands pretty full at home, Paige."

"I make time for what's important, and when I set my mind to something, I make it happen. I'll make this happen, Margaret. Please."

The woman studied her for a full thirty seconds while Paige worked hard to telegraph her resolution. Her lungs seemed frozen in place as her heart kicked against her ribs.

Margaret let out a sigh that seemed to come from her toes. "I really think you're biting off more than you can chew here. Maybe if Riley's family stepped in to help a little more."

Surely the woman wasn't going to make her choose between running the shelter and caring for Riley.

"I *am* Riley's family. You don't need to worry about that. I can do this. Not only will I get additional funding, I'll go over the expenditures and cut every spare cost. I'll initiate a fee for lost pets and charge for every service we offer if I need to. Just give me a chance, Margaret. Three months, that's all I'm asking."

Margaret's eyes searched hers for a long moment. "All right. I think I can talk the board into three months."

Paige's breath tumbled out.

She was in a fog as she walked Margaret out. After the door fell closed behind her, Paige turned and let her weight sag against it.

Three months to raise thousands of dollars. What had she gotten herself into?

Chapter 5

*R*iley maneuvered through the Roadhouse doors on his crutches. The local hangout was noisy for a Thursday night. Loud TVs broadcasted the Red Sox game, and the chatter of patrons rose above it all. It was only the spicy aroma of hot wings that drove him forward.

"Are you sure you don't want your wheelchair?" Paige let the door fall shut behind them.

"I'm sure." He was sick and tired of looking up at everybody.

He scanned the restaurant for his brothers, finding them in their usual spot, a large corner booth. He headed that way, working the crutches carefully as his therapist had shown him. His missing leg threw him off balance. He'd almost taken two nasty falls while Paige was at work this week. Not that he was going to tell her that.

He greeted his brothers energetically as he approached, and they scooted over to make room.

"Why don't we get a table," Paige said. "There's an open one right here."

"What for?" Beau asked. "We always sit here."

"I just thought"—her eyes darted off Riley—"it'd be, you know, easier."

Warmth rode up Riley's neck. "It's all good." He backed up to the seat, shifted his crutches to his good side, and lowered himself into the booth. The act took a good thirty seconds, and a sweat broke out on his forehead with the effort.

Remember when sitting wasn't an event?

Riley stowed his crutches beside him and picked up the menu. "I'm starving. Where are the girls?"

"Playing pool," Beau said. "Or trying to."

Riley spotted them in the far corner. Eden stood back while Lucy lined up a shot.

"Hey, now," Zac said. "Lucy's gotten a lot better. We beat you last week, if you'll recall."

"Dumb luck."

Zac rolled his eyes.

Paige popped up. "I'm going to the ladies' room. Order me the buffalo chicken salad, will you?"

Riley watched her retreat for a moment before turning his attention to the menu.

"Since when does she use public bathrooms?" Beau said, frowning after her.

It irked Riley that his brother knew her so well, but Beau and Paige had dated for months, after all. Nothing like watching the love of his life fall for his older brother. He'd joined up because he couldn't have what he wanted most, but enlisting had only ensured he'd never get it. The irony wasn't lost on him.

"She's not using the restroom," Riley said. "She's pretending to use the restroom while she clears a path for me just in case I need to go." Just like she'd removed all the rugs from the main level of her house, tucked away each stray cord, and moved every item he could possibly need to waist level.

"She's just trying to be helpful," Zac said.

Riley's jaw tightened. He didn't want Paige's help or her pity. He didn't want the woman he loved looking after him as if he were an invalid. He wanted to be functional and independent. He wanted his flipping leg back.

"Hey," Beau said. "You're doing great. Already getting around on those things like an old pro."

Yeah. He was a real pro. A month ago, he could run five miles in full battle rattle; now he had to learn to walk again like a toddler.

He plastered a smile on his face. "All in good time, right?"

"You'll be back to lobstering before you know it," Beau said.

Riley's eyes cut to his as he gave a mirthless laugh. "Yeah right."

"Well, why not?" Zac said. "Amputees do all kinds of things these days. Look at that Olympic runner."

Riley scowled at him. Even walking across the room on his own steam seemed like a fairy tale at this point. His future looked about as bright as a black hole.

So much for all the "plans You have for me," huh, God? Prosper not harm? Hope and a future?

Right.

"What?" Beau said. "There's no reason you couldn't go back to fishing."

What planet did his brother live on? "Yeah, with my luck I'd lose a hand in the rig. No thanks. I'd like to keep the rest of my limbs, thank you very much. I don't really have any to spare at this point."

The girls returned to the table, exuberant, squishing into the other side, alleviating the growing tension.

"Where's Micah?" Zac asked. Eden almost always had her seven-year-old son in tow.

"My dad took him fishing. In other words, they'll throw their lines into the water for about fifteen minutes, then give up and go get ice cream."

"Smart guys," Lucy said. "Nothing better than a big ol' scoop of ice cream. Unless it's two."

Zac nudged his wife's shoulder, giving her a fond look. "I remember a certain someone who put a scoop right in my lap. As I recall, the incident led to a rather sweet and lengthy first kiss."

She smiled at him, her eyes going soft. "A girl's gotta do what a girl's gotta do."

Riley absently massaged his stump. Zac and Lucy's history was long and twisting. They'd been engaged until she ditched him a week before their wedding. Then she turned up with amnesia months later and didn't remember anything but being in love with Zac. Riley had missed all that while he was in the sandpit. But the two seemed to have come out of it on the other side somehow.

The newlyweds were still looking into each other's eyes like they were the only ones in the room.

Beau shifted. "All right, you two, get a room."

Zac gave a cocky smile and made to stand. "If you insist."

Lucy elbowed her husband, laughing. "Stop that now."

Beau scowled at Eden. "How many days till our wedding?"

"Hang in there, babe," Eden said. "Just two more months."

Beau closed his eyes. "*Months*. Why are we waiting so long again?"

"So she has time to realize what a big mistake she's making," Zac said.

Beau shot his brother a look as Paige returned, scooting in opposite Riley. She greeted the girls.

"Is it true what I heard about the shelter?" Lucy said, her tone full of dismay.

Riley's eyes fixed on Paige. They'd been alone together all week, and she hadn't even hinted at a problem. "What about the shelter?"

Paige gave a tight smile, her eyes flittering around the group. "We're experiencing some financial difficulties, that's all."

"Charlotte said they were going to shut it down," Lucy said, referring to the owner of Frumpy Joe's. "That the board decided yesterday."

"Is that true?" Riley asked. But he already knew it was by the look on Paige's face. "Why didn't you tell me?"

"It's not so dire as that. They're giving me three months to turn things around. It'll be fine."

"What are you going to do?" Eden asked.

"Find new sponsors, head up a fundraiser, and apply for grants."

Riley frowned at her. "When are you going to find time for all that?"

"Evenings and weekends. I can get some of it done during slow times at work. Lauren will help with the grants—she's a whiz at paperwork. It'll all work out. You'll see."

Riley's gaze narrowed on Paige. He saw all right. Saw the way her eyes tightened at the corners, the way her brows furrowed, the way her fingers fidgeted with her napkin.

"If you need help with the fundraiser, let me know," Eden said. "I can add a page to the shelter's website and do anything else you need."

"Count me in too," Lucy said.

"Thanks, girls. I appreciate it."

The server came over and took their orders. Riley's stomach twisted in hunger as another server passed with a steaming basket of atomic wings. It had been too long.

"How's PT going?" Beau asked as the girls settled into their own conversation.

"Good. Guy that's helping me reminds me of a drill instructor I had back in boot camp."

"Sounds fun," Zac said.

"Anything that gets me back on my feet." *Foot.*

"Let me know if you ever need a ride," Beau said.

The conversation shifted to the Red Sox game. Riley fixed his eyes on the screen and pretended to listen.

He'd been down since this morning when he'd passed the harbor on his way to therapy. It hit him like a sucker punch. Seeing the lobstermen getting their boats ready, recognizing the markings on the buoys, remembering when he was one of them. Remembering his own colors out there, bobbing in the water. He should be out there right now, hauling traps, seeing how many legals he'd caught.

He felt a yawning ache to be out at sea, the briny wind in his face, working the way his father, and his father before him, had. Lobstering was in his blood.

But it was all over now. Beau and Zac had only made it worse, making it seem as if he could just stick on a prosthetic limb and jump back on a boat.

It was a dangerous trade even for an able-bodied man. He'd lost boots and gloves when they'd gotten tangled in the line. Most lobstermen did. Thankfully he'd never had a body part entangled, had never been dragged overboard. But a prosthesis wouldn't allow for the dexterity needed to avoid that. Or if it did, it would take years to develop.

Something in the girls' conversation tweaked his ear, and he listened in, his eyes still on the TV.

"Isn't he the one who bought your picnic lunch at the auction last summer?" Lucy was saying.

"That's the guy," Paige said. "We went out once after that, but he was just coming out of a long-term relationship and he told me he needed to take some time. Then about a month ago he asked me out again."

His stomach twisted. Who was she talking about? And why hadn't she mentioned it to him?

"Friday'll be our fifth date."

Fifth? He turned a dark look on Zac, who was too busy watching the game to notice. *Thanks for the warning, buddy.*

"So where are you going?" Lucy asked.

"I don't know. He's going to surprise me."

"He has the dreamiest brown eyes," Eden said.

"Like a puppy dog," Lucy added. "Has he kissed you yet?"

Riley clenched the napkin in his lap, fighting the urge to cover his ears. He was glad when the Red Sox scored the tying run and the patrons erupted in applause, causing him to miss Paige's response. He didn't want to imagine some other guy's lips on hers. He'd had the privilege only once, and he remembered every detail. That was the only image he wanted in his brain.

"Those shoulders were made for crying on, sugar," Lucy was saying. "He goes to our church, doesn't he?"

"Yeah, the early service though."

Early service. Brown eyes. He was still drawing a blank.

"Strong faith, strong shoulders . . . what else could a girl want?" Lucy said.

Riley set his teeth, glaring at the TV screen.

"Doesn't his mom own the Mangy Moose?" Eden asked. "I was in there this spring looking for a trinket for Micah and chatted with her awhile."

"Yeah, that's her."

So they were talking about Dylan Moore. He was a lobsterman born and bred, just like Riley. Only he still had both legs. And dreamy brown eyes, apparently.

"You'll have to let us know how the date goes."

The conversation shifted to Eden and Beau's upcoming wedding, and Riley's thoughts drifted away. It had been hard enough watching Paige's relationship with his brother get serious. Then they'd broken up on the eve of his departure, and he'd had to leave her for months on end, not knowing if he'd come home to find her involved with someone else. But in all of those scenarios there had been at least a sliver of hope for him.

Now he had to watch some moron take her out, wine and dine her, knowing there was no hope of a future for the two of them. Because even if her feelings did change—and that was about as likely as a midnight sunrise—he'd never saddle her with the man he'd become.

Somehow he was going to have to get used to the idea of her with someone else. Because if there was anyone who deserved the love of a good man, it was Paige.

Chapter 6

*R*iley's head was practically spinning just watching Paige dart around the house in her yoga pants and T-shirt. In the kitchen, back with a glass of water he didn't need, up the stairs.

She stopped in the middle of the staircase, frowning. "What was I doing? Oh yeah, my clothes! Oh my gosh, I'm losing it." She dashed up the steps, calling over her shoulder, "You need a blanket? It's a little cool in here. I'll shut the windows. You can turn on the heat later if you need to."

It was pointless to respond. She'd been like the Energizer Bunny since she'd gotten home from work. Her date was due to arrive in—he checked his watch—five minutes. His hands tightened on the sofa cushions. This really blew.

The floor creaked overhead with her hurried movements. A few minutes later she reappeared, those tanned legs making quick work of the stairs. She wore a pale blue shirt that matched her eyes and shorts that revealed too much skin. Her hair flowed straight over her shoulders like a waterfall of spun gold. She was stunning. Breathtaking.

His heart ticked too quickly as the words teased at his lips. But he seasoned them with a hefty dose of friendship. "You look nice."

"Thanks. Did I tell you Zac brought over some wings? And there's pizza in the freezer, your favorite kind. Not to mention twelve varieties of casseroles from your fan club."

"Got it."

"I meant to put together a fresh fruit salad," she called from the kitchen. "But I didn't have time."

"I'll make it later."

"The toilet keeps running when it's flushed. You know how to fix it when that happens?"

"Of course I do. I'm not an idiot." He failed to keep the edginess from his tone.

She stopped on the kitchen threshold, a frown tucked between her brows. "What's wrong?"

"Nothing."

She folded her arms and stared him down.

Fine, she wanted to get it out there, he'd get it out there. "You're fussing over me like a mother hen. I don't need a babysitter."

"I'm not your babysitter, Callahan. I'm your friend."

Yeah, she was his friend. And only his friend. He didn't need the reminder. Or maybe he did. Maybe that's what his mood was really about. This stupid date was stirring up a lot of crap.

He clamped his teeth to keep the verbal garbage inside. It was getting harder and harder.

Paige leaned against the doorframe and heaved a sigh. "I'm not doing anything for you that you wouldn't do for me. In fact, this is the first time I can remember that you've been on the receiving end. It's always been you taking care of me. You coddling me when

Casper got hit by a car, you fixing my furnace and changing my oil. Remember that night when I was seventeen and got stupid after my dad died? You were there for me. You took care of me."

His steeled himself against the memory of the night. Against the helpless weight of her in his arms, the pliable brush of her lips. Oh yeah. He'd taken care of her all right.

"Well, I don't need you fussing over me. You're going to be gone a few hours—I think I can manage that long." A disturbing thought occurred. Was she planning to be gone longer? He tried to shove the thought down, but it kept bubbling to the surface. He tried for a casual tone. "Unless you're going to make this an over-nighter or something."

Paige frowned at him from the doorway. "Of course not. What is up with you?"

He gawked at her. "Me? I'm not the one running around here like a chicken with its head cut off. You're nervous as heck. Dylan Moore got you all hot and bothered or something?"

She narrowed her eyes. "No, I'm not hot and bothered, and you're being a real jerk, you know that? Maybe you should just go back to avoiding me."

Riley gave a wry laugh. "We live in the same house, Paige."

"And yet you've barely spoken to me for twelve hours."

The doorbell pealed as they stared each other down for a long beat, neither giving an inch.

When she finally moved toward the door, he suddenly wanted to wrap the quilted throw around her lower half. Instead he gathered his crutches. Dylan already had him by a couple inches. He wasn't going to make it even worse.

He pulled to his feet and turned toward the door in time to see Dylan's eyes sweep over Paige's body with a flicker of male appreciation. He fought the urge to gouge out the man's dreamy brown eyes with the blunt end of his crutch.

"Wow," Dylan said. "You look beautiful. Gorgeous."

Paige's smile widened, her eyes lighting up like he'd just made her entire week. "Why, thank you."

You should've been the one to say it, idiot. He wanted to punch himself in the face.

Dylan finally tore his eyes away from Paige long enough to notice him. "Riley. Hey, dude. Heard you were back. Good to see you, man."

Riley balanced on his crutches and shook Dylan's hand, making his grasp good and firm. "Good to be back."

Dylan winced slightly as he pulled away.

"Let me go grab a sweater," Paige said. "I'll be right back."

She dashed up the stairs.

Dylan's eyes followed her until she disappeared. Then he turned a congenial smile on Riley. The guy didn't even see him as a threat. And why would he? Riley's mood took a turn for the worse.

"So . . . ," Dylan said after a long, uncomfortable moment. "How's it going? You know, the therapy and everything?"

"Peachy. Where are you taking her tonight?"

Surprise flickered in Dylan's eyes, and his mouth worked a minute.

Okay, maybe he wasn't being very friendly. But he was digging deep just to keep from wrapping his hands around the guy's thick neck.

"Ah . . . thought we'd take the ferry over to Folly Shoals and hit the Seafood Shack. It's the perfect weather for a boat ride."

"She gets motion sick."

The sparkle in his eyes dimmed. "Oh. Well, I guess we'll stop for some Dramamine on the way."

"And she's allergic to shellfish." Didn't this guy know anything about her?

A tinge of pink moved into Dylan's face as his eyes narrowed. "Well . . . they have a varied menu. I'm sure she can handle herself."

"I'm sure she can." Riley continued to eye the man. *And you'd better treat her right, Sparky, or I'll be the one handling you.*

Dylan shifted. His cheeks were mottled pink. "Listen, is there a problem here?"

Riley stood stock-still despite the growing ache in his stump. "Nope. No problem."

"'Cause it seems like there's a problem."

"Long as you treat her right, there's no problem at all."

"Well, *Dad*, you don't have to worry about—"

"All right," Paige called as she descended the steps. "I'm ready to go."

Riley held eye contact with Dylan, drilling his message in deep.

When Paige neared the guys her eyes toggled back and forth between them. She gave a nervous laugh. "Everything okay here?"

Riley aimed one last look of warning at Dylan. "Wicked awesome."

As Dylan ushered her toward the door, she tossed Riley a *What was that?* look.

He gave her a tight smile. "You kids have a good night, now."

Paige shot him a look, which he pointedly ignored.

By the time the door shut, Riley's energy was spent, and his stump was a throbbing ache. He dropped onto the sofa, dreading the long evening that stretched ahead.

He turned on the TV to ESPN, but five minutes later his mind had wandered back to Paige. He wished he hadn't asked where they were going. Now he could envision every second of their date, right down to the drugstore run.

He remembered the look that had come over her face at Dylan's compliment. *He* wanted to be the one making her feel good, making her smile, making her eyes dance. He wanted to be the one holding her door and making sure the chef cooked her dinner with care.

Darkness flooded through him. He picked up the throw pillow and whipped it across the room. It landed against the wall with an unsatisfying soft *whump*.

Get a grip, Callahan. You can't have her.

He punched his useless thigh. *Is this Your idea of entertainment, God? Watching a cripple lose the woman he loves to another man?*

Again.

He closed his eyes and took a deep breath. He could do this. He just had to focus on his recovery. Work his butt off, get his prosthesis, work his butt off some more, and then he could leave here and let Paige get on with her life. As would he.

He had a new life awaiting him. A new job in Georgia, where his platoon buddy Noah was just waiting on word from him.

The thought left a hollow ache in his middle. If only this had never happened. If only his feelings for her had never changed. His mind wandered back to that day. How many times had he wished he could somehow go back and make things different?

It had begun the second Paige returned from summer camp their seventeenth year. Her mom always sent her away to various camps during the summer. To enrich her life, she said. And Paige's dad went blithely along like he did with all her mother's decrees.

Paige had three back-to-back camps, one of them lasting a whole month, much to Riley's dismay. He'd spent his summer mowing grass at the Christmas tree farm and helping his dad plant new seedlings. Some days, when his chores were caught up, he went out with his dad on the lobster boat. It had been the only good thing about the whole summer.

Paige arrived home only a week before school started. When her mom finally let her leave the house, she arranged to meet up with Riley at the inlet pier where the Warrens moored their rowboat.

He showed up early, eager to see her. He knew she'd want to go gliding up the inlet while they caught each other up on their summers. And afterward, he hoped she was up for a game of basketball. His brothers had been too busy to give him the time of day, and he wanted to be conditioned for tryouts when basketball season rolled around. He liked playing with Paige, especially since he'd shot up four inches over the last year.

His legs hung over the end of the pier, his feet dangling a few inches from the water's smooth surface. The boat's hull bumped rhythmically against the piling, making a scraping sound, and a seagull sailed overhead, giving a lonely cry. The sun was just low enough to dapple the sky with gold by the time he heard her footsteps on the wooden pier.

"'Bout time you got here." He turned, and the smirk on his lips shriveled up and died.

The sun sparkled off her summery blond hair, and her tanned skin glowed as if it had been kissed by the sun. The slim, straight lines of her body had given way to subtle curves, highlighted by her snug T-shirt and shorts. Her legs . . . had they always stretched so long and shapely? And since when did she paint her toenails?

She tweaked a brow as she neared. "Cat got your tongue, Callahan?"

He blinked. *Snap out of it, man. This is Warren. Your best pal. Your buddy.*

"Hey, Warren," he said as he got to his feet. Unfortunately the view was just as nice from up there. She reminded him of the gorgeous blond chick from that *Sisterhood* movie she'd made him watch twice the summer before.

Her smile widened as she approached, and she threw her arms around him. "I missed you!"

Her breath tickled the hair over his ears, making his heart kick into overtime. He sure hoped she couldn't feel how hard it was pounding.

"You too."

She even felt different—all soft against his chest. His mouth went dry. She smelled like sweet flowers—the really pretty kind. He fought the urge to bury his nose in her hair.

What the heck is wrong with you? If she knew what he was thinking she'd slug him in the arm. Hard.

Paige pulled away, leaving him teetering somewhere between relief and disappointment.

Her face had matured as well, he saw, now that he was up close and personal. The gentle curves had given way to refined planes and intriguing slopes. She had a fresh sprinkling of freckles on her nose, and her lips seemed fuller.

Or maybe he'd just never noticed them before.

Those lips curved in a saucy grin. "You're staring."

Heat crept into his face. He set his hand on the back of his neck. "Well, you changed. You—you got taller." And lots of other -er words he didn't even want to think, much less say.

She shrugged. "A couple inches." She narrowed her eyes, studying his face hard, and it was everything he could do to stay still under her scrutiny.

"Are those whiskers? You trying to grow some facial hair, Callahan?"

He rubbed his stubbly jaw. "What do you mean, trying? This is a bona fide beard." There. That sounded pretty normal.

She laughed. "I don't know if I'd go that far, but it's a valiant effort." She stepped around him and climbed gracefully into the boat. "Let's go. I've been looking forward to this for weeks."

Riley was distracted the whole evening. He tried to act normal, but inside he felt anything but. When she suggested they pass on the basketball, he was all in favor. He needed time alone to dissect—and eradicate—these weird thoughts.

But time didn't help. Something had shifted. He'd noticed the changes in her, and he couldn't unnotice them. Over the coming days the observations somehow led to a shift in his feelings. Worse, Paige seemed just fine. He'd had enough interactions with girls that he'd notice if she was giving off vibes. But she treated him as she always had—as her best buddy, Callahan.

All that fall and leading into the winter, he wished for things to go back to normal. He begged God to make the new feelings disappear. But no matter how many times he beat himself up over it, they remained, stubborn and strong.

He hid them behind familiar jabs to the arm and high-fives and behind safe words like buddy and pal. Paige seemed oblivious, and thank God for that. Because if she found out, it would only make everything awkward. She'd probably put distance between them or feel sorry for him, and he couldn't stand the thought of either of those things.

He had three choices, and he worked them endlessly until he wanted to bang his head against the wall. One: he could tell Paige how he felt and risk losing her forever. Two: he could distance himself from her and deprive them both of their relationship. Three: he could go on pretending nothing had changed and continue to suffer in silence.

He didn't like any of the options, but there was only one that left him any kind of relationship with her. And he didn't even want to imagine his life without Paige.

Chapter 7

"A re you feeling okay?" Dylan asked.

Paige glanced up from the salmon she was picking at with her fork, forcing a smile. "Of course. I'm fine. This is delicious." She took a bite. "How's your lobster?"

"Excellent."

He wiped his mouth and took a swig of his Coke. "Anyone adopt an animal this week?"

"Just one. A cat." She thought of all the homeless animals in the kennels and Dylan's big empty yard. She should talk him into a dog. The brown Lab would be a good match for him, and he had the space for her. But somehow she couldn't find the energy for the conversation.

"Are you sure you're not feeling sick?" He eyed her. "You seem . . . kind of quiet tonight."

"The Dramamine did the trick. This was a nice surprise. I love Folly Shoals. It feels like a world away from Summer Harbor."

And yet her mind had remained onshore the entire time, all through their long walk along the harbor and their delicious dinner. She couldn't get Riley out of her head.

43

As much as he tried to put on a smile for everyone else, it was clear he wasn't doing all that great. He'd been on edge tonight, and truth was, she felt all kinds of guilty for leaving him alone when he was clearly struggling. Not only had she left him, but she'd been impatient with him.

He'd been like a wounded animal, guarded and snarling at her efforts to help. She'd treated so many animals with care and patience, giving them not only treatment, but comfort. Yet what had she done with her best friend in the world? She'd snapped at him, then left him to fend for himself.

Deep down she was still peeved at him for leaving *her*. It was stupid, she knew. But somehow that didn't stop the feelings.

Guilt pricked hard. She set her fork down on her plate, her appetite completely gone.

Dylan planted his elbows on the table, clasping his hands at his jaw. "What's wrong, Paige?"

She tried for a smile. "Sorry. Guess I am a little distracted."

"Anything you want to talk about?"

She looked into his brown eyes—they really were kind of dreamy. And thoughtful. He was a good listener. She'd dumped her work worries on him. He'd listened patiently while she'd gone on about fundraisers and donation drives. Why not this? Riley was a big part of her life, especially now that he was back in Summer Harbor.

She let loose a sigh. "It's Riley. I'm worried about him. He puts on this jovial act and tries to pretend everything's okay, but I'm not buying it."

Dylan released a skeptical puff of air. "That was jovial?" There was a sarcastic edge to his voice she hadn't heard before.

She gave him a withering look. "He's been through a lot.

Sometimes he lets his guard down and gets a little prickly. Like tonight. I didn't handle it well." She tossed her napkin onto her plate. "I didn't handle it well at all."

"Don't be so hard on yourself. You're letting the guy stay with you. You're practically his nursemaid."

"Don't you dare say that in front of him. He's independent to a fault. And of course I'm helping him. He's my best friend."

"Are you sure?"

Her eyes darted to his, questioning. "What do you mean, am I sure?"

Their gazes tangled. His brown eyes didn't seem so dreamy at the moment. They seemed shrewd, harder somehow.

Her shoulder muscles tightened, and heat flushed through her body.

"I mean . . . ," he said slowly. "Are you sure that's all he is?"

She sat back in her chair. "Of course I'm sure."

"You just seem awfully distracted by someone who's supposedly just a friend."

She narrowed her eyes thoughtfully on Dylan's face. Was he one of those jealous, possessive guys? Was his question a red flag or just a rational concern? In high school there had been a couple guys who didn't understand her friendship with Riley, who seemed put out when she spent time with him. But she and Dylan were adults. Surely they were beyond the petty insecurities of the teen years.

She pushed back her plate and met his gaze head-on. "Look, Dylan. Riley and I go back a long way. He's like a brother to me, and I'd do anything for him, as he would for me. If you're uncomfortable with me having such a close male friend—"

Dylan put his hands up, palms out. "No, no. I'm sorry. I didn't mean to go all possessive guy on you. He's your friend. You want to be there for him. I get that."

"I appreciate that."

But observing his unrepentant face, she wondered if he really did get it.

In any case, the polish had quickly worn off their date, and suddenly she only wanted to be at home with Riley. She wanted to apologize for losing her temper and make everything right between them again.

She checked her watch. "I hate to be a fuddy-duddy, but would you mind if we caught the next ferry back? It's been a long day."

She knew her tone sounded a little peeved, but you know what? She was peeved. She had enough stress in her life right now without a guy she'd barely begun dating getting all jealous over Riley.

Dylan stared at her for a long moment, his jaw knotting up more with each second that passed. Finally he set his napkin on his plate. "Fine. We'll catch the next ferry." He lifted his hand as the server passed nearby. "Check, please."

❧

What was he doing? Last place Riley should be was out here in the darkened living room, waiting for Paige like some overprotective father. He'd even turned on the porch light, though it was barely dark.

Number one, fat chance she'd come home this early. Number two, what did he hope to accomplish? Did he really think seeing some guy kiss her was going to make matters better?

Maybe it would finally drill into his head once and for all that she was out of his reach.

Or maybe you're just a glutton for punishment.

A crackle of gravel sounded, and he peered through the slit in the blinds. Lights swept across the room, then went out.

Well, well, well. An early night. Considering they'd gone all the way to Folly Shoals, he hadn't expected her home till at least eleven. He couldn't quite smother the glee that rose inside or the smirk that curled his lips. Had something gone wrong? Or maybe Dylan Moore, lobsterman extraordinaire, was worried about his beauty rest. Stupid schmuck.

A car door slammed, then another. Riley edged over on the couch so he could follow them to the porch. Dylan was walking a good three paces behind Paige, but once they were on the porch he narrowed the gap.

Riley had to shift up on his knee and lean in to see them under the golden glow of the porch light.

Something about Paige's posture seemed stiff. Maybe it was her squared shoulders. No, it was the stubborn jut of her chin. He couldn't see Dylan's face in the shadows. They spoke briefly while Riley's heart boomed in his chest cavity. He held his breath, as if the quiet might help him hear their conversation. But the house was too well insulated. Why hadn't he thought to crack a window?

His heart stuttered as Dylan leaned in, the back of his head mercifully blocking what appeared to be a good-night kiss. Riley's fingers tightened on the sofa cushion.

He sucked in a lungful of oxygen, trying to get his emotions under control. *She's not yours, Callahan.* It didn't seem to matter how many times he told himself that, his heart wasn't buying it.

The door whooshed open.

Riley dived away from the window. His stump caught on the sofa cushion, and his good leg got caught up under him, making him lose his balance. He grabbed for a hold, but it was too late. He toppled downward, landing on the floor with a heavy thud.

"Riley!" Paige was at his side before he could get his bearings. Heat flooded his face, his entire upper body. *Seriously, God?* He gritted his teeth. "I'm fine."

His stump was upright against the sofa, pulsing with pain. He pushed up on his elbows and swiveled his body away from her.

Paige grabbed his arm. "Wait. Are you hurt? You're too heavy. Let me get Dylan."

"No." Hadn't he suffered enough humiliation for one day? "I don't need his help." He pushed back, rolled over, and used his arms and good leg to lever himself off the floor.

Paige reached out for him as he teetered.

He jerked away. "I can do it myself!"

He was huffing and puffing by the time he was upright. A sheen of sweat dampened his back, and heat settled like warm pools into his cheeks.

"Are you okay?" The pity in her eyes made him want to hit something.

He hobbled toward his crutch. "Wicked awesome."

"I'm really starting to hate that phrase."

He grabbed his crutches and propped them under his arms, ignoring the pain in his leg. "I'm going to bed."

"Riley, don't. Let's talk."

He swung his crutches forward. "Tomorrow."

"Please?"

The need in her voice was the only thing on planet Earth that could've stopped his escape right then. He stopped in his tracks, giving a hard sigh. His heart was racing like he'd just done fifty push-ups.

"You're home early," he taunted. "What's wrong? Did the dreamy Dylan Moore not live up to your expectations?"

She walked around until she faced him. The porch light filtered through the blinds, giving her face a golden glow. Those baby-blue eyes . . . They sucked him right in every time. His eyes flickered down to her lips. The ones that had just hosted Dylan Moore's.

His jaw clenched. *What did you expect, Callahan? That she was saving herself for a man who can barely pick himself up off the floor?*

She touched his arm, and he flinched as a jolt went through him.

She withdrew her touch. "I'm sorry about earlier. I was . . . impatient and short-tempered. I should've been more patient with you."

"I don't need your pity, Paige."

She gave him a flinty look. "It's not pity. It's compassion. I love you, you big jughead."

He gave a hollow laugh. "Yeah."

"What's that supposed to mean?"

He hobbled away.

"Where are you going?"

"To bed."

She skirted around him again, blocking his path. Great. A hundred-and-ten-pound girl could now outmaneuver him. He'd just reached a new low.

He gave her a dark look, forbidding himself from softening under the look in her eyes.

"You can push me away all you want, but I'm not going anywhere."

He'd seen that look in her eyes before. It was the one she got when there was an emergency call at the shelter. Like she was on a mission. Like she was rising to the challenge.

He bristled as a fresh flood of heat washed into his face. Gritting his teeth, he locked in on her eyes and lowered his face until they were a breath apart. "I'm not one of your animals, Paige. I don't need you to save me."

He held eye contact, making sure he'd driven his point home. Then he shouldered past her, using his crutch to edge her out of the way.

He swung through the bedroom door and gave it a push. It closed behind him with a loud slam.

Chapter 8

Saturday morning found Paige in a back booth at Frumpy Joe's, opposite Eden and Lucy. The three of them were unlikely friends. First of all, Paige had been dating Beau when Eden came along and stole his heart. And a year and a half ago Lucy had left town a week before her wedding to Zac, leaving him brokenhearted and thus a sworn enemy of the Callahans. But then she'd turned up all lost and confused last summer, and the two of them had ironed everything out.

Paige had let both girls off the hook long ago. Forgiveness wasn't so hard when she witnessed the perma-smiles on Beau's and Zac's faces.

The girls ordered, then settled in, starting with an overview of Paige's date with Dylan. For some reason she skipped over the awkward conversation they'd had about Riley and focused on the romantic aspects. When their need for details was exhausted, they moved on to the reason for their meeting.

"What we need," Eden said, "is a fundraiser to get you through the short term. Then we'll work on finding new sponsors."

"How about a picnic auction like we put on last year for the firehouse?" Lucy said.

"I think we need something fresher," Paige said.

"A spaghetti dinner?" Eden suggested.

"The Rotary Club just had one of those." Lucy tossed her long dark hair over her shoulder. "How 'bout a bachelor auction? One of the sororities did that while I was at Harvard. They raised a boatload of cash."

"That's an idea," Paige said.

"We should do it." Eden clapped her hands. "Oh, this sounds like a ton of fun."

Paige shot her a look. "Simmer down, Miss Future Callahan. You don't get to join in the reindeer games."

"Trust me, it'll be more entertaining as a spectator." She arched a delicate brow at Lucy. "This is a prime opportunity for matchmaking."

"I'm not sure I like where this is going," Paige said.

"Relax. I've been taking notes from Aunt Trudy."

Paige rolled her eyes. "Heaven help us all."

Eden and Lucy began pitching ideas back and forth while Paige jotted them down. After a while the topic shifted toward Eden's upcoming wedding, and Paige's thoughts scattered as she doodled beside her copious notes.

She'd slept horribly, waking every couple hours to stew over the words she'd exchanged with Riley. At five o'clock she finally gave up. She'd been hoping to clear the air before she left, but he'd still been in his room. By the time she'd met the girls she was buzzing with caffeine.

"Earth to Paige . . . ," Lucy said.

Paige looked up to find both women staring at her. "Sorry, what? I drifted off."

"What's the big frown all about?" Eden asked. Her gaze bounced off Lucy, then returned to Paige. "You're not . . . Would you rather we not talk about my, um, wedding?"

"What? No." Paige put her hand on Eden's. "Hey, I'm nothing but happy for you and Beau. You two were always meant to be."

Eden couldn't really help that she'd captured Beau's attention practically the minute she arrived in town, in all her desperate-fleeing-woman glory. Beau had always been a sucker for a woman in distress.

It was true Paige was hurt when Beau broke up with her. But time had a way of healing wounds and bringing clarity. Beau was completely wrong for her. They were definitely lacking in the sparks department. And Paige was holding out for sparks.

"Is it the auction then?" Lucy asked. "Are you not keen on the idea?"

"No, no, it's a great idea. I'm just . . ." She sighed as she pulled her hand back and began picking at her napkin. "Things aren't going great with Riley, that's all. He's been irritable, which is completely understandable. He doesn't want any help from me, and I just feel like I keep doing and saying all the wrong things. I thought I knew him so well, but right now I feel like I don't know him at all."

"Aw, sugar," Lucy said. "I'm sure that's not true. He's been through an awful lot. War alone can cause a lot of issues, but to top it off he's dealing with the loss of his leg and the trauma from that. He'll be faring better in time, sure enough."

"I know that, and I'm here for him as long as he needs me. But it's so hard to find a balance between helpful and smothering. No, there is no balance. He doesn't even want 'helpful.' It's like he wants to be all alone in this. He's done nothing but push me away lately."

"Is he getting counseling of any kind?" Lucy asked.

"Starts next week. Maybe that'll help."

"I bet it will," Eden said. "It's sure helped me cope with the remnants from my first marriage. Emotional trauma takes a toll, but he'll come out of it. You'll see."

"Hey!" Lucy said. "We should get Riley to be one of our bachelors."

Paige squirmed in her seat. "I don't know. I think he needs to focus on his therapy. Besides, with the mood he's been in, he might scare away all the single ladies."

"Are you kidding me?" Lucy said. "What's more appealing than a handsome, broody marine? The ladies'll be fighting over him. I bet that would perk him right up."

"Maybe she's right," Eden said. "Having a little female attention might be just the ego boost he needs. Plus he'd be raising money for a good cause. Feeling productive is great for the mood."

"Yeah, but . . ." Paige searched for a valid excuse and came up empty.

"I could ask him if you want," Lucy offered.

"No, that's okay. I-I can do it."

"Why don't we come up with a list of names," Eden said. "We'll divide them up and ask them this week. Next time we meet we'll have a list of willing victims—er, participants."

"I think you had it right the first time." Paige gave a playful grin.

But inside, the thought of asking Riley to be one of the bachelors made her feel anything but playful.

Chapter 9

*R*iley secured the towel at his waist, leaned against the bathroom counter, and wetted the razor. After last night's debacle he felt the need for a clean slate of some kind, and his face was the easiest target. The mirror began fogging up, so he opened the door leading into the bedroom.

He'd been a real jerk with Paige last night. Why was it everything seemed so different, so clear, in the morning? Just because he was all knotted up over her didn't give him the right to be nasty. She didn't know the close proximity was hard for him. That watching her go out with Dylan was torture. She was only trying to help him.

The razor scraped as he drew it along his stubbled jaw. He rapped it against the sink, drawing in a deep breath of the humid air. Somehow the bathroom always smelled like Paige after he showered. The bedding smelled of her, too, no matter that it was freshly washed. Living in her private space was its own special kind of torture.

He wondered where Paige was this morning, hoped he hadn't chased her from her own house. He'd gotten through his exercises and was feeling restless. He was tired of being cooped up. The thought of facing people didn't thrill him, but he had to get out of here, find something to do. Was it too soon for a job?

Hard as it was to admit, he didn't know if he had the stamina for that. After the exercises and shower, he was beat. His heart was pounding hard just from standing upright, and his stump was throbbing.

Plus, he couldn't drive, and he couldn't walk far, making him dependent on others for transportation. He gave the razor an extra hard rap against the sink, rinsed his face, and blotted his freshly shaven cheeks with a towel. Much better. If only he felt as normal as he looked.

Now for the exquisite treat of getting dressed. He grabbed his crutches and hobbled into the bedroom.

His eyes darted toward a movement in the open doorway. Paige froze at the threshold, one hand poised to knock.

"Oh. Sorry."

Her eyes slid downward, and he looked away before they could drop past the towel and fasten on his naked stump. Now there was a sight sure to please. He wished he could tug his towel south to hide it, but that would expose other areas she had no interest in seeing.

He gritted his teeth, continuing toward the bureau. "How was your morning?" he asked, pleased his tone sounded more agreeable than he felt.

"I had—" She turned her head and cleared her throat. "I had breakfast with the girls—Lucy and Eden."

"That's great." He pulled open a bureau drawer. His gaze flickered up to the mirror where he could see Paige avoiding eye contact. Her fingers fiddled with the top button of her shirt.

Was she uncomfortable at the sight of his bare stump, or just feeling awkward after their argument the night before? The tape of his ugly words played one more time in his head.

"Listen, Paige. I'm sorry about last night. I was a jerk."

"Riley . . ." Her eyes darted to his and then away.

He faced her, skivvies and cargos in hand. "I know you're trying to help. I was just in a mood."

"Well, who wouldn't be? My gosh, you've been through so much."

He tossed his clothes over his shoulder and hobbled toward the closet. "That's not your problem."

"Of course it's my problem. Whatever you're going through, I want to be there for you. I'm here if you want to talk, and so are your brothers. And I'm sorry too. I'm sorry I was so short-tempered."

"I appreciate that. But right now, I think we just need to come to an agreement that if I need help, I'll ask."

She gave him a look. "You know you won't ask."

"Yes, I will." He opened the closet door. It hit his crutch and bounced back. He hobbled out of its way and reached for it again. He toppled forward, nearly losing his balance before he caught himself on the doorframe.

"See?" Paige had taken a few steps forward. Her palm rested against her chest, which rose and fell quickly.

"See what? I got it opened."

"You almost fell!"

"*Almost* being the key word."

She huffed, crossing her arms. Her eyes shot daggers at him.

He smothered a smile. He'd take her temper any day over the nervous Nellie she'd been when she walked in. He loved the way it made the silver flecks flash in those blue depths.

"It's not funny."

"Lighten up, Warren." The empty hanger pinged around as it released his shirt.

"You're so stubborn."

"We established that years ago."

"You know, some people work on their flaws once they become aware of them."

He turned with a smirk, his shirt in hand. "Who says it's a flaw?"

She lifted her chin. "Anyone who knows someone stubborn."

He moved toward the bed and dropped his clothes there.

She eyed the pile. "Do you need some help with—?"

She stopped at his stony look, pressing her lips together as if keeping the words from escaping.

"I'm getting dressed now—all by myself."

She only stared back, her own brand of stubborn in those sea-blue eyes.

Feeling ornery, he raised a brow, reached for the knot of his towel, and gave a little tug.

"Callahan!" She whirled away, but not before he saw the flush rise to her cheeks.

A chuckle rose up his throat, foreign yet familiar, filling the room as the door slammed shut. And man, did it feel good.

Chapter 10

The fiftysomething woman knelt in the grass beside the dog. His tail wagged wildly, his tongue lolling out to the side. If Paige had ever seen a dog smiling, this one was now.

She squatted beside the two of them, ruffling the dog's fur. "He's a mixed breed, been with us for a couple weeks. He's healthy, neutered, had all his shots. He's very playful and affectionate, as you can see."

Mrs. Miller drew her hand back and sighed. "I don't know. I kind of had my heart set on a Yorkie."

The dog nudged his nose under the woman's hand, begging for attention.

"He really likes you. And he's got a great temperament. He'd be a good companion. Do you have grandchildren? He's terrific around kids. A family was just in yesterday checking him out."

Mrs. Miller stood, brushing the dog fur off her slacks. "I do have grandkids, but I don't think this is the right one. He's got long hair, and he's shedding pretty badly. Plus, he doesn't exactly seem like the sharpest knife in the drawer, if you know what I mean."

Paige suppressed the urge to cover the dog's ears and dug

deep for extra patience. "Did you see the black Lab? They're very easily trained and quite affectionate. He already knows basic commands."

"Oh no, I don't want something that big. I have a small yard."

"Our female sheltie might be a good fit then. She's extremely smart and great with kids. Shall we bring her out and see how you get along?"

Mrs. Miller hitched her bag on her shoulder. "I don't think so. I like the idea of rescuing an animal, but I don't think there's a good fit here."

Paige followed Mrs. Miller to the lobby, doing her best to encourage the woman to keep an open mind.

When the door finally closed behind her, her receptionist, Lauren, shut the file drawer. "Well, you can't say you didn't give it your all."

"I was really hoping she'd take one home."

"We are getting a little full back there."

And the daily care was costing a pretty penny. Paige had sat down the night before and looked over their budget. There weren't many more corners to cut. She had to find homes for some of these dogs. And scrounge up some new benefactors. And plan the fundraiser. Her head spun. She was glad it was almost quitting time. She was looking forward to a nice quiet dinner with Riley. After that she could work on the sponsor letter she was sending out.

"Hey, Paige, you have a few minutes?" Something about Lauren's tone set off warning flares.

"Sure." She leaned her elbows on the counter. "What's up?"

Lauren's eyes flickered down at the empty desk as she seemed to search for words.

Lauren had been manning the shelter's desk since she'd

graduated from high school four years ago. She was more than a receptionist, really, and it occurred to Paige that it was past time for a raise. But she dearly hoped that wasn't what this was about.

Lauren looked up with her wide brown eyes. "I'm really sorry to do this to you, but . . . I found another job."

The bottom dropped out of Paige's stomach. "You're quitting?"

Lauren winced. "I don't want to. I really don't, but with the shelter in such dire straits financially, and its future so up in the air, I had to find something more stable. I have a car payment, and I just bought my cute little house, and they were looking for someone to manage the sheriff's office."

"Oh, Lauren." Paige sighed. "You're worth a lot more than you're making now. I wish I could afford to pay you more."

"I know you do. But this is a really good opportunity for me, and I just can't afford to turn it down."

"Of course you can't. I wish you the best, really." She was trying hard to be happy for the girl.

"I'd like to help you find and train my replacement, but we'll have to move fast. I can only finish out the week, and I really had to fight for those days."

"Oh boy. All right. Well . . . I'll write an ad to place tomorrow." After she wrote the sponsor letter and filled out a stack of grant forms and created a GoFundMe page. "I'm sure it'll all work out."

Lauren rolled out from behind the desk and stood. "Thanks for taking this so well. I was really dreading telling you."

Paige dredged up a smile. "Well, you're not just an employee. You've become a friend. Sheriff Colton got himself a real winner, and I'll make sure he knows it."

Lauren hugged Paige, then gathered her things and left.

Paige fell into the spot the girl had vacated, her breath leaving her body in a big gush. Great. Just great. Where was she going to find another Lauren, and for the low wage she could afford? She was sure Sara, their other staff member, couldn't work more hours. She was taking a full load of online courses and barely holding it together now.

Paige's phone vibrated in her pocket; she pulled it out, eager for something else to think about, and found a text from Lucy.

Brendan Marquart agreed to be a bachelor! Have you asked Riley yet?

The bachelor auction. One more thing on her to-do list.

She'd been planning to ask him Saturday morning after she apologized. But it totally slipped her mind after one look at his muscled torso. And those arms. He'd always been brawny, but now he seemed chiseled out of stone.

How many times had he whipped off his shirt during a game of basketball? She'd thought nothing of it. Now she found herself wondering what it would feel like to run her hands over his biceps, feel the softness of his flesh stretched over the hardness beneath. The thought left her disturbed, feeling like all kinds of perv.

What was wrong with her? She shook her head and texted back. That's great! I haven't asked Riley yet.

What are you waiting for?

Good question. She'd had all weekend. But every time she started to ask, something stopped her.

She was only trying to protect him. What if no one bid on him? Or worse, what if women felt sorry for him? He'd hate that. But she was probably worrying for nothing. She couldn't even imagine him agreeing to this. Not now.

The right timing. I'll ask in the next couple days.

She stashed her phone in her pocket.

Right now she had bigger fish to fry. She got out a blank sheet of paper and starting working on an ad for the paper.

❧

"What are you doing?" Paige said.

Riley turned from the smoking grill to see her slipping through the sliding door. It squeaked on the track, making a sparrow flutter from the tree branches overhead. Dasher slinked up to Paige, her gray tail swishing.

"What?" he said. "No 'Hi, honey, I'm home'?"

"You're going to burn your arm."

He smirked. "Well, then, we'll just cut it off too."

"That's not funny."

"Lighten up, Warren." He shifted his weight on the crutch and flipped the steak with his free hand. "Still like yours medium?"

"I was going to broil those in the oven."

"A waste of good meat. You're getting medium if you don't answer."

"That's fine." She took a step forward, then stopped and shuffled around, no doubt fighting the urge to take over.

"If you just can't help yourself, go set the table. Already tossed a salad."

"My, aren't you industrious today." She picked up Dasher and disappeared through the doorway, leaving it open.

"Just hungry and bored," he called.

Man, was he bored. Beau had offered to take him out on a buddy's boat, but the thought of being back on the water was depressing when he couldn't be doing what he wanted to be doing.

Just being outside helped though. Breathing the salt-laden air, hearing the wind whisper through the trees.

It beat the nightmares filled with dry air, gritty sand, and the still body of his comrade lying nearby in a pool of blood. His latest dream had been so real. More memory than dream.

Tex's lips moved, wordlessly at first, while Riley tried to stop the flow of blood from a gaping stomach wound. When he realized the futility of his efforts, he gave up and focused on comforting his friend.

"I got you, buddy. It's going to be okay," he said. Lied. What else could he do?

Tex's lips moved again. "Why—why me?" His body quivered one last time, then stilled, his eyes staring blankly at the evening sky.

Riley had awakened with a shudder, his heart racing, his body covered in a sheen of sweat. The words repeated over and over in his mind. *Why me? Why me? Why me?* It wasn't what his friend had really said. Those were Riley's words. Riley's question.

"Callahan!"

He whirled around, trying to clear the crud from his head, realizing it wasn't the first time Paige had called. "Yeah?"

"Inside or outside?"

"Outside."

He checked the steaks, making an effort to shake the memory. Push the darkness away. Maybe the nightmares were going to intrude on his sleep, but he'd be darned if he was going to give them headspace during the day.

Twenty minutes later he pushed his plate back and massaged his aching leg under the table. The steaks had been perfect, and the conversation nice. Paige had asked about his first counseling session. It hadn't gone as well as he made out, but seeing some of the worry dissipate from her eyes was worth the exaggeration.

In truth, he'd spent the hour avoiding the subject of his missing leg and the trauma surrounding its loss. He didn't want to talk about his stupid decision to enlist or the fact that he'd lost his vocation right along with his leg. He was thankful Dr. Lehman didn't push. Even so, his back had been damp with sweat by the time he left.

What could the man possibly know about what he'd been through? Riley had read his bio online. The guy had it all: education, a loving wife, three kids. All his limbs. The hour had felt like a month. He wasn't sure he could bring himself to go back.

A squeak sounded as Paige's fork connected with her plate. Half her T-bone remained, and she seemed more interested in pushing her food around than putting it in her mouth.

Come to think of it, she'd been asking all the questions since she'd gotten home. He began to wonder if the worry he'd seen in her eyes had nothing to do with him.

"Your steak cooked okay?"

Her eyes flickered up. "It's perfect. Delicious." She took a bite as if to prove it and followed it up with a swig of iced tea.

She resumed pushing her food around the plate.

One more squeak, and he grabbed her hand.

She looked up, wide-eyed.

"What's going on?"

"Nothing." She set down her fork and began fiddling with her necklace. "Why do you ask?"

He studied her face. Lines etched her forehead, and a telltale frown crouched between her brows. "You're stressed out."

"No, I'm not."

He gave her a look.

"You don't know everything."

"Maybe not, but I know you. It's too much, all this fund-raising and stuff on top of your job."

"I can handle it."

"Paige . . . maybe you should just . . ."

Her eyes tightened. "Just what?"

"I know how much the shelter means to you, but maybe you should just—"

"Quit?" She thrust her plate back, her eyes colliding with his. "Is that what you were going to say? Because if it is, then you really don't know me at all." She started to stand.

He tightened his grip on her arm. "Hey."

"I'm not giving up the shelter. I'm not giving up on those animals. They need me. When have I ever failed at something I put my mind to, huh? Can you answer me that? I'm going to fix this."

He put his palms up. "Okay, okay. Settle down. Good grief."

She slowly relaxed into the seat, her eyes finding the checked cloth of the table. "Sorry."

"Why don't you tell me what's going on? Maybe I can help."

She set her elbows on the table and palmed her eyes. "Lauren quit today."

He frowned, suddenly wanting to throttle the mousy girl who'd been Paige's right hand for years. "She quit? Just like that?"

"She's finishing out the week. I can't really blame her, with things so up in the air. She got a job with the sheriff's office."

"She's leaving you in the lurch."

"I'll just have to find someone else. I wrote up an ad for the paper. It's just one more thing, you know?" She tucked her hair behind her ear. "But I'll find someone, and it'll be fine."

An idea popped into his mind and quickly grew roots. Was

this a temporary solution to Paige's problem? To his own bore-dom? He could fix both with one move.

And work side by side with the woman of your dreams? Are you an idiot?

But she needed his help. And he wanted nothing more than to erase those worry lines on her forehead. She was so selfless, want-ing nothing more than to save those animals, giving of herself for him. He wanted to do something for her.

"I know someone who's perfect for the job," he said. "At least temporarily."

Her eyes brightened. "Really? Who?"

He planted his elbows on the table and clasped his hands. "Me."

Her mouth twisted as she gave him a long look. "You."

He bristled at the look on her face. Nice. Did she think he was incapable of answering the phones and running a credit card machine?

"What, you think I can't do the job? I'm missing a leg, not a brain."

She gave him a glum look. "Will you stop that? I know you're perfectly capable, I just don't want you to overdo it and set your-self back."

"Overdo? I'm bored to death. You'd be doing me a favor. Just for a while. Until you find someone permanent."

She scratched her head. Fiddled with her necklace some more. He could see the indecision all over her face.

Really? "Come on, Paige. I want to help. I owe you big for let-ting me crash here."

She narrowed her eyes. "Stop it. You don't owe me anything."

"Okay, then. I just want to help out. The way you're helping me. You're always saying 'that's what friends do.' Well . . . it's my turn."

She looked him over skeptically.

"What, it only applies to you?"

"Of course not. I just—" She sighed hard. "I don't want anything getting in the way of your recovery. Or our friendship."

Something was already in the way of their friendship, but she didn't need to know that.

"It'll be good for me. I need something to do, something to keep my mind busy. It's mostly sitting, right? Nothing I can't manage physically."

"That's true."

"As for our friendship, hey, we've weathered a lot worse. I don't think working together for a couple months is going to shake that foundation."

She pulled her lower lip in, working it with her teeth. She really did have nice lips. They were full, especially the lower one. And the prettiest shade of pink. He knew for a fact they were soft and pliant and capable of the most exquisite give-and-take.

He dragged his eyes away as heat pooled in his cheeks. He focused on the napkin in his hand, trying to steady his heart rate.

"You're right," she said.

He looked up at her.

"I don't know why I'm being so cagey about this. The job's yours if you want it, until I find a permanent replacement. But I want you to start part time—and you have to promise you'll tell me if it gets to be too much."

Riley scanned Paige's beautiful face. The clouds had lifted from her blue eyes, leaving them clear as a June day. Her lip had escaped her teeth, the pink color deepening. His eyes traced the chin he'd always thought so cute.

He forced a smile as he extended his hand. "Deal." Her hand was small and delicate in his grip, and he wondered what the heck he'd just signed up for.

Chapter 11

Riley drew the plastic wand out of the bubble bottle, held it up, and blew. The two dogs in the yard with him bit at the iridescent bubbles, their jaws snapping like mad. They went for the same bubble and collided, but it didn't even faze them.

It was his second week at the shelter, and he'd slowly bumped up his hours. He had the hang of the office stuff, but when he was caught up he enjoyed entertaining the dogs. Poor mutts shouldn't be stuck inside on a nice summer day.

He blew another round of bubbles, watching the dogs bound around, snapping, tails wagging. Somehow happy despite the fact that they were lost or abandoned. Didn't they know things weren't all that great? That they lived in a kennel, and their future was completely up in the air? If not for Paige, it would be even worse.

Paige.

She was part of the reason he preferred the outdoors and the company of the animals. He'd overestimated his ability to be around her all day. He'd somehow imagined her shut away in her office with a stack of paperwork, but it wasn't like that at all.

She was always breezing past the reception desk, her flowery scent trailing like an alluring shadow. Leaning over his desk, her hair teasing the back of his neck. Calling him in to see what one of the animals was doing, her laughter ringing out like a beautiful melody. In fact, she was rarely in her office at all.

Just when he'd think he couldn't take it anymore, she'd stop at his desk and tell him how relieved she was for his help. With gratitude shining in those baby blues, what was he supposed to do?

Movement caught his eye, and he looked up as she came outside, leading a boxer on a leash. She stopped in her tracks, taking in the sight.

Then she burst out laughing. "What are you doing?"

"Entertaining our guests."

He blew out a fresh round of bubbles. The mixed mutt jumped up, going for a large, wobbling bubble. She snapped at it, and the bubble splattered in her face, making her sneeze. Both dogs turned to Riley, tongues lolling, waiting for the next batch.

Paige laughed again. "Where on earth did you get that?"

"At the bottom of the lost-and-found box."

"That is ingenious."

She let the boxer loose, and he moped over to the other side of the lawn, sniffing at the grass.

"I was thinking . . . ," Riley said. "What if you did a volunteer drive? A few volunteers would cover this position, and then you wouldn't have to pay anyone."

The picnic table wobbled as Paige sat on the other side. "Not a bad idea. Lauren actually started as a volunteer. I also thought about trying to find a student who might be willing to intern."

"That's smart."

"A little late though. Summer's already under way."

"Wouldn't hurt to check the local colleges anyway."

The bell rang, signifying a customer, and Paige stood. "I'll get it. And I'll take these two back inside. Would you mind bringing Bishop back in when he's finished?"

"Sure." It was cute the way she named some of the animals.

The dogs trotted next to her as she strode toward the building. Riley watched her go, admiring her purposeful gait and, yes, the gentle sway of her hips. Hey, he wasn't dead.

The boxer, finished with his business, wandered over and plopped at Riley's foot. A moment later he looked toward the building Paige had disappeared into, then looked up at Riley with soulful eyes.

"You got it bad too, eh, buddy? Yeah, I get it."

The boxer blinked, looking away. Now here was a creature that knew how things stood. They weren't good, and he got it. No faking it here, or frolicking around like life didn't suck some serious egg.

Paige had mentioned earlier that the dog needed a bath. It was almost quitting time, but he could take that item off her to-do list easily enough, make sure she got out of here at a decent hour. The family was meeting up at the Roadhouse for supper.

He grabbed his crutches and stood, collecting the leash off the table. It was a challenge to use a leash when it took all his remaining limbs just to hobble around.

He gave the dog a look. "Am I going to have to put this on you, or are you gonna stick close by?"

The dog stared back with those solemn brown eyes. *I got nowhere better to be*, they seemed to say.

"Good enough."

The boxer followed as he entered the shelter. Riley led him to the back corner of the building where the walk-in tub was. He grabbed a towel and looked for the shampoo bottle, but didn't see it. Must be in the supply closet. He turned on the water to warm it up, plugged the drain, and hobbled out of the room and down the long hall.

The boxer's claws clicked on the tile behind him. Unlike the other animals, this one gave Riley the room he needed to maneuver. He gave the mutt another point for intelligence.

He entered the supply closet and located the industrial-size bottle of shampoo. He was just reaching for it when he heard Paige's laughter ring out. Then a male voice.

He shuffled to the doorway and listened.

❧

Paige took a whiff of the fresh flower arrangement, trading a smile with Dylan. She'd been surprised to find him waiting in the lobby. He'd never stopped in before, and their texts had been sporadic since their last date.

"They're beautiful. Thank you."

"I didn't feel good about how our date ended last week. I'm sorry if I was—out of line."

His regretful tone and dreamy brown eyes gave her mood an instant lift. The gesture of flowers didn't hurt either.

She gave a saucy smile. "So these are apology flowers?"

"Apology flowers . . . you're-really-special flowers . . . can-we-go-out-again flowers . . ."

"That's asking an awful lot from a bunch of blooms."

"What can I say? I like to shoot for the moon."

Paige turned, setting the vase on the countertop in front of Riley's slightly cluttered desk. It was great having him in the office. He was a fast learner, and he knew her so well he could intuit what she needed before she even asked.

But beyond that, something seemed to be shifting in her. She found herself seeking him out sometimes, wanting his opinion or even just his reaction.

She gave herself a mental shake. She just wanted him to feel needed and appreciated. His self-esteem had taken a huge hit. The loss of his leg weighed heavily on him, she could see it in his eyes.

"Shoot," Dylan said. "I knew I should've gone for the roses."

She turned, realizing he'd taken her silence for rejection, and offered a smile. "Roses are so predictable."

He took a step closer. "Does that mean you'll go out with me again?"

For some reason Riley's face flashed in her mind, his green eyes beckoning.

Beckoning? What was the matter with her?

She had to get rid of these silly thoughts. And what better way than the handsome man standing right in front of her? A man who wasn't her best friend. A man who actually seemed to be entertaining the thought of kissing her.

"I'd like that."

He moved closer, the toes of their shoes almost touching. "I'll call you next week?" His voice was deep and quiet in the stillness of the lobby.

"Sounds like a plan."

The familiar tap-shuffle of Riley's gait reached her ears before he entered the room, Bishop on his heels.

Riley's gaze toggled between them as the guys greeted each other. Then his eyes settled on Paige. "You 'bout ready to shut down for the night?"

She checked her watch. They still had an hour before they had to be at the Roadhouse, but she wanted to grab a shower. "Sure."

Dylan nodded at Riley as he took a step back. "I should get going. I'll call you about Friday."

"Sounds good." She walked him to the door and let him out, conscious of Riley behind her. When she turned, he was staring at the flowers on the counter.

He jerked his eyes back to her. "I'll put the dog back, then we'll head out."

She watched him go, feeling oddly torn. Then she shook her head. *Stop it, Paige. You're being weird.*

So weird. Her girlfriends had always thought it odd that she had a guy for a best friend. "Doesn't the girl/guy thing get in the way?" they'd asked. They'd gush about how attractive Riley was and marvel that Paige didn't even seem to notice or care.

But lately she was noticing. Noticing the sharp turn of his angled jaw, the deep olive tone of his sun-kissed skin, the amber flecks in his pensive green eyes. His build wasn't exactly a turnoff either, with those broad shoulders and corded arm muscles.

She walked to the window air conditioner and turned it on. Cool, stale air blasted her warm cheeks. She leaned against the window ledge.

It is not okay to be thinking this way, Paige Warren. He's your friend—your best friend. He doesn't have corded muscles or pensive green eyes.

Except he did. And now that she'd noticed, she couldn't seem to go back to seeing him the way she had before.

Okay, fine. He's a good-looking guy. He's well built. That doesn't change anything.

So why was she standing here dithering over this, needing an air conditioner to cool her cheeks? *Gah!* She raked her fingers into her hair and tugged.

"Ready?"

She whirled around. The sight of her purse hanging from Riley's shoulder made all her previous thoughts tumble from her head.

"Goes great with your outfit," she said with a smirk. "You can borrow it sometime if you like."

"I prefer your white one," he deadpanned. "It makes me look tanner."

And just like that they were back on familiar ground.

Chapter 12

*I*t was Friday night, and the Roadhouse was packed. The dozen or so TVs hosted the Red Sox game, but Paige didn't care much about baseball. She did, however, take great delight in squeezing into the big corner Callahan booth. Dinner with the family was among her favorite things.

Riley settled in beside her, propping his crutches against the booth. They were the last ones to arrive, save Zac, who was in the kitchen, probably dealing with some crisis.

A pool game was under way in the back room, and someone had started a country song on the jukebox, making all the sports fans scowl as they strained to hear the game. Laughter, chatter, and the clinking of silverware filled the room, and the tangy smell of buffalo wings prevailed.

They ordered and settled into conversation, topics surfacing as quickly and randomly as air bubbles in a pot of boiling water.

"How's the center going?" Eden asked Lucy.

Lucy, who'd inherited her great-aunt's fortune, had put the money to use on a community center. She'd converted the old firehouse into a pretty nifty hangout that mostly served kids and teenagers.

"Terrific," Lucy said. "I scrounged up another volunteer. Ellen Mays is going to help out on weekends. And she's going to snap some professional photos for the website."

"That's great," Eden said. "Let me know when you have them, and I'll put them up."

Zac appeared, squeezing into the other side of the booth next to Lucy. "Sorry. Got caught up in the kitchen."

"Everything okay?" Miss Trudy asked.

"Just the normal Friday night chaos. Did you order for me?"

"A big ol' basket of hot wings," Lucy said.

"Perfect." He dropped a kiss on his wife's lips, then murmured something too quiet to hear. His palm found the curve of her cheek and he went in for another kiss.

"Here we go again," Riley muttered.

Eden cleared her throat. "So . . . Paige . . . how are things coming with the bachelor auction?"

"Great. The community center is the perfect venue—and for the unbeatable price of free. Zac agreed to provide appetizers and drinks for free, and we have about—"

"Hey . . ." Zac stopped making eyes at his wife long enough to frown at Paige. "Nobody said anything about free."

"That got his attention," Beau said.

"Give me a break," Zac grumbled. "I haven't seen my wife all day."

"A whole twelve hours?" Riley said.

"So, anyway . . . ," Lucy continued. "We have a venue, food and drinks, we're working on advertising plans, and we'll all pitch in with the decorations."

"I'm making the bidding paddles," Miss Trudy said.

"And I added a page about the auction to the shelter's site," Eden said. "Once we have pictures of all the bachelors, I'll put those up, and we can post the link on our Facebook pages."

"So what's the verdict?" Lucy asked, eyeing Riley. "Is your picture going to be up there, Riley?"

He frowned. "What?"

Lucy's eyes darted between Riley and Paige. "Oh. Sorry. I thought surely you'd have asked him by now."

"I've been—busy." Right. Like she hadn't had a chance, what with working together and living in the same house and basically being together 24/7.

Riley nailed Paige with a look. "What's she talking about?"

She shifted in her seat. "We thought, you know, you might be willing to help out with the auction."

"As a bachelor," Lucy added enthusiastically.

Paige aimed a scowl her way. This was not the way she'd wanted this to go down. She'd wanted to warm him up to the idea. Maybe hint around about it and give it a chance to sink in before she went in for the kill. Yeah, that's what she'd been waiting for.

"Um . . . ," Riley said. "That would be a big fat no."

At his answer some of the tension eased from Paige's shoulders, and she frowned at her reaction. She'd effortlessly talked three other single men into entering the auction and had been thrilled with their consent.

"Why ever not?" Lucy asked.

Riley's body stiffened as he wiped his palms down his pants. "I can think of about twenty reasons."

"Well, we have to have at least one Callahan or the ladies'll be disappointed," Miss Trudy said. "And these two are taken." Her gaze swung to Beau, who was nuzzling his nose in Eden's hair. "Clearly."

Riley gave Paige a dark look, as if this was somehow all her fault. "Ain't happening." His voice was low and growly.

"But we only have eleven bachelors," Lucy said. "And we need an even twelve. Our theme is the Twelve Men of Summer."

"Not my problem."

"Come on, man," Beau said. "Take one for the team."

"You know what?" Riley shifted from the booth, his movements rigid and jerky as he gathered his crutches. "You take one for the team. I need some air."

After turning another sour look on Paige, he hobbled away, through the restaurant and out the front door.

"Whoops," Lucy said.

"Well, he can't go far," Zac said, earning a scowl from Paige.

She scooted toward the aisle. "I'll go talk to him."

Miss Trudy set a hand on her arm. "Now, now, give the boy some space. He needs to cool off."

A while later, as they finished their food, Paige was still trying hard to keep Miss Trudy's advice in mind.

Zac had slipped off to the kitchen again, and Lucy had gone to the restroom, when Sheriff Colton came by the table. Beau invited him to sit a spell, and when Miss Trudy didn't budge, Paige scooted over, making room on her side.

The sheriff took off his hat as he sat, revealing his shaved head. He'd been coming around Miss Trudy for years, blushing and stammering, but Miss Trudy wouldn't give him the time of day. The others had found out only recently that the two had been secret high school sweethearts.

"How's the visitor center going, Trudy?" The sheriff eyed her across the table, his usual flush working its way up from under his collar.

"As usual." Miss Trudy took a delicate sip of her clam chowder.

"Our class reunion's coming up," he said. "The emails have been flying back and forth. You planning to go?"

"I haven't decided yet."

"Should be a good group of us. Sure be nice if you could make it."

"You should go together," Beau said.

Miss Trudy shot him the look of death. A long pause hung in the air.

"Oops . . . ," Beau offered into the gaping silence.

"I'd be honored to escort you, Trudy." The deep pink had worked its way up into the sheriff's cheeks, making them clash with his fiery red mustache.

Miss Trudy tossed down her napkin and stood. "If I decide to go, I can get my own self there, Danny Colton." Back ramrod straight, she grabbed her purse and stalked off toward the exit.

The sheriff shrank in his seat, his face finding an even deeper shade of pink.

Beau gave a nervous chuckle. "Was it something I said?"

Chapter 13

*R*iley shuffled into the shelter behind Paige, who held the door for him. Things had been awkward between them since the night before. The thought of being on that stage beside all the other bachelors—whole, healthy bachelors—was enough to darken his already foul mood.

What had the girls been thinking? Who'd want to go out with him now? Oh, he'd get plenty of bids all right—pity bids. His skin heated at the thought.

He ignored the pain in his stump as he hobbled over to the air conditioner. Paige headed toward her office, flicking on lights. He was getting ready to punch the On button when a shriek reached his ears.

He turned as fast as he could and hobbled toward the hallway, coming to a stop a couple feet in, right behind Paige.

The tips of his crutches were covered in water. The dampness began seeping into his shoe.

"What in the world!" Paige dashed ahead, splashing through the inches of water.

Riley struggled to follow her. Dogs were yapping in their kennels, but he passed the door, looking for the source of the flood.

At the end of the hall he came to a stop at the utility room, where Paige was shutting off the spigot.

Her hands turned, palms up. "What—? How—?"

Riley tore his eyes from her shocked face, staring at the overflowing tub. Yesterday came rushing back. The boxer in need of a bath. Going for shampoo. Hearing Paige and Dylan in the lobby.

Had he turned on the water? He couldn't remember. Surely he wouldn't have left it running.

"The animals . . ." Paige pushed past him, splashing up the hall, and disappeared into the kennel.

Riley followed, his heart pounding, his thoughts spinning. No. He did not do this. He couldn't have. His eyes scanned the hallway where water inched up the woodwork and into all the rooms along the way. The carpet in Paige's office, the boxes on the floor in the supply closet. The bags of dog food, kept on the floor . . .

He entered the room where Paige was, the cacophony growing louder as he pushed the door open.

"Help me get them outside."

The water was barely into the cages. Paws were wet, and the cats were distressed, but no damage had been done in here.

"They're fine," he said.

Paige shot him a look. Tears trembled on her lashes. "They're not fine! They're terrified!"

He opened a tabby's cage while Paige passed with two dogs in her arms. He dumped one crutch so he could carry the cat outside. He didn't know why he bothered. The tabby clung to him for dear life, its claws going right through his shirt and into his skin.

Paige returned, putting two of the more aggressive dogs into higher kennels and grabbing the boxer and a mixed breed. By the time they had the animals outside, Paige's cheeks were wet with tears.

Riley's gut clenched. This was all his fault.

Paige put the boxer in a run and closed the door. She picked up the little mixed breed, who was still shivering, and cuddled her close.

Paige raked her fingers into the hair at the nape of her neck and squeezed. "I don't understand. How could this have happened?"

The weight in his chest grew heavier. He had to tell her. "Uh, Paige, I—"

"You were outside before we left, and I didn't use the tub all day yesterday. Could someone have broken in and done this?"

"Paige, I—"

"Should I call the sheriff? The front door was locked, but they could've come in another way. Did I leave a window unlocked? Why would someone do this? I should call the sheriff."

She pulled her phone from her pocket.

"Paige." Riley grabbed her arm, unsteady on his crutch. *"Paige."*

She finally looked up at him, mid-dial, and the sight of her panicked blue eyes cut right through him. After everything she'd done for him, this was how he repaid her? She was going to hate him. And she should. This was going to cost her a fortune she couldn't afford, and it was all his fault.

"What?" She was looking at him, something like hope filling her eyes and, man, how he hated to disappoint her.

He swallowed hard, then forced the words out. "This is—this is my fault, Paige."

She studied him, confusion in her eyes, waiting.

"Yesterday after you left me out here, I decided to give the boxer a bath. You'd mentioned he needed one. But there was no shampoo by the tub, so I went to the supply closet." And then he'd heard Dylan's voice and gotten all jealous. But he couldn't tell her that. "I got . . . distracted. I must've turned on the spigot and forgotten to shut it off."

"But how— I can't— Are you—?"

He watched helplessly as the emotions in her eyes shifted from confusion to denial to frustration. Her face grew flushed, and finally her lips pressed together. A sure sign she was holding back what she really wanted to say.

"I'm sorry. I'll help you get it cleaned up. I'll stay here as long as I need to. I'll pay for all the damage."

"Do you have any idea—?" She clamped her lips against the words that obviously wanted to tumble out.

"Go ahead and say it. Say whatever you want." He deserved it. He was a real idiot. Who left a spigot running all night?

She drew in a long breath, her shoulders rising then sinking as she blew it out. "It was an accident." Her voice trembled like she was holding on by a thread.

"That's not what you were going to say. Not what you want to say."

He needed her to be real with him. They'd always been honest with each other, and he sure didn't need her holding out on him now just because he was a cripple.

"It doesn't matter."

His jaw flexed. "Yes it does."

She set the dog down. "We should get this cleaned up. I have a Shop-Vac in the—"

"Stop it."

She huffed at him. "Stop what, Riley?"

"Stop treating me different. You never held back on me before, why hold back now? I was an idiot, so call me a flipping idiot."

"You're not an idiot." She turned to go inside.

He took her arm. "I flooded your shelter."

"It was an accident."

"It was stupid. Just say it."

She jerked her arm loose. "Stop it."

"Just say it!"

"Fine! You're an idiot. Are you happy now?" She nailed him with a look before she spun on her heels and headed back inside.

Strangely enough, he wasn't happy at all.

Chapter 14

The shelter was eerily silent at o'dark hundred. Riley lined up the drywall sheet in the hallway.

He and Paige had worked all day to clean up the mess—his mess. It had taken half the day to Shop-Vac the water and sort through the things that had been sitting on the floor. The bottom of the drywall in the hallway had been ruined, as had the carpet in Paige's office. Beau and Zac had helped, removing the wet drywall and replacing the carpet. The upholstered chair in her office was ruined, along with stacks of files.

They'd opened every window and brought in all the fans and dehumidifiers they could borrow. They'd worked through the day in strained silence. He'd had to force her to stop for lunch, and the weariness in her slumped shoulders when they'd locked up for the night made him want to kick the nearest wall. He'd decided right then that as soon as she was asleep he was coming back to hang the new drywall.

As it was, the supplies they'd purchased were almost five hundred dollars, not including the carpet, and they'd lost at least that in dog food and supplies. Paige said her insurance would cover it, but Riley felt personally responsible.

He heard a low whine and stopped his efforts to listen. He should check on the animals. His body needed a break anyway. He maneuvered himself off the floor. Man, his stump ached like a big dog, and his back and other leg were sore too. He'd already taken his pain meds.

Fatigue pressed on his shoulders as he hobbled stiffly toward the kennels on his crutches, feeling every ache and pain. He hadn't been so worn out since the Crucible at boot camp. Nice to know one day of normal physical activity now left him as exhausted as fifty-four hours of field training had before.

He opened the door and moved into the dimly lit room. It was quiet except for the boxer's whimper and a crude snoring sound coming from another one of the kennels.

Riley leaned down and released the latch on Bishop's kennel, encouraging the dog to come out.

"What's wrong, bud? Can't sleep?" The dog stared up at him, his eyes like coal in the dimness. Riley scratched behind the dog's ears until his legs grew tired.

"All right. Come on, boy." The dog followed him down the hall, his claws clicking on the tile. If he was going to be here all night, he might as well have some company.

❧

Paige slipped from her car and headed toward the shelter. She'd slept fitfully, worrying over the shelter and then over Riley.

She'd left him at home in bed, going so far as to slip into his room and turn off his alarm. She'd stopped at Wicked Good

Brew for her caffeine fix, not wanting to wake him with the coffee grinder. He'd worked far too long and hard yesterday, refusing to leave until she did.

She'd asked him many times to go home and rest or, at the very least, take a break. But he was so stubborn. She knew he was angry with himself for leaving the faucet on. Shoot, she'd been angry with him too.

But her ire morphed quickly into concern when he refused to stop. She hoped he hadn't done anything to set back his recovery. He was supposed to get fitted for his temporary prosthesis in two weeks, and she knew he was looking forward to that. But if he had swelling or got an infection it would have to be postponed. It was important for him to get upright and independent again. The sooner he was able to walk, the better for his mental health.

She slipped the key into the lock and twisted. The door opened with its familiar creak. She hated to work on a Sunday, but she needed to get a couple hours in before church. Having closed the shelter yesterday, she was behind. There were at least a dozen messages on her voicemail, and a couple bills were going to be late if she didn't get them into tomorrow's mail. To say nothing of the work she had yet to do to repair the water damage.

The dogs, hearing her entry, began moving restlessly, barking and yapping, eager for food and attention.

A strange chalky smell drew her attention, and she frowned as she made her way through the lobby, fearing another disaster.

Oh please, God, not something else.

It took her a moment to realize the smell was coming from the hallway. The new drywall was hung and seamed, the mud still in the process of drying.

Who in the world had done that? And when? Unless there was a home improvement fairy no one had told her about—

The bell jangled as the front door opened, and Paige whirled around. Riley hobbled through the door. He'd walked the three blocks on crutches?

She entered the lobby, taking in his bloodshot eyes. His short hair was smooshed on one side, and a pillow crease marred his left check.

His eyes homed in on her, and he frowned. "Did you turn off my alarm?"

"Maybe." A niggling suspicion was blooming in her mind, and she crossed her arms. "Did you come back here last night?"

He lifted a brow. "Maybe."

It was him? He'd not only worked all day yesterday, but half the night too?

Her pulse sped as heat flushed through her body. *"Riley . . ."*

"Paige."

She nailed him with a look as she thought of how much time it must've taken to hang the drywall. And heaven knew what else he'd done during his midnight madness. She didn't even know how he'd managed on one leg.

She stalked toward him. "You are going to set yourself back, you foolish man. Is that what you want? I was going to handle all this today, as you darn well know."

His jaw ticked. "It was *my* mistake."

She threw her hands up. "You're impossible, you know that?"

"A simple thank you will do."

A simple— "Gah!" She spun on her heels. She needed to get away from the stubborn man before she said something she'd regret.

Chapter 15

Fitful nights were starting to become a habit. Paige turned over and tossed the sheets off, noting the time: just past one.

There was a new uneasiness between her and Riley that was as unsettling as it was frustrating. She probably owed him an apology for calling him an idiot after the flooding, though he'd practically begged her to do so. Why had she let him get to her?

She'd worked Sunday afternoon and had gotten caught up. Riley had finally gone home at three o'clock, when it was apparent there was nothing more he could do. She hoped he'd taken a nice, long nap.

He had supper on the table when she got home. The meal was an awkward affair filled with stilted comments and punctuated silences. She couldn't help but notice the way he winced when he moved, but she knew better than to say anything.

She rolled to her back and was just considering some chamomile tea when she heard a scream.

Paige jumped from her bed and dashed toward the stairs. Riley must be having a nightmare. She took the stairs quickly and headed toward his room. A low groan greeted her as she hit the threshold.

She slid to a halt, remembering the way she'd startled him awake the night of his arrival.

"Riley," she said into the darkened room. "Wake up."

Another low moan carried across the room.

"Riley!"

"I'm—awake," he gritted out. His breathing was loud and irregular.

She flipped on a lamp, illuminating the room.

His hands clenched the sheet, and a sheen of sweat coated his forehead. "Cramp," he groaned.

She rushed to his side. "What do I do?"

"Heating pad." His eyes squeezed shut. "Dresser."

She found the heating pad and fumbled with the cord until she had it plugged in behind the nightstand. She flipped it to High and stood helplessly, waiting for it to heat.

Riley clutched his stump, his back arching as he breathed through a spasm. His face looked carved from marble. He sucked in a shallow breath and held it.

She'd never felt so stinking helpless. Tears burned the backs of her eyes. "What can I do? Tell me what to do."

Seemingly lost in pain, he grabbed his stump and pressed his fingers into the flesh.

Massage. Hadn't she read something about this?

She brushed his hands away and pulled back the sheet. "I'll do it."

He pushed at her hands, but she fought back. "Let me!"

He gave up, grabbing fistfuls of sheet as she began massaging the flesh. His stump was bare, the compression bandage lying on the nightstand. The muscles spasmed under her hands, knotting and jumping. She wondered how long he'd suffered before she'd heard him.

Riley squirmed. Paige pressed harder into his quivering flesh, praying she wasn't doing more harm than good. How long would it take the heating pad to warm?

He'd had some cramping since his return, but nothing like this. It was all those hours of work at the shelter. She'd known he was overdoing it. She was angry at herself for not insisting he quit, and she'd be angry at him, too, if she didn't feel so darn bad for him.

A groan tore from his lips before he clamped them shut.

Her eyes stung with tears. "Oh, Riley." She redoubled her efforts at massage. "Is this helping? Do you want me to quit?"

He jerked his head.

She continued to massage, the minutes crawling by until her hands began to ache with the effort. Still she kept on.

Was it better? His eyes weren't squeezed quite as tight. His knuckles were still white against the blue sheets, but the muscles of his thigh didn't feel as hard and knotty.

"Heating pad," he whispered a few minutes later.

She grabbed the pad, relieved to find it nice and warm, and placed it over his stump, pressing down as if she could force the heat into his spasming muscles. The end of his stump was bare, and for the first time she saw the pink scarring on the tender flesh.

It seemed unfathomable that weeks ago a doctor had sliced away his leg. It felt so violent and cruel. And she was suddenly filled with the intense desire to kiss that wounded, vulnerable part of him.

Riley batted her hands away. He grabbed the sheet and jerked it up over his stump. His breaths were regular and quick now, his eyes open and avoiding hers.

"Better?" she asked.

He nodded.

"Do you need some meds? A glass of water?"

"No. I'm fine now." But the troubled, angry look in his eyes did nothing to reassure her. "Thanks. You can go back to bed."

What if it happened again? What if she didn't hear him next time? Maybe she could get one of those baby monitors for his room. Yeah, he'd love that.

"Are you sure you're okay? What if you get another one?"

He looked at her for the first time since she'd entered his room, his eyes glittering darkly in the low light. "I'm *fine*."

He didn't sound fine. But pushing him, she'd found lately, was the surest way to upset him. And after seeing him in such awful pain, that was the last thing she wanted to do.

Chapter 16

$\mathcal{R}$iley grabbed the mail from the floor in front of the shelter's door slot. The act of bending down with crutches was a real bear. He'd just been casted for his temporary prosthesis and would have it in a couple weeks. He couldn't get rid of these crutches soon enough.

After standing upright and regaining his balance, he flipped through the letters, mostly junk, then dropped them on Paige's desk.

He could hear some dogs barking as he passed the kennel, but he was in no mood to deal with them. Lately he couldn't seem to pull himself out of the funk he'd fallen into the night of his cramp a couple weeks ago.

He was angry that she'd seen him so weak and vulnerable. Angry that she'd seen his ugly flesh. That everything that used to be easy was now so hard. And what did he have to look forward to once all this rehabilitation was behind him? A menial job a world away from Summer Harbor and the people he loved.

There was so much darkness inside, it welled up and came gushing out at the worst times. Paige, being so convenient, had become the recipient of his ugliness. He'd been negative and surly, and he knew she was about at her limit. He could tell by the way she'd clamped her lips down this morning when he'd snapped at her.

She'd had a date with Dylan Saturday night. Riley had arranged a boys' night out with his brothers to take his mind off it. But even that failed to lift his spirits.

They didn't deserve his rudeness, and neither did she. Paige had done nothing but help him. But somehow he couldn't seem to stop himself, and that only fed his anger. His feelings for her only added to his frustration. Why couldn't he pull himself out of this vicious cycle?

He'd stopped going to counseling after that first session. Couldn't bring himself to go back. Just what every man wanted—some stranger staring at him, waiting for him to share his deepest feelings. How could anyone understand what he'd been through?

He hadn't had the nerve to tell Paige he'd quit. She still dropped him off every Tuesday night like clockwork. Fortunately the counseling center was right around the corner from the Sugar Shack, where he'd begun indulging in a weekly homemade cinnamon roll. He took it down by the harbor and watched the lobster boats coming in for the day, remembering when he was out there. When he was following in the footsteps of generations of Callahan men. When he had a real purpose.

Riley kept himself busy for the remainder of the afternoon—proofing a couple ads, answering the phone, and taking stock of the medications.

When closing time came, he flipped the sign in the window and went to find Paige. She'd steered clear of him most of the day. And after the way he'd spoken to her this morning, who could blame her?

He found her at her desk, shoulders slumped, head in her hands, fingers plowed into the thickness of her hair.

The sight of her defeated posture, so unlike her, flooded his veins with worry. His own frustrations, all the stuff he'd been dealing with since he got home, ceased to matter.

"What's wrong?" His voice vibrated with tension.

Her head snapped up, the vestiges of worry replaced by surprise. Her hair was ruffled from her busy fingers, and if he wasn't mistaken, her eyes were a bit bloodshot.

"Nothing." She lowered something in her hand. A letter. She folded it up carelessly, then glanced at her watch. "Is it that time already?" The cheerful note rang false.

"Something's wrong." He gestured toward the letter. "What's that?"

"Nothing. It's nothing."

But he could see by the way she tried to make the letter disappear that it wasn't nothing. His eyes fell to the empty envelope on the desk, and he remembered it from today's mail.

"It's from the insurance company. What did it say?"

She stood and began gathering her things. "It's just a letter. Not a big deal. Did you call the vet about the spaniel? We should probably get him to check for an ear infection, don't you think?"

She probably would've gone straight out the door if he weren't blocking the exit.

He crossed his arms—not an easy feat with a crutch—and stared her down for a full ten seconds before he spoke. "I think you should tell me what's going on."

She stared right back, her chin lifting a fraction of an inch. Her lips pressed together.

"I'm not moving until you tell me."

She started to go around him, but he shifted his weight to block her. He had the advantage; she wouldn't take chances with his balance.

She scowled at him. "You're a bully."

"Tell me."

She gave him a withering look.

He held his ground, and half a minute later her façade began to crack. The tightness around her eyes softened. Her lips relaxed. Her shoulders sank.

"They're dropping me," she said finally.

His jaw clenched. This was all his fault. The flooding was all on him, and that's why they were dropping her. He closed his eyes. He was such an idiot. He'd done nothing but make things worse for her since he'd come back. She'd be better off without him. They all would.

"Hey . . . it'll be fine." She infused the words with an enthusiasm he knew she didn't feel. "I'll find another company. You'll see."

He turned and hobbled down the hall, his crutch hitting the floor hard with each step. "And they'll charge you an arm and a leg. Ha! Isn't that fitting?"

"Riley, stop it . . ."

"Stop what? Stop making trouble for you? Stop being a huge pain in the—"

She grabbed his arm, turning him. "You're not a pain."

His skin felt hot. He couldn't even look at her. He was too angry at himself. And this time he wasn't taking it out on her.

"It was an accident. This kind of thing happens all the time with businesses. I'll ask Zac for advice. It happened to him a while back. It'll be fine."

His head was swimming, darkness swelling. And, as if his

missing leg just wanted in on the action, a sharp stab of phantom pain darted up his leg. He needed to get away before he lashed out at her again.

"Sure," he grated out, turning.

But she tightened her hand on his arm, stopping him. "Riley . . . we'll get through this. I promise. I know it's hard right now, but I-I love you."

His eyes flickered back to hers, looking deeply, wishing for something that just wasn't there.

"We should go." This time when he turned away, she didn't stop him.

Chapter 17

$\mathcal{P}$aige carried her empty plate to the sink, leaving Riley at the table. One more awkward and silent supper in the bag. He'd been disturbingly quiet since the day before. She preferred the Riley who lashed out to this tense, quiet version who seemed coiled up and ready to spring. Even so, either was preferable to the fake cheerful thing he'd done upon his return to Summer Harbor. At least this was real. Honest.

She opened the dishwasher and grabbed the dirty cookware from the stove top, aware of the scrape of his chair on the floor. She stopped herself—barely—from grabbing his plate off the table. He wouldn't welcome her help.

She'd thought therapy the night before might help him sort out his feelings, but he'd come away just as pent up as when she'd dropped him off.

"I'll do these." Riley had managed to sneak up behind her. She drew in a whiff of his spicy sent and imagined she felt the warmth of his chest at her back.

Warmth of his chest?

She pressed forward against the front of the sink. "I got it."

"Move."

If she thought his tone brooked no argument, the scowl on his face left no room for misunderstanding. She set down the plate she'd been rinsing and dried her hands. "Fine." She tossed the towel and spun to leave, but he grabbed her arm.

"I changed my mind . . . about the bachelor thing."

She couldn't think past the tingles shooting up her arm. "What?"

"The auction. Go ahead and sign me up."

Realization of what he was saying made the tingles fizzle away like the remnants of a firework. She fought the cloud of dread that threatened to engulf her and smirked at him. "Has a cold front passed through hell recently?"

"If you think it'll bring in a few extra dollars, I'm game. It's the least I can do."

A few dollars? Her eyes scrolled over his face. Even frowning, he was the handsomest man she'd ever known. Those deep-set green eyes, the straight slash of his brows, the rugged planes of his face. All of it somehow softened by a fringe of dark lashes. And that was just from the neck up.

Half the women in Summer Harbor would be lining up for a chance with him. The Callahan brothers were the town's most eligible bachelors—or had been. Now there was only one left, and he was a broody, handsome marine.

She swallowed hard. "You don't have to do this, Callahan. We've got it covered."

"I want to."

"You don't look like you want to."

The muscles in his jaw flickered. "Well I do."

She imagined him on that stage surrounded by dozens of swooning women. She imagined a tall, svelte redhead taking his hand and leading him from the stage. She imagined them disappearing off into the sunset.

Her heart kicked hard, making her breath catch in her lungs before it raced faster. She should've found their twelfth bachelor.

"Paige?"

She redirected her focus. "I was going to ask Mary Ann's cousin."

"Well, now you don't have to."

She cocked her head. "Riley . . . are you sure you want to do this?"

"What, stand on a stage and make a fool of myself? Even I can do that right."

She was so tired of the way he put himself down. She smacked his arm. Her hand practically bounced off his solid bicep.

Something in his eyes shifted as he gave her a long, searching look. "Or maybe you're afraid I won't raise as much money as Mary Ann's cousin."

Was he really that clueless? "Don't be ridiculous."

A flush climbed his neck as his gaze fell to the floor. He shifted his weight to his crutch. "Maybe you should go ahead and ask him."

She sighed hard. "No, Riley. You'll round out the roster very nicely. I'll tell Eden to add your name to the website."

His eyes lifted to hers again. His nose flared. "Now you just feel sorry for me."

She threw her hands up. "Gah! You're impossible."

"Seriously, if he'll bring in more money for the shelter, ask him. I don't blame you."

"You idiot. What is wrong with you? Don't you know women will be lining up for a date with you?"

His eyes narrowed to slits. "Yeah, 'cause every woman is dying to go out with a gimpy loser."

She put her hands on her hips and glared right back. "You know, it's really too bad you can't see yourself the way everyone else does. Maybe when a dozen women are waving their paddles in the air it'll finally sink in."

Before he could respond, she whirled away and stormed up the stairs. Let him do the dishes. Let him stand there and stew about what she'd said. Maybe some time alone would do him good.

She pulled out her phone to text Eden. Sign Riley up for the bachelor auction.

She hit Send before she could second-guess herself.

Her heart was beating a million miles per hour. What was wrong with her? Why did it bug her so much to think of Riley with other women? And those tingles . . . what were those about? Hadn't one Callahan man been enough for her? Now she had to go for Beau's brother too? Her *best friend*?

You are one sick woman, Paige Warren.

She'd done a lot of soul-searching after Beau had broken up with her. They'd never been meant to be. They'd been missing that spark, that something special. It didn't take her long to figure out the main appeal had been his family. The Callahans had what she'd never had—and had always dreamed of. A real family. A place to belong.

Did she want it so badly she was now manufacturing feelings for Riley? She shook her head. Pathetic. Just pathetic.

A text buzzed in, and Paige looked at the screen.

Yay! I'll add him to the roster. That is awesome!

Paige sighed as she closed the program. Yeah. It was flipping awesome.

Chapter 18

*R*iley looked down at the temporary prosthesis as the technician gave it one final tweak. He couldn't believe this day had arrived. He'd hardly slept last night in anticipation of standing upright, of walking again.

The prosthesis felt tighter than he'd expected. It hit him that this bulky piece of equipment was going to be part of him for the rest of his life. The thought made his heart thump against his ribs.

"All right," the prosthetist said. "Let's give this a try."

Riley's breath hitched. He grabbed the parallel bars and pushed to a stand, his weight balanced between his arms and legs. It felt awkward, but he was upright and on his own two feet—even if one of them wasn't real.

Using his arms to brace his weight, he took his first unsteady step. It felt strange. He was grateful for the bars.

"Looking good," the technician said. "How's it feel?"

"Good. I think." He wasn't sure how it was supposed to feel.

He walked down the length of the bars slowly, carefully, his arms trembling. He turned and came back. It was tedious. It was exhausting. But he was walking. He was really walking.

"How's it feel?" Beau shot Riley a look from the driver's seat of his pickup.

Riley looked down at his prosthesis. He looked a little like a robot.

"Like I've got a fake leg attached to me. There's a lot more to it than I expected. All the donning and doffing stuff . . . desensitization . . . stretching and strengthening . . . I hope I remember it all."

"It's in the take-home stuff if you need a refresher. And you can always call if you have questions."

"I have an appointment with the physical therapist later this week." He was going to work his butt off to get back on his feet. "I thought I was done with those things." He gestured to his crutches in the back.

"Give yourself time. You're young and strong, so that helps. Did he say how long it would take to walk without them?"

Riley shrugged. "It's one of those everyone-is-different kinds of things. But I read some people can walk after a couple weeks. I plan on being one of them."

"I have no doubt you can do whatever you set your mind to."

The sooner he became self-sufficient the sooner he could drive. The sooner he could move to Georgia. "At least I'll be on my feet for your wedding."

"I'm just glad you'll be there."

"Unlike our other brother, who didn't bother waiting for my return."

Beau spared him a look. "Stop crying. We Skyped you in."

Riley looked down at his prosthesis and wondered whether the thing would be his friend or foe. He'd been looking forward to this day for weeks, but he hadn't expected to feel so awkward and clumsy. The prosthetist said the fit was critical, told him what to watch for in the way of problems, and warned him he'd likely need to come back regularly for adjustments as his stump shrank. Now there was a pleasant image.

"Don't forget the tux fitting is Wednesday."

"I won't."

He was happy for his brother. Anyone could see Eden was better suited for him than Paige had ever been. He was sure he'd feel that way even if he weren't in love with Paige himself. But he had to admit it was a huge relief to know it was Eden, not Paige, who was becoming his sister-in-law.

He remembered the sheer misery of being on the sidelines while they dated. Was it any wonder he'd resorted to joining the Marines?

And look at him now. Just when Paige was finally available, when he was finally back from overseas, he was unfit for any woman, least of all her.

Not that she had the slightest clue how he felt. She'd never guessed, not in all these years. He must be one heck of an actor. There had only been one close call.

He'd thought the gig was up that night of their eighteenth summer, after her dad died. He asked her over after the funeral, but she wanted to be alone. He was worried about her in that little house, alone with her mother. Not that Darleen would ever physically hurt her. But she'd offer no comfort either. He'd told Paige to call him later, but it was after nine o'clock and he'd heard nothing.

He tried to call, but there was no answer. Worried for her, he borrowed his dad's truck and made his way to the place she went when things were bad at home. He parked along the street and followed the grassy trail back to the pier on the inlet where the Warrens moored their boat.

He was relieved to see the boat still tied up, and a few seconds later the pier came into view. Paige sat at the end, tucked into a ball, facing the water. The vestiges of twilight streaked the sky with pinks and purples, silhouetting her small frame. Water rippled against the shoreline, and the boat bumped rhythmically against the dock.

His shoes thumped quietly on the wood as he moved down the pier. She must've been lost in thought, because she didn't seem to notice the sound or the way the dock shimmied under his weight.

She lifted something and, when her head tilted back, the silhouette of a dark bottle came into view. It took him a second to configure the facts and arrive at the only reasonable conclusion.

How many parties had they been to where Paige only nursed a can of Coke? He knew for a fact she'd never even tasted an alcoholic beverage. Her family had taught her from an early age that drinking was a sin, and though Riley's own perspective was a little less conservative, he knew Paige would never resort to drinking unless something was terribly wrong.

Her relationship with her dad had been complicated. And now he was suddenly gone, and she had all these unresolved feelings. Clearly she wasn't thinking straight.

When he reached the end of the pier, he grabbed the Jack Daniels from her hands. "What are you doing?"

She looked up at him with eyes that were so sad he almost regretted his sharp tone. "Riley." She patted the space beside her, losing her balance and nearly toppling over. "Have a seat."

The bottle was almost empty. He sighed, lowering himself to the end of the pier and setting the bottle out of her reach.

"Where did you get this? You shouldn't be drinking. You could've fallen in the water."

"It's only a few feet."

She clasped her arms around her knees, staring at her toes as if mesmerized by the peeling pink polish.

"You should've called me."

"I couldn't." She belched and covered her mouth belatedly.

"Why not?"

"Darleen took my phone."

He frowned. He'd never heard her call her mom by her first name. "What happened?"

A duck swooped low across the inlet, feet reaching forward, before it came to a graceful landing on the water.

Paige shifted beside him. "She's not my mom."

He set his arm around her shoulder. "She's not much of one, that's for sure. But it'll be okay. You start college in a month, and you'll be gone most of the time. You won't have to see her much."

"No . . ." She shook her head dramatically as she turned toward him. "No, I mean, she's really not my mom. My dad ch-cheated on her when they lived in Augusta, and he got me."

"What?"

"Yep." Her lips popped with the "p" sound. "He had an affair with some woman, and she got pregnant, and then Mo—*Darleen*—found out, and all hell broke loose." She leaned around him, looking, her forehead scrunched up. "Where's my bottle? I want my bottle."

He grabbed her shoulders to keep her from falling over. Looked her in the eye. It couldn't be true. But even as he struggled with disbelief, in so many ways, it made sense. The way Darleen treated her as an afterthought. The way her dad stood by and did nothing about it.

"If that's true, where's your real mom?"

Paige lifted her shoulders. "She died when I was two. Dad talked Darleen into taking me in, and they moved here to start over."

"She told you all this? *Tonight?*"

He wanted to throttle the woman. She couldn't have waited until things had settled down? Until Paige was no longer caught up in a vortex of grief? But no. It had always been about Darleen. She couldn't wait ten seconds after her husband died to spill the truth.

"I'm not hers," Paige said softly. "She never even wanted me."

The forlorn sound of her voice plucked at his heartstrings. He tightened his arm, pulling her into his chest. He wanted to protect her from all this. He wanted to rewind time and stop Darleen from shooting off her mouth.

Even as he wanted to rail against Darleen, he mentally stepped into her shoes. Paige must've been a daily reminder of Donald's betrayal. A bigger person could've separated the two, could've loved the child anyway. But they both knew Darleen wasn't that person.

He clenched his jaw hard. Paige deserved so much better. And she sure hadn't deserved to hear the news from a bitter woman who'd done nothing but make her feel like an outsider—and on the same day as her dad's funeral.

It had always angered him that Paige's dad didn't stand up to Darleen. Not when she grounded Paige unfairly or when she gambled away Paige's babysitting money. Now he knew why. Donald was living out a penance for his betrayal. But he hadn't been the only one paying the price.

Paige started to pull away. "What'd you do with my bottle?"

"Shhh." He tucked her back in tight. "You don't need that now. I'm here."

"My legs feel all tingly."

"I know." He kissed the top of her head, breathing in the sweet, flowery scent of her.

He had to take care of her. There was no way she could go home like this. Darleen would ground her for a year. Shoot, she might even kick her out of the house now that Paige's dad wasn't there to stop her.

He'd have to bring her to his house. His dad wouldn't be thrilled about her condition, but he wouldn't turn her away.

The sun's warmth was long gone, and Paige shivered as a cool breeze swept across the inlet. He rubbed her arms to warm her as he stared into the heavens. What would happen now that the truth was out? Would she even be welcome in her own home?

Help her, God. Remind her she's loved. So much. He set his chin on her head.

A few minutes later her weight began to sag against him. He looked down to see her eyes had closed.

"Paige?"

"Mmmm."

"Come on. It's getting dark."

She buried her face into his chest.

"Paige. We need to go." He jostled her until she lifted her head. Then he stood and helped her to her feet, steadying her when she wobbled.

"Where we going?"

"My house."

She didn't argue as he led her to the truck or on the short drive back to his place. He called his dad on the way home and explained what had happened. When they got there, his dad opened the door, compassion in his eyes.

"Take her on up to your room. You can take the couch."

Paige had grown quiet in the car, closing her eyes a lot, probably drifting off. She was still quiet as he led her up the stairs and turned into his room. The last bit of daylight filtered through the curtains, giving him enough light to see by. He bypassed the light switch and led her straight to his twin bed. She wavered on her feet as he pulled back the covers.

He unzipped her light jacket and helped her out of it. She wore a T-shirt and a pair of shorts that would be comfortable enough to sleep in. A moment later she flopped onto her back with a sigh. Her blond hair fanned out on his pillow, her lashes black shadows against her cheeks.

He slid her sandals from her feet and pulled the covers to her shoulders. "Get some sleep," he whispered.

"Stay." She grabbed his hand, her eyes flicking open. "Please? Just for a minute."

He'd never been able to deny her anything. Certainly not after a day like today. He sank down on the edge of the bed, turning so his knee was propped near the pillow's edge.

"I don't want to be alone," she said.

He tightened his hand on hers. "You're not alone. Not ever."

Her eyes grew glassy, and her breathing turned ragged. "I don't know what I'd do without you, Riley." She grabbed the collar of his shirt and pulled him down. She held him against her chest, clamping her arms around his head.

Her heart thudded in his ear, the warmth of her skin pressing against his cheek. The sweet, flowery scent of her tugged at his senses.

Her hands moved sloppily over his head. "You're a good friend, Callahan."

Friend. He swallowed hard. It was difficult thinking in those terms with his face smashed up against her—

"You're the only one who's there for me. Don't know what I'd do without you."

"You won't have to find out, honey." His words were garbled against her chest. He flattened his palms against the bed and pushed.

But she grabbed his face, holding him inches from her.

"Thank you." Her eyes were smoky blue in the dim light. Her breath teased his lips an instant before she touched them with her own.

It was barely a brush. Soft and quick. And not nearly enough. Their breath mingled between them. His heart kicked against his ribs, his good judgment evaporating in a flood of want.

He lowered his mouth to hers one more time. Her lips were soft and yielding. Responsive. A thrill shot through him, and he brushed her lips again. Warmth surged through him, urging him to continue with his slow exploration.

She was kissing him back. The wonder of it kindled a fire deep inside that flared outward to the tips of his fingers. He trembled with hope.

Her fingers moved into his hair, stirring every follicle to life. If this was a dream, he didn't want to wake up. He wanted to stay here forever, kissing this girl.

He slowly became aware of the faint taste of alcohol on his lips. He remembered the bottle—almost empty. Guilt nagged at the edges of his conscience, pulling him further and further away from his most excellent dream until the distance brought clarity. Reason.

What was he doing? She was tipsy, if not outright drunk. He

was taking advantage of her. Even if she didn't seem to mind—and she didn't. He hung on to the thought long enough to extend the kiss a few delicious seconds. Then he reluctantly pulled back.

His breath came fast and shallow. The air in the room felt stifling.

Her hands fell away, and he missed them immediately. Her eyes remained closed, her breaths feathering his lips with little puffs. He brushed the hair back from her face, wishing she'd open her eyes and look at him for just a second. Acknowledge what had happened. Admit that something had changed.

But her eyes remained closed.

A long minute later her breathing began to even out, growing deep and steady. Ignoring the sting of disappointment, he eased off the bed and pulled up the covers. When he got downstairs, the TV was off and the lights were out. His dad had put a quilt and pillow on the sofa for him.

He lay in the dark, the quiet swimming around him as his mind rewound the last few minutes. No question, she'd kissed him back. She'd even kissed him first.

But her kiss had been more like a friendly peck. And the alcohol was a factor. She'd been under the influence, possibly doing something she never would've dreamed of, never even wanted.

When she woke up, was she going to be horrified? Maybe. And what excuse would he have? He was completely in his right mind. She was going to know his feelings went far beyond friendship.

And what if that wrecked their relationship? The very thing he'd been carefully avoiding for a whole year, and he'd undone it all in one night. In a moment of weakness.

He tossed and turned for a long time and must've finally fallen asleep, because next thing he knew light was shining through the living room curtains. He heard a clank in the kitchen and sat up, the smell of coffee reaching his sleepy brain cells.

He checked the time. His dad would already be out on the water, and Beau and Zac had classes, which meant—

Paige came through the kitchen door, wincing against the daylight, a mug of coffee in her hand. "You're up." Her voice grated across her throat. "I brought you coffee."

"Thanks." He shifted the quilt.

She set down the mug and lowered herself onto the coffee table across from him. Her hair was wild and messy around her face. She had black smudges under her eyes, and he figured he had to be crazy in love because he thought she was just about the sexiest thing he'd ever seen.

She massaged her temples. "Remind me never to drink again."

"Headache?"

"The headache of all headaches."

He started to sit up. "I'll get you some—"

"I already took ibuprofen."

He sank back against the sofa cushions.

"Sorry about rooting through your medicine cabinet, but I was desperate. I drank two glasses of water, and I'm still thirsty, and my mouth feels like it's stuffed with cotton balls."

His eyes dropped to her lips, sticking there for a long moment. He pulled them away before she noticed, a flush rising into his neck at the memory of those lips on his.

"Did that really happen?" she asked.

His eyes darted to hers, his heart kicking his ribs hard. "What?"

"I still can't believe it's true. Everything she told me."

Oh. That. He had to put aside his own fears and focus. Her eyes looked so sad. He stifled the urge to pull her into his arms again. "I can't either. I'm sorry. I can't believe she told you like that."

"I wish they'd told me a long time ago. I feel like my whole life has been a lie. I don't even know who I am anymore."

"That's not true. You're still the same person you've always been."

"I guess now I know why she hates me so much. At least there's a reason. I always figured it was me. That I was just too much trouble."

"She doesn't hate you," he said. But deep inside he wondered if it was true. "And you're not a bit of trouble. Shoot, one of us Callahans alone is more trouble than three of you would be."

"Did you text her and tell her where I was?"

"Yeah. Hope that's okay."

"What'd she say?"

"Not much. She probably knows what she did was inexcusable."

She played with the hem of her shirt. "Did—did your dad see me like that?"

He swallowed hard, his heart beating up into his throat. "You don't remember?"

She closed her eyes in a long blink as if searching her memory files. "Not really. I remember walking with you down the dock, then the next thing I remember is waking up here."

Relief flooded him. She didn't remember the kiss. Didn't know he'd kissed her like she was his long-lost lover.

"Dad was cool about it, but you've definitely got a lecture coming. I hope you don't mind, but I told him what happened with Darleen. He won't say anything to anyone."

"That's fine. I trust him. I can't believe I drank all that." Her blue eyes locked onto his, softening. "Thanks, Callahan. For taking care of me."

His heart skipped a beat. "Anytime."

"Would you mind taking me home? Darleen'll be at work, and I just want to go back to sleep."

She was quiet as he drove her home a while later. His thoughts spun with everything that had happened. A weight had settled heavily in his midsection and wasn't budging. He tried to tell himself it was relief that she didn't remember the kiss.

But then he remembered the way she'd responded to his touch, so sweetly, so eagerly. Despite her drunken condition, hope had sprung to life last night, filling him with anticipation. But now the new weight inside crushed every last bit of hope, pressed down until his lungs could barely expand.

"We're here."

Beau's voice called him back to the present. Somehow they'd arrived back in Summer Harbor and were pulling into Paige's driveway. The drive was empty, and he was momentarily glad she was still at work.

He thanked his brother for the ride and moved awkwardly up the porch steps using his crutches. The house was warm, smelling of Paige's sweet perfume. He opened a window, letting a fresh breeze chase away the fragrance.

The memory of that kiss was like a kick in the pants. He couldn't go back and change his decision to enlist. He couldn't wish his leg back on his body. All he could do was work with what he had—however little it might seem.

Improvise, adapt, overcome. It was time he applied the philosophy to his life.

Paige was never going to feel the same way about him, and even if she did, he wanted more for her now. She deserved so much better than half a man. He looked around the living room, seeing Paige in every piece of art, in every throw pillow and flower arrangement.

He was going to do everything he could to get back on his feet. It was time to move on with his life, and he couldn't do that until he put some miles between himself and Paige.

Chapter 19

rumpy Joe's was filled with the usual rush of morning customers. Paige didn't mind the ambient noise of silverware and chatter. Somehow the familiar sounds of chaos helped soothe her troubled spirit.

Across from her, Lucy set down the laminated menu. "All right, sugar, what's ailing you? You've hardly said a peep since I sat down."

The server brought her glass of orange juice. "Thanks," Paige said before the woman scurried away.

She had been distracted. Riley had been acting so strange this week. Somehow she thought she'd see a little of the old Riley again once he got his prosthesis. A hint of hope or eagerness.

Instead he was all dogged determination with his exercises and stretching. He was walking without his crutches now, only a slight unevenness to his gait. He fell into bed exhausted each night. And he seemed to have built a cement wall around himself to keep her out. When she woke him from a nightmare, he pretended he was fine and asked her to leave. When he startled from a loud sound, he brushed off her concern.

She was glad to see the surliness go, but the disconnectedness made her feel like an outsider looking in. You'd think she'd be used to the feeling.

"I'm just in a funk," she finally answered with a sigh. "I don't know why—things are going well at the shelter. I found a new insurance company with decent rates, I've got three new sponsors, and I finally found a girl who can take Riley's position in about a month. Best yet, she's happy with the salary I was paying Lauren."

Lucy's brows notched up. "That's awesome. See, we're getting there. Cheer up."

"We still have to raise enough funds at the auction to tide us over until we receive the new donor funds and find a couple more benefactors with big bank accounts. And hopefully at least one of the grants will come through."

"We still have what, a little over a month? We can do it. You should be thrilled, and instead you look like someone ran over your puppy."

Paige tried for a smile. "You're right. I've prayed my heart out for this, and God's answering my prayers. I should be more grateful."

Lucy tucked her brown hair behind her ear. "I wasn't trying to lay a guilt trip on you. I was subtly hinting for you to spill your guts."

"I'm not used to subtle. You pretty much have to hit me over the head with a brick."

"I thought that's what I was doing when I said 'spill your guts.'"

She was dying to talk to someone about these weird feelings she was having for Riley. Since Lucy's return to Summer Harbor, she'd proven herself a trustworthy friend. As long as . . .

Paige bit her lip. "You can't tell Eden. Or even Zac."

"Okay . . ."

"It's personal, and I'd just die if anyone else found out."

Lucy set her hand over Paige's. "Hey. You can trust me to keep my lips on lock-down."

"I know that, I just—" She just needed to get it out there. Stop hoarding these feelings. Maybe it was one of those things that would disappear once she acknowledged it. The thought gave her courage.

"I've been having these weird feelings that come and go—okay, mostly come—ever since Riley got home." The words came out in a rush, and she met Lucy's gaze, wincing.

Lucy raised her brows. "Feelings like . . . more than friendly feelings?"

"Feelings like my heart beats faster when he's close, and my mouth gets all cottony, and I'm suddenly noticing the smell of his cologne, and the cut of his biceps, and his beautiful hands, and the way his deep voice is so darn sexy—come on, tell me you haven't noticed these things."

Lucy gave her a look. "Um, I haven't noticed these things."

Paige's shoulders slumped. What was wrong with her? "Women have been bringing food over for Riley, you know? *Single* women. Well, guess who brought him a tuna casserole last week? Roxy Franke."

"And . . ."

"I keep forgetting you're from away. Roxy's this girl he dated in high school. You should've seen her practically drooling all over him. I wanted to shove her perky little nose right in the casserole."

Lucy chuckled. "Paige. Your feelings are evolving. It's not unheard of, you know."

"I already dated his brother, for pity's sake. I'm starting to think I have a Callahan addiction."

"Well, if you have to have an addiction . . ."

"He's my best friend. He calls me by my last name. I'm his buddy, his pal, his *bro*."

Lucy smirked. "I'm pretty sure even Riley has figured out you're a girl."

"You know what I mean." She covered her face. "Gah! I just want it to go away. I want things to go back to normal."

"How do you know he's not sweet on you too? Maybe there's something there. You guys would make a great couple."

Paige gave her a look.

"You should pray about it. Maybe it's no coincidence he couldn't recuperate at the farm. Maybe God put the two of you up close and personal so you could see each other in a new light. You should talk to Riley about it."

Paige dropped her hands. "Oh no. That is not happening."

"Obviously you're compatible. You've been friends for years. Maybe his feelings could shift too."

"Or maybe he could think I've gone totally *insane*."

The server approached and took their orders. When she left, Lucy's brows were puckered thoughtfully.

Paige thought she'd feel better after she'd spilled the beans, but she didn't. If anything, she felt more agitated than before. And the feelings sure weren't gone. She took a sip of her OJ and noticed her hands were shaking.

Get a grip, girl.

"You should at least think about touching on the subject with Riley. Y'all are close. You share everything."

"Well, not this. He doesn't feel the same way, and it'll only make things awkward. He'll feel sorry for me and conscious of everything he says and does. Or worse, he'll think I just feel sorry for him, and before you know it he won't even want to be around me."

"Not possible."

The thought of losing Riley made her gut tighten into a huge knot. It had about killed her when he'd left for the military. What would it be like to lose him for good? He and the Callahans were the only family she had.

"We're under the same roof, not to mention we work together. The poor guy wouldn't even be able to get away from me."

"I know, but . . ." Lucy tapped her chin. "Maybe you can make that work in your favor."

That piqued her interest. "Like how?"

"Like make him see you in a different light. Make him see you as a woman."

"And how am I supposed to do that?"

Lucy's gaze scrolled over her face until Paige felt like crawling under the table.

"What? Why are you looking at me like that? Do I have drool on my face?"

"I was just . . . You're a natural beauty, sugar. That gorgeous mane of blond hair, those blue eyes. You have great skin. But maybe a few little tweaks wouldn't hurt. Take your hair out of that ponytail for starters, and give the top a bit of lift, you know? Maybe a little mascara, a little lipstick."

Paige gave her a wry grin. "Careful, your Southern roots are showing."

"I'm just saying. Maybe if you make him see you in a new way . . . Hey, the wedding! It's the perfect opportunity. You'll be all spiffed up. Do you have a date yet?"

"I was thinking about asking Dylan."

"You have to ask Riley."

"I'm not asking him on a date!"

"Think about it. You'll be looking all beautiful, there'll be romance in the air, and dancing . . . it's the perfect opportunity. Do you have your dress picked out?"

"I was going to wear slacks and a blouse."

Lucy's eyes widened in horror. "Oh, honey." She shook her head. "No, no, no. We're going dress shopping. And you're coming over to my house to get ready for the wedding. By the time we're finished with you, Riley won't know what hit him."

Paige couldn't get Lucy's words out of her head the rest of the weekend. Riley spent a lot of his free time with his brothers, and part of her felt relieved. There was a strange tension in the air. Or maybe she was only imagining it.

She spent the extra time mulling over what Lucy had said. Mulling and praying. Lucy didn't think her feelings for Riley were out of bounds. Maybe Paige was making too much of it. Maybe all those people who'd said men and women couldn't be just friends were right.

Maybe she should do something about it.

One thing was sure. Paige was right about her ponytail. And about her general appearance. She couldn't remember the last time she'd put on mascara, much less lipstick.

It wouldn't hurt to show him a different side of her, and the wedding was the perfect opportunity. She was even going to ask him to be her date. It made perfect sense. What woman wanted to attend a wedding alone, much less the wedding of her ex-boyfriend?

She'd ask him tonight when he got home from the Roadhouse. She'd planned to ask him after church, but she'd chickened out.

Come on, Warren. Make this happen.

The growl of an engine sounded outside the window, followed by the popping of gravel on the driveway. She peeked out the curtains. The headlights of Beau's truck stopped in front of her house. A car door slammed, and her heart began racing in her chest.

"Well, here goes," she said to Dasher, who blinked at her with knowing eyes.

A minute later the door opened, and Riley came through.

All her bravado drained away at the sight of his scowl.

She clutched Dasher more tightly. "Hi. Did you have fun?"

"Sure." He set down his crutch, which he still needed for steps, and walked into the kitchen, his gait looking amazingly even. He was getting more independent every day. All he needed was a full-time job, and he'd be moving out of her house. She swore she could hear a second hand ticking in the background.

The faucet kicked on, and he reappeared a few seconds later with a glass of water.

"Beau getting excited about the wedding?" she asked.

He gave her a long, assessing look, and she wondered if he thought she was still hung up on his brother.

"He's pretty impatient," he said finally. "If it were up to him, they would've been married a year ago."

"I'm really happy for them. They make a good couple." Too obvious? She bit her lip.

He seemed to relax a little.

Maybe not.

"Think I'm going to turn in." He headed for his room. "Good night."

She couldn't let another day go by. The wedding was only five days away, and what if he asked someone else? Someone like Roxy Franke.

"Wait!"

He turned, his brows raised.

Dasher mewled, and Paige released her death grip on the cat. "Um . . ." *Just do it already, Paige.* "Speaking of the wedding . . . You got a date yet?"

His lips pressed together. "No."

She breathed in a fresh batch of courage. "Well . . . I don't either. We should, um, go together." Her stiff shrug felt anything but casual.

He frowned at her for a long second. "I thought you'd go with Dylan."

"No. Nope. I'm free as a bird." Her little chuckle sounded forced. And nervous. She wondered if he could see her heart pounding through her shirt.

"So . . . ?" she said.

"You should probably ask someone else. Someone who can dance with you."

"You're getting around great. Come on. We're both going. We may as well go together."

He shifted, ran his fingers through his hair as his gaze cut away. "I don't think so."

She knew that look. He was trying to think of an excuse. He didn't want to hurt her feelings. Her face burned. But time was running out, and this was feeling increasingly like a last chance.

"Come on. We always said if one of us didn't have a date, we'd be each other's backup."

He gave her a droll look. "We never said that."

"Well . . . we should have. I hate going to weddings alone. It's humiliating. And this isn't just any wedding, you know . . ."

A shadow shifted on his face as his jaw twitched. "Right." He stuffed his hands into his pockets as his eyes left hers to dart around the room.

Her mouth had gone dry, and prickles of heat poked her under her arms. She'd die on the spot if he knew how fast her pulse was racing at the thought of rejection.

He exhaled a hard sigh. "Fine. We'll go together."

He continued to his room, closing the door behind him with more force than necessary. But even his obvious reluctance couldn't squelch the bud of hope that bloomed inside her.

Chapter 20

Zac exited the tuxedo shop's dressing room, running a finger around the inside of the collar. Riley could hardly believe it was time for the final fitting. Beau's wedding was only two days away.

"I feel like a penguin," Zac said.

From a nearby stool, Riley scanned his brother from head to toe. "You look like one too."

Zac's eyes flickered over Riley's identical tux as he hiked a brow. "Don't know how to break it to you, bro . . ."

"Oh, stop your whining," Beau called from inside his dressing room. "The ladies love a well-dressed man. You should be thanking me."

Zac considered himself in the full-length mirror, his countenance brightening as he shifted to and fro. He stood up straight, his tall frame eating up every inch of the mirror.

"You're going to break that thing," Riley said.

"He's got a point, you know," Zac said. "Lucy's going to like this. She's going to like it a lot."

Riley rolled his eyes.

"At least I've got a date. Who you going with, Romeo?"

Riley barely held back a grimace. He'd been having big regrets since he'd agreed to be Paige's date. But what was he supposed to do? It was obvious she'd feel humiliated if she had to go alone. And yeah, part of him had been relieved she wasn't going with Dylan. He sure hadn't been looking forward to watching that all night. Still . . .

"Well . . . ?" Zac buttoned his top button and shifted, admiring himself. "Don't tell me you're going alone."

He sighed. "I'm going with Paige."

Zac's eyes met his in the mirror, then he turned around. A moment later he strolled over, lowering his voice.

"Has there been a new development there?"

"Sure," Riley whispered. "She doesn't want to show up at her ex's wedding without a date. There's your new development."

Zac made a thoughtful face. "*She* asked *you*? That's interesting."

"Convenient would be a better word for it. Not to mention painful. Now I have to spend a whole night reminding myself she's just my friend."

He had to get out of Paige's house. Out of Summer Harbor. Just a little more work with his leg, and he'd be able to operate his motorcycle safely. His replacement at the shelter was starting in a month. There'd be nothing holding him here then.

"You're looking at it all wrong," Zac said. "This is an opportunity."

"For her to see me as the gimpy date who can't even spin her around the dance floor?"

"Don't be such a Debby Downer. This is your chance, man."

"It's too late for that."

"What do you mean it's too—"

"Anyone know how to put these on?" Beau emerged from the dressing room, messing with the cuff links at his wrist.

Riley nodded toward a middle-aged employee. "That lady helped me with mine."

"Man, these things take forever to get into," Beau said.

Zac smirked. "Bet it won't take Eden long to get you out of it."

Beau gave him a harsh look as he gestured toward the dressing room Eden's dad was using.

Zac held up both hands, palms out. *Sorry*, he mouthed around a laugh.

Beau smacked him in the back of the head before he walked away, which only made Zac laugh harder.

Chapter 21

The doorbell rang, and Paige's heart skipped a beat. "It's Riley."

"Of course it's Riley." Lucy put one final spritz of hairspray on Paige's hair. They were in her and Zac's apartment above the Roadhouse, which was closed for the day. Zac was already at the church with Beau, and she and Riley were getting there early, too, since he was a groomsman.

Lucy gave Paige's curls one last poof. "There we go. You are absolutely gorgeous. If Riley can't see that, he's blind. I'll get the door. Wait a few minutes, then you can make a grand entrance."

"But I don't want to . . ."

Lucy was already gone, her heels tapping down the stairs.

Paige met her worried gaze in the full-length mirror. Her blond hair cascaded over her shoulders in glossy waves. Her makeup, while (thankfully) minimal, made her skin look flawless and somehow drew attention to her eyes. The rosy lipstick made her lips look full. She'd never looked better. But was she setting herself up for failure?

She stepped back, letting her eyes fall to the dress Lucy had finally agreed to after Paige had tried on what felt like a million options. It was fitted enough to show off her curves and sported a modest scooped neckline. The teal blue set off her golden brown skin. The straps were wide enough to allow for a regular bra, but left more of her arms showing than she was used to.

"You have great arms," Lucy had said when Paige had complained at the boutique. "Slim and toned. And those legs!"

She heard Lucy and Riley's muffled voices downstairs and wondered if she'd waited long enough. She was so bad at this boy/girl stuff.

"It's just Riley," she said to her mirror image. But somehow that knowledge only made it worse.

❧

Riley pulled at his collar. Supposedly the tux fit him to a T, but he thought a suit of armor might be more comfortable. At least the pants covered his prosthesis. At the bottom of the stairs Lucy attempted to make small talk, but he was so nervous he could hardly follow her from one subject to the next.

It seemed forever before he heard a shuffling at the top of the stairs. He turned, and his breath left his body at the sight. It was Paige. Good ol' Paige. Only tonight she looked like an angel. He wouldn't have been the least surprised if she sprouted wings and flew down the staircase.

She'd done something with her hair. It was falling past her shoulders in curls, and that dress . . . It called attention to all the right places, stopping just above her knees. He'd seen her legs before; she wore shorts when they played basketball. But that was different. Way different. And those heels . . .

He felt a compulsive need to swallow, which made no sense. His mouth was as dry as moon dust. As she descended the steps, his eyes flittered back to her face. Man, she was beautiful. Her eyes looked wider than usual, and they seemed to sparkle somehow.

She bit her lower lip, drawing his attention there. She had the most luscious lower lip. Full and pink and utterly kissable. How many times had he imagined soothing it with his own after she'd bitten it, just as she was now?

Behind him, Lucy cleared her throat.

Realizing Paige had reached the bottom of the stairs and he was still gawking wordlessly, he dragged his eyes from her lips.

"Look at you." He cleared the hoarseness from his voice. "Don't you clean up nice."

He winced. *Wow, you sure have a way with words, Callahan.*

If she was disappointed with his stupid comment, she didn't show it.

"You're wearing a dress," he said.

She lifted a brow. "Your powers of observation are astounding."

"I don't think I've ever seen you in a dress."

"Probably because I've never worn one." She tilted her chin up at him and flashed a smile that about made his good knee buckle.

Aw, man. It was going to be a long night.

A while later Riley stood beside Beau and Zac listening to Pastor Daniels ponder aloud the virtues of love and marriage. From the other side of Eden, her attendants, Miss Trudy and Lucy, looked on.

The chapel's lights were dimmed, making the sanctuary feel

smaller and more intimate. Candlelight flickered on the altar, and the fragrant scent of lilacs wafted through the air.

Eden looked beautiful in her simple white gown. It being her second wedding, she hadn't splurged on a fancy dress or numerous floral arrangements. The long engagement hadn't been about planning for a grand wedding, but planning for a grand marriage.

It had been Beau who'd insisted on the tuxes, and as Riley swallowed against the tight collar, he wondered if it was merely to make his brothers suffer.

He shifted slightly on his prosthesis, careful of his precarious balance. He'd been practicing walking in the fancy shoes since he'd picked up his tux two days ago. He hoped he didn't do something stupid like fall on the way down the aisle. Even standing here so long was testing his agility.

Pastor asked Beau and Eden to face each other as he continued with his thoughts on Christian marriage.

Riley caught a glimpse of Eden's face and knew a moment of complete joy for Beau. Her love was shining on her face for the world to see. She'd come a long way in the past year. After her emotionally abusive marriage, she'd needed time to find herself, to become strong again. Beau had been supportive of her efforts. So patient.

Riley's only regret was that their parents weren't here to see this happy moment. His eyes cut over to the empty spaces on the front pew where two white roses lay in memorial to them. They'd be so happy for Beau. He was the true big brother, always looking out for everyone else. No one deserved happiness more.

He swallowed against the lump in his throat as his eyes shifted to Paige in the next pew back. She was looking at him, her eyes a little glassy, as if she'd read his thoughts. She probably had.

Her lips tilted upward as their eyes caught and held. A moment of sweet communion suspended between them like a wispy vapor. Would anyone else ever understand him the way Paige did?

"Eden . . ." Pastor Daniels's voice boomed in the chapel. "Repeat after me."

Riley tore his gaze from Paige and watched as Eden repeated her vows, her eyes firmly planted on her groom.

"I, Eden Martelli, take thee, Beau Callahan, to be my lawfully wedded husband. To have and to hold from this day forward, for better, for worse, for richer, for poorer, in sickness and in health, to love and to cherish till death do us part."

He couldn't see Beau's face as he repeated back the vows, but his voice was low and unwavering. His love for Eden was as strong and steady as hers for him.

He felt a pang of longing that started as a surface wound and burrowed deep until he ached from the inside out. He'd never have that with Paige. He was just her buddy. Her pal. Maybe she even had feelings for Beau still. Maybe that was why she'd been desperate for a date tonight.

The ache bloomed until it pressed against his lungs, making his breaths quick and shallow. He kept his eyes on Beau, not daring to look at Paige for fear she'd see his every thought.

Somehow he got through the rest of the ceremony. He made it down the aisle without tripping, endured the receiving line, and made it through a short photo shoot.

By the time he reached the reception hall at the community center, his jaws hurt from holding a fake smile in place. White twinkle lights, candles, and some kind of poufy fabric draped here and there made the place feel intimate and romantic. Lucy had done a terrific job.

The bride and groom were announced and applauded, then the strains of "The Way You Look Tonight" began to play. Riley watched from the corner of the room as the happy couple, all eyes on them, shared their first dance.

When the song was over, other guests joined the bride and groom on the dance floor. He scanned the transformed interior and found Paige sitting at a round table near the dance floor with Aunt Trudy.

He made his way through the crowd, stopping to chat with neighbors as he went. Several of them hadn't seen him since his return and inquired about his injury and his prosthesis. They weren't happy until he'd filled in all the details, and by the time he arrived at the table, his mood had hit a new low.

It took an effort to smile at Paige. "Sorry it took so long."

"No worries. We were just catching up."

His eyes swung to his aunt. "You look pretty, Aunt Trudy," he said over the loud music. It didn't escape him that it was a nicer compliment than he'd given Paige.

"I passed pretty about twenty years ago, but I appreciate your saying so."

He shot Paige a look. "She never could take a compliment."

"Hey, Paige."

A guy he didn't recognize set a hand on Paige's shoulder. He had dark hair, pushed up at the front, and reminded Riley of a young Tom Hanks.

"Let's dance."

She gave him a polite smile. "No thanks. I'm kind of tired."

"Aw, come on. It's a great song."

"Maybe later."

He shrugged and squeezed through the crowd on the dance floor, disappearing into the throng.

"Who was that?" And hadn't he noticed Paige's date was sitting right here?

"Scott Lewis. Remember him? He was a couple grades behind us."

"A couple? Isn't he like eighteen?"

"More like twenty or twenty-one. Too young for me, though."

"It's just a dance," Aunt Trudy said. She missed the dim look he gave her. "You should have some fun. You're only young once."

His heart twisted at the thought of Paige with another man. He didn't know if he could stand seeing some other guy's hands on her again.

But he was leaving soon, and what did he want for her? An empty house with nothing but cats for company? She deserved to find someone. Maybe not Scott Lewis, but someone.

"She's right," he forced out, his throat tightening with the words. "You should dance."

"You're my date. You dance with me."

"It's all I can do to stay upright. I saw Dylan earlier. You should ask him."

She gave him a long, hard look. Something shifted in her eyes. Hardened. The corners of her lips tightened as she stared him down.

He lifted his shoulders and gave her a *What?* look.

She lifted her chin. "Fine. Maybe I will."

"You should."

She turned her back to him and set her tiny handbag on the table. "Could you watch my bag for me, Miss Trudy?" And then she was gone.

Chapter 22

*R*iley watched Paige as she scouted out Dylan at the punch bowl. The man's face lit up with a smile as he caught sight of her approach.

They talked through three songs, gradually shifting toward a corner, out of the way. A few minutes later Dylan seemed only too happy to abandon the spot, pulling her onto the dance floor. As if the universe was conspiring against Riley, the band segued to a slow song.

Dylan took Paige into his arms, resting his hands on the curve of her hips. They swayed together, Paige's hands resting on his shoulders. She looked comfortable in his arms, content.

The ache that had begun during the wedding ceremony spread through Riley's body. If only it could be him. If only he'd been patient enough to wait out Paige's relationship with Beau. If only he'd been there for her as she'd grieved the loss. Maybe her feelings would've changed. Instead he'd run away.

Dylan leaned close to catch something Paige said, taking the opportunity to gather her closer.

Every muscle in Riley's body went tense as he forced his eyes away. Was he some kind of masochist, that he had to watch?

It should be him out there with her. He should be healthy and whole and working to win her over instead of watching from a distance while someone else wormed his way into her heart. He tugged at the tight collar as a suffocating heat rose up his neck. Was there any air in this place?

"Don't you think it's about time you told her?"

His eyes flew to Aunt Trudy. She was giving him one of those looks. Her lips tight, one of her sparse brows cocked at an angle.

He made himself settle casually back in his seat. "Told her what?"

"I may be old, but I'm not blind."

"I don't know what you're talking about."

"Don't you give me that. I've watched you pine away for her for years. Watched you die a thousand deaths while she was with your brother. Now's your chance, young man, and you're wasting it. You know you Callahan men only love once. It's proven true for generations."

"Stay out of it, Aunt Trudy."

She crossed her arms, scowling. "I've never known you to be a coward, but I'm starting to wonder."

His spine stiffened as heat flooded his face. A coward? He'd gone off to war. Had watched his friend bleed out. Had lost a flipping leg. He clamped down on the words and focused on Aunt Trudy instead.

"That's pretty ironic, coming from you."

"Don't you sass me, young man."

"Sheriff Colton's been after you for years, and you've turned him down time and time again. Despite the fact that you clearly have feelings for him."

A flush rose to her cheeks. "That's altogether different."

"And why is that?"

Her mouth opened, then closed. Then opened again. And closed. "It just is," she said when she finally collected herself. She snapped her head away from him.

"The only difference is . . ." He leaned forward, planting his elbows on the table. "It's easier to tell someone else what they should do than to do it yourself."

As if the universe was also conspiring against Aunt Trudy, Sheriff Colton wandered over. He lowered himself into the empty seat on the other side of her and greeted them both.

Riley felt sorry for Colton's bad timing. Aunt Trudy had already turned her back to him. He took pity on the man. "I heard the reunion went well. Must've been nice seeing all your old friends."

Sheriff Colton straightened his tie. "It was good to catch up with the gang. Hadn't seen some of them in ten years or more." His eyes drifted to Aunt Trudy. "You're looking awfully nice tonight, Trudy. I like your dress."

She muttered something Riley couldn't hear.

"Can I get you something to drink?"

"I can get it myself."

Zac and Lucy stepped off the dance floor and took a seat at the table, bringing some much-needed distraction. Riley complimented Lucy on the decorations, and they made small talk until Zac and Lucy became absorbed in each other again. Across the table Miss Trudy was still giving the sheriff the cold shoulder.

The music shifted to a faster song, and Riley's eyes found Paige and Dylan on the edge of the dance floor. His whole body sighed in relief as they separated and began dancing independently as the jiggy beat of "Country Girl" filled the space.

His eyes slid over to Dylan. He moved effortlessly to the beat, taking Paige's hand and spinning her until she laughed. On top of everything else—looks, money, and working legs—the man had rhythm.

Riley's eyes swung back to Paige, to the smile on her face. The joy sparkling in her eyes. The ache inside about made him double over. If he loved her—and he did—shouldn't he want this for her? Shouldn't he want her smiling and laughing and happy? Even if he wasn't the one making it happen?

Aunt Trudy's rising voice drew his attention back to the table. "Well, you're the one who left me, Danny Colton! Don't you forget that!"

A pink flush rose into Colton's face, clashing with his red mustache. "It was the NBA, Trudy. What did you expect me to do? Turn the Celtics down? It was my dream."

"If you loved me you would've told me that instead of keeping it all a big secret!"

Two angry slashes formed between his brows. "You knew I loved you."

"Could've fooled me. Seemed you couldn't leave me in the dust fast enough!"

His face turned mottled red. "And what about you? I'd barely unpacked my bags in Boston before I got word you'd married Tom Barclay. *Tom Barclay*, Trudy! How do you think that made me feel, huh? So much for your love."

"I was pregnant, you big buffoon!"

Colton blinked at her with slack-jawed shock.

Aunt Trudy's eyes widened as if she just realized what she'd said. She snapped her mouth shut.

"Shazam," Zac said quietly.

"Oh boy," Riley muttered.

Aunt Trudy sprang to her feet and dashed away.

A half second later, Colton scrambled off in the opposite direction. His height made him visible even as he skirted the crowd. He went out the front door.

"I'll go talk to her," Lucy said.

Zac helped her up. "I'll come with you."

Riley stared after them long after they disappeared into the crowd.

Aunt Trudy had been pregnant when she'd married Uncle Tom? But she'd never had any children. She must've miscarried after the wedding. Surely she wouldn't have given the baby up for adoption after going to the trouble of getting married. Besides, there was no keeping something like that a secret in a town the size of Summer Harbor.

And clearly this was the first Colton was hearing of the child they'd conceived.

Riley palmed the back of his neck. What a mess. Colton was ticked Aunt Trudy had moved on so quickly, and Aunt Trudy was angry that Colton had deserted her in her time of need. Maybe now that the truth was out they could finally work through it.

He didn't know how long he sat there pondering the pair of them. He was dimly aware of toasts being made and more music and dancing as he sat guarding Paige's little purse.

Sometime later Paige flopped into the chair next to him. Her cheeks were flushed, her hair tousled and sexy. "Whew! That band is really good, isn't it?"

"Run out of dance partners?" He didn't mean to sound so grumpy, but why'd she even ask him to be her date if she was going to spend the night dancing with every guy here?

"I needed a breather." She fanned her face. "It's hot in here." She chugged down the punch she'd brought with her. "Where's Miss Trudy?"

"She went out for some air."

"Is she okay? I saw the sheriff over here."

"There was a—quarrel. Lucy and Zac went after her."

"What happened? Did they—" Her eyes narrowed at some spot over his shoulder, then toggled up to his, widening. "Oh no. Dance with me."

"Thought you were tired."

"Scott won't leave me alone, and he's headed over here."

"So ask Dylan."

"He had to leave. I need you to dance with me right now, Callahan."

"I couldn't dance when I had *two* legs."

"Funny." She popped to her feet and grabbed his hands.

He let her pull him up. For just a second he forgot about his leg, and he wobbled a moment.

Paige, on some kind of avoidance mission, didn't even notice.

Ten seconds later they were in a shadowed corner of the dance floor. The sultry strains of "I Don't Dance" began floating through the room. His heart cheered the slow song selection while his brain sent up warning flares.

Paige came closer, her hands sliding up his lapels and stopping at his shoulders. He set his hands at her waist, praying he wouldn't fall as they shifted their weight slowly from one foot to the other.

The heat of her body seeped through the thin material of her dress. Her fingers moved at his collar, sending a hum of electricity down his spine.

"Thanks for the rescue," she said. "He's a nice enough guy, but he's way too young for me."

He looked down into blue eyes that were filled with gratitude, and something inside him puffed up. *You're no hero, Callahan.* But the way she was looking at him made him feel otherwise.

"No problem." Except his heart was beating a million miles per hour, and he was having thoughts he was pretty sure she'd smack him upside the head for.

He couldn't seem to tear his eyes away from hers.

"See, you can dance."

"The song title would suggest otherwise."

"You're doing great. You've been working really hard. I can hardly even tell a difference."

"My gait's not quite right."

"You're being too hard on yourself. You should be proud."

A couple box-stepped nearby and Paige pressed closer, avoiding a collision. Riley's hands slid around her back before he'd given them permission to do so. One of her arms had wound around his neck, and the other hand lay flat against his heart. He hoped she couldn't feel how fast it was beating.

"So what happened with Sheriff Colton?"

Hoping to distract himself from her proximity, he told her the whole story. Paige gasped when he told her the secret.

"She married your Uncle Tom because she was pregnant? With the sheriff's baby?"

"Apparently."

"Oh, wow. She must've miscarried, right?"

"I guess so."

"No wonder she's so crotchety with him."

"He didn't even know about the baby. You should've seen the look on his face. He was shocked. Devastated."

"And Miss Trudy just walked off after that?"

"More like ran. I don't think she meant for it to come out. She was pretty flustered."

"Oh, poor Miss Trudy. Poor Sheriff. We should do something." He gave her a look. "We are. We're staying out of it."

"But—"

"It's none of our business."

She closed her mouth, but he knew Paige. She wouldn't leave well enough alone.

$\mathscr{P}$aige frowned at Riley. Everything in her wanted to see Miss Trudy and Sheriff Colton get their happily-ever-after. But her frown didn't last long. How could it, when she was staring into Riley's deep green eyes from inches away?

His hands burned against her back, and it was taking everything in her not to press closer and lay her head against his chest.

He let go with one hand and reached for the chain around her neck, gently pulling. The ring she wore on the necklace slid from under her dress, sending a shiver down her arms.

He held the ring in his palm. "Still wear it, huh?"

She nodded. It was the only thing she had of her dad's. He'd worn it every day. It was *his* father's airborne ring from World War II.

"He would've been proud of you, you know." Riley dropped the ring, letting it slither back under her dress.

"Thanks." She didn't want to think of her dad tonight. It only reminded her of how alone she was. Of being abandoned. First by her dad's death, then by Darleen's departure.

And let's not forget Riley. He abandoned you too.

Over his shoulder she could see Beau and Eden dancing, their foreheads together, their eyes closed. They seemed so happy, so in love. Paige felt a conflicting mix of joy and envy. Sometimes it seemed like everyone had someone except her.

Her eyes fell to Riley's lapel, where a white rose was pinned. All the Callahan men were wearing one, plus Eden's dad. Miss Trudy and Lucy wore lovely matching corsages made with sweetheart roses. They were family.

"What's wrong?" Riley's voice vibrated against her hand.

She smoothed his already-smooth lapel. "Nothing. I was just thinking about the wedding."

"You were frowning."

She gave him a wry smile. "I'm a single woman in my midtwenties. Weddings do that to us."

"There's half a dozen men in this room who'd snap you up in an instant if you gave them a second look. You'll find someone, Warren."

She didn't want just someone. She wanted *him*. Any uncertainty about her feelings for him had dissipated the instant his arms had closed around her. He was home. Maybe she was a little confused about that family thing. Maybe that played into it somehow. But she was definitely in love with him. And that knowledge scared her to death.

"Don't be sad." His arms tightened around her.

Giving in, she rested her head against his chest, curling her fingers into his lapel. They were barely swaying, his thighs brushing hers. He was so big and strong. He made her feel safe and cherished.

She wanted to freeze this moment in time, stay in it forever. If she closed her eyes she could even pretend they were really together. That he loved her the same way she loved him.

But that wouldn't be real. She'd only be lying to herself. Maybe Riley had noticed she was a woman, but it didn't matter. He wasn't interested in her the same way. She remembered Lucy's advice to talk to him and barely contained the dry laugh. Hadn't he practically begged her to dance with someone else? Hadn't she had to force him onto the floor with her?

The joy of the evening seemed to drain right out of her, leaving her limp and depressed. The poignant strains of the melody tugged at her emotions.

Riley was independent now. He'd surely be moving out soon, and his time at the shelter was almost up too. It would be good for him to manage on his own, to find something productive to do. She should be happy for him.

But those same things would take him farther away from her.

And maybe that was for the best. Maybe these stupid feelings would go away if they weren't together 24/7. The thought brought a strange mixture of hope and sadness.

Who was she kidding? She turned into his chest and breathed in his familiar spicy, clean scent. She'd gotten used to having him around. She wanted to keep him like a sweet stray puppy. Wanted to love him and take care of him.

Her hand slid down until her palm lay over his heart. How had her feelings changed so quickly? And how on earth would she keep him from guessing? She wasn't exactly known for her poker face.

And she knew Riley. If he found out, he'd do whatever he had to do to make it easier on her. He'd withdraw from her, put distance between them. He'd skip family outings so she could go without feeling uncomfortable.

And she couldn't allow that. He needed his family now more

than ever. Was she going to have to give up not just Riley, but the only family she had? It seemed too much to bear all of a sudden.

Her breath felt stuffed into her lungs, and she couldn't seem to empty them properly. Her eyes burned, and she blinked trying to get herself under control. But all those emotions were roiling inside. She was going to burst with them. She needed to get out of here before she lost it.

She pulled away from Riley, trying for a smile as she averted her eyes. "I-I'm going to get some air. It's too hot in here."

"Paige . . . ? What's wrong?"

She pretended not to hear as she made a beeline for the back door. She kept her eyes down, praying no one would stop her. She was a hot mess, and one look in her eyes would give that away.

When she reached the door she opened it, stepping out onto the deck. There were twinkle lights even out here, but thankfully she had the space to herself.

She walked to the balustrade that overlooked the broad inlet and slipped into the shadows, her hands finding the wooden railing. The air was laden with salt. The water kissed the grassy shoreline in rhythmic ripples. It was a sound that had always soothed her before, but it wasn't working tonight.

She drew in a deep breath of cool air, letting it invade her body before she blew it out in one shaky exhale.

So this was what a broken heart felt like. She'd thought that's what she had when Beau broke up with her. She knew better now. This was so much worse.

Get a grip, Paige. This isn't a tragedy. Nobody died.

But it did hurt. It hurt badly. Like when her dad died. Like when Darleen moved away the second her dad died. She actually ached in the center of her chest as if her heart really had broken in two. She placed her palm there as if she could hold it together somehow. Why didn't anyone want her?

The music grew louder as the door behind her opened. She hoped whoever it was wouldn't see her over here in the shadows. Or maybe it was just a couple looking for a nice quiet place to—

"Paige?"

She blinked away the tears that had gathered even as her heart kicked into gear. She had to get it together. And quick.

She turned and tried for a smile, hoping the shadows would hide the anguish that had rolled in like a heavy fog. She squeezed the handrail until the wood cut into her palms. "Feels much better out here. All those warm bodies in there . . ."

Her voice faded away as she ran out of steam. Her eyes found the moon, hanging over the cove like a glowing ball. Maybe Riley would see she was fine and go back inside.

But his footsteps were getting louder, his gait sounding a little uneven on the wooden planks. All the standing during the ceremony and dancing had probably tested his stamina. And now she'd dragged him outside to check on her.

He stopped beside her, a hairbreadth away, his hand close to hers on the railing. A breeze wafted across the deck, teasing her with his spicy scent.

"You okay?" His voice, so deep and delicious, scraped over her, raising chill bumps.

She shivered.

"You're cold."

"No." She winced, realizing she'd just given away a perfectly good excuse for her reaction. "The breeze feels good after all that dancing."

They stood in silence, listening to the night sounds, so

familiar. Her family had kept their boat just down this inlet, around the corner. She and Riley had spent so many hours out there talking, swimming, rowing.

"I never know what to say to you at times like this," he said.

"Times like what?"

"When that sad look comes into your eyes. When I see you looking around at everyone else, at other families, and your chin gets that little dent."

"Oh."

"I know you got royally gypped in the family department. But you'll always have us Callahans. Always have me. You know that, right?"

Her eyes burned. She swallowed hard against the growing lump. She'd always have him. But not in the way she wanted.

"Do you ever hear from Darleen?"

Paige gave a short laugh. "No."

It shouldn't hurt. The woman had never been her real mom, not in any way that counted. But she was the only mom Paige had ever known. And she had just walked away that summer. Moved back to Augusta where her sister lived.

"Your dad loved you. I know he didn't stand up for you sometimes, but he did love you. If he hadn't, he wouldn't have brought you into his family, put up with all Darleen's animosity."

"I know that." She'd settled all this a long time ago. She was at peace with her upbringing. But that hollow space inside remained, despite the Callahans' efforts to include her.

That wasn't her biggest problem, however. Not right now, with Riley inches away and a sultry breeze blowing in off the harbor. She drew in a breath, the snug bodice of her dress hampering her lungs' expansion.

Her eyes flickered over the dress. So much for capturing his attention tonight. So much for making him see her with different eyes. So much for the curls and the makeup and the sexy kitten heels.

He'd never see her as anything more than his poor little orphaned friend. Her eyes filled with tears until the darkened seascape went blurry. She swallowed against the lump in her throat, trying to get control.

"Hey . . ." He took her chin in his hand and turned her toward him. Their eyes caught and melded. The pity there only made her feel worse.

"Don't cry, honey."

He pulled her to him and, weak as she was at the moment, she went right into his arms. The endearment warmed her from the inside out. So much better than him calling her by her last name. Why couldn't things be different? Why couldn't he want her the way she wanted him?

She clutched at his back and buried her face into his chest. He felt so good, so strong. For the hundredth time she whispered a prayer of thanksgiving that he'd come back alive. She'd come so close to losing him over there. Maybe he'd never be hers, but he was still alive. Still here. His heart beating against her cheek. And that was enough. It would have to be.

He set his chin on top of her head. His sigh stirred her hair, making every follicle tingle. "I'm sorry I've been such a tool lately."

"You haven't been."

He gave a wry laugh. "Liar."

"Okay, maybe you have been. But I understand. You've had a lot to deal with."

"And I've been taking it all out on you."

"It's okay."

"Not *just* you, though. I'm a nondiscriminating kind of guy. I take it out on all my close friends and family."

She gave a little laugh. Only Riley could make her laugh at a time like this. It only made her love him more.

He rubbed her bare arm and another shiver passed through her. The roughness of his jaw tugged at her hair as he laid his cheek against her head.

"I hate it when you cry," he said softly.

"I hardly ever do." Despite her best efforts, her voice wobbled.

"That's why I hate it so much. If you *are* crying, I know you must really be hurting."

She felt a prick of guilt. He didn't need to be worrying about her. He had enough stuff of his own to deal with. Worse stuff. She was so selfish.

"I'm fine. It's just the wedding. Weak moment." She blinked back the tears and pulled away, but his arms didn't loosen enough to go far.

Her chin wobbled despite her efforts, and she bit her lip to still it.

His thumb swept across her cheek, leaving a trail of heat. Their gazes caught and held. Something flickered in the depths of his eyes, making her heart do a slow roll.

She couldn't have looked away if she tried. And why would she want to when he was finally looking at her in a way she'd only dreamed of?

Or was she imagining things?

His thumb had stopped its slow, delicious movement, making her aware of how close he stood. Of his body's warmth. Of their breaths mingling between them, a tantalizing taste that only left her wanting more.

He leaned closer. Or maybe she did. Their breaths became one, and then their lips touched. Soft and reverent. Heart-stopping.

It should be weird, some part of her brain argued. He was her best friend. But it wasn't. His kiss was everything she dreamed it would be. Supple yet strong. Commanding yet gentle. Familiar yet new.

Her heart, as if making up for lost time, raced in her chest. She slid a hand up his arm, delighting in the feel of soft flesh over solid muscle.

His fingers slid to the delicate skin of her neck, making a shiver of delight pass through her. He cupped her face, his touch making her insides melt even as his lips did things that made her knees threaten to buckle.

Riley. This was *Riley*, and he was kissing her. Surely it had to mean—

"Paige? It's time for—"

They sprang apart.

"Whoopsie." Lucy stood on the threshold, her eyes darting between them. "Uh, sorry . . . they're, um, cutting the cake. I'm going now."

"We'll be right there." Riley didn't sound the least bit shaken.

It seemed impossible, given her own condition. The way her heart pummeled her ribs, the way her breath quivered in her throat.

She dared a look at him as Lucy disappeared, but he was already heading for the door, his eyes averted. "We should get back to the party."

Chapter 24

*R*iley accelerated through the green light. His hands gripped the steering wheel so tightly they were starting to hurt. He shifted his leg. It was so fatigued, his stub aching. He probably shouldn't have insisted on driving tonight.

Paige sat in the passenger seat, practically glued to the door. A terrible awkwardness had climbed into the car with them and seemed intent on thickening with each moment that passed.

After they'd come in off the deck, it had been easy enough to get lost in the crowd. He somehow made conversation with friends and neighbors as the evening wore on. Until, at last, Beau and Eden made their exit in a flurry of flying birdseed and confetti. They were off to Key West for a week.

And he was stuck here dealing with a real mess. A mess he'd made all by himself. He had no one else to blame. Paige had been upset and emotional, and he'd taken advantage of her, just like that night when she'd been drinking. Tonight he'd taken one look at those vulnerable blue eyes and he was a goner.

He clenched his jaw. *Idiot.* He had to fix this somehow. But he had no idea how.

His mind went back to the kiss. To the feel of her lips on his. The taste of her. Everything had been good in his world for those few seconds. So right. He allowed himself to relive every brush of her lips. Every touch of her hands. Every whisper of her breath. He wanted to cement each detail into his mind. They'd have to keep him for the rest of his life.

Because as right as it had felt, he'd only caught Paige at a weak moment. He didn't dare entertain the idea that she actually wanted the kiss. It would be purely wishful thinking. She deserved so much better than he had to offer. Surely she knew that.

He remembered the sight of her dancing with Dylan. Her joy as he spun her around and around. That memory was seared in his mind also. It was the one he should hold the closest. Dylan made her happy. Riley only made her sad.

"So . . . ," Paige said, finally breaking the heavy silence. "Are we just going to pretend that didn't happen?"

Her voice sounded small in the confines of the car. He felt a pinch of guilt. He'd confused her, but good. And no wonder.

He squeezed the steering wheel. "Look, Paige . . . that shouldn't have happened. I don't know what . . ." He sighed. "It was just the wedding. Weak moment."

Her words from earlier came tumbling out of his mouth. They seemed to fit. It was as good an excuse as any. Besides, there was no need to make a mountain out of a molehill.

"Let's not make a big deal of it. It was just a kiss." It about killed him to say it. To make light of the best thing that had happened to him in forever.

"Just a kiss."

He couldn't tell much from her tone of voice. And he sure wasn't going to look at her.

"So I think you're right," he said. "We should just pretend it never happened."

The long silence clawed at him until it was all he could do to keep from looking at her. He forced his eyes to stay on the spot where his headlights converged on the road ahead.

"Sure," she said, a hint of something—relief?—in her voice.

A few minutes later he turned into Paige's drive and shut off the car. By the time he made it to the front door, she was already upstairs. He loosened his tie as he limped into his bedroom and shut the door.

He had to get out of town. He would call Noah this week and set a date to move down to Georgia. He had to get out of here before he wrecked things even worse than he already had.

❧

Lucy tugged on Paige's arm, pulling her from Miss Trudy's newly renovated kitchen and into the hallway. The savory smells of pot roast and baker's yeast lingered in the air, and the oven dinged as the dinner rolls reached completion.

Miss Trudy was busy in the kitchen, and Zac and Riley were outside, hovering around Riley's motorcycle, which they'd pulled from the barn. He was planning to ride it home. Aunt Trudy had hated the thought of him riding it even before he'd lost his leg.

"I have to get the food on the table," Paige said when they reached the end of the hallway.

"I can't believe you haven't called me," Lucy whispered.

"Um, I just saw you last night."

"Exactly. Or more importantly, I saw you . . ." She raised her finely arched brows. "*And* Riley . . . So, now that we've got a minute, go ahead. Tell me everything." She crossed her arms, waiting expectantly.

Paige lifted her shoulders. "There's nothing to tell, really."

Lucy gave her a look. "Uh, I beg to differ. His lips were all over yours, sweetie pie."

The memory of Riley's kiss hit her like a rogue wave, and a random shiver passed through her. She tried for an air of nonchalance. "It didn't mean anything. He said it was 'just a kiss.' That it was the wedding, the romance and everything. You know how that can work on the mind."

"Just a kiss. The wedding."

Okay, maybe it was more than that. Remembering the moments leading up to the kiss, she winced. "He wants to forget it ever happened."

Lucy's face fell.

"I think he just felt sorry for me. And . . . I think I might've actually kissed *him*. So it was, you know, all me."

"Um, I'm not sure what kiss you're talking about, but the one I walked in on looked pretty darn mutual."

"I was upset right beforehand. I was crying. He only kissed me back because . . . It was probably his way of . . . of comforting me or something."

Lucy laughed. "Comforting you."

"Seriously. I was feeling lonely last night. I was upset about my feelings for Riley, but he thought I was sad about having no family, and I let him believe it because I sure couldn't tell him the truth. And then I went and kissed him. What was he supposed to do? Push me away? You know Riley. He's got a tough front, but he's a softie inside. He'd never reject me like that."

Lucy arched a brow. "So it was a pity kiss."

"It wasn't even that, because *I* initiated it. It was a pity response." She closed her eyes as if she could block out the thought. "And it was so awkward afterward. Terrible."

Lucy touched her arm. "That was my fault. I barged in on you."

"I don't mean then. I mean afterward. At the reception and all the way home. By the time I got home I just wanted to crawl into bed and pull the covers over my head. Actually, that's what I did."

She pressed her fingers into her eye sockets. This morning had been just as bad. There'd been enough space between them in the pew to seat a family of five. And he'd hardly said two words to her. She didn't hear a thing Pastor Daniels said during the sermon.

"I don't know . . . ," Lucy said. "I caught him staring at you after church today when you were talking to Sheriff Colton."

"Of course he was. He was trying to figure out what planet I'm from."

"You're perfectly human, Paige."

"Well, no more kissing for me. And no more fussy hair or fancy dresses either, so just keep your womanly wiles to yourself." She started to walk away.

Lucy caught her arm. "But you didn't say . . . the actual kiss . . . How was it?"

Paige couldn't help the warm feelings that rushed over her at the thought of the moment their lips had met. Any more than she could help the forlorn smile that followed. Maybe it hadn't meant anything to him. But one kiss was all it had taken for her.

"It was amazing."

Chapter 25

*R*iley ran water in the sink for the supper dishes. He and Paige had gotten back to some semblance of normality over the past two days. Their relationship still seemed a little stilted, but what did he expect? He'd kissed his best friend.

They went through the motions at home and at work. He'd only been relieved tonight when she said she was going to the grocery after supper. It was past time to make that phone call.

He turned off the water and grabbed his cell, taking care with his leg as he shifted back to the front of the sink. Noah should be off work by now, though he and his wife, Josie, might be in the middle of supper. He dialed the number, then held the phone at his shoulder while he picked up the first plate and began scrubbing.

Dasher wove between his legs, her gray tail flicking high. She looked up at him, then slinked away as quietly as she'd come.

"Oo-rah!" Noah said.

Riley grinned at the familiar greeting. "Oo-rah!"

"Long time, no hear, Tank! How you doing, man?"

"It's all good. My brother just got married over the weekend. Lucky guy's in Key West right now."

"Good for him. She the one who was married before?"

"Yeah, she really went through it with that guy. But she's a great match for Beau."

"Have you heard from any of the guys?" Noah had just been finishing his tour when Riley started his. They'd bonded quickly though.

"Eddie and Fin called me a while back to see how I was doing," he said, referring to a couple guys in their platoon who'd finished their tours. "Seems like they're adjusting all right."

"Fin still moony-eyed over that Suzy he was missing?"

"Oh yeah. I expect he'll be putting a ring on her finger soon as he can buy one he thinks is worthy of her."

"It'd help if money didn't burn a hole in his pocket so fast."

They caught up on other details, careful to skim over the parts of the sandpit neither of them wanted to rehash. Noah seemed to be happy in his marriage, and his home improvement business was doing well.

"How's your recovery going?" Noah asked. "You getting mobile yet?"

"Oh yeah. Got my temporary prosthesis, and I'm staying busy. Still helping Paige out at the shelter." He'd never revealed his real feelings for Paige, though Noah had once come across the picture of her that he'd carried.

"Well, when you get tired of working with the puppies, we could sure use you here."

Noah's family owned the home improvement company. He'd been begging Riley to come work for him.

"Dad's itching to make his retirement official, but the work keeps coming in. I'm still at the office now, and I gotta say, paperwork is the pits."

Riley ran water over the plate he'd washed. "That's why I called.

I'm about ready to move down there. My replacement at the shelter comes in a few weeks, so I should be able to get out of here then. That apartment over your garage still available?"

"Yeah, man. Absolutely. It'll be great to have you around. You sound pretty good."

"I'm doing great. The prosthesis is working out. I'm walking and everything." He didn't mention the soreness or the blisters or the hours of therapy and exercises he'd endured. Or the cramps and nightmares that plagued him. Oh, and the broken heart. He didn't mention that either.

"Tank . . . you sure you want to do this? Leave your family and everything? I mean, don't get me wrong, I'm gung ho to have you down here. But you got a life there, and from everything you've said, it sounds like a pretty good one."

Riley thought about Paige. About Paige and Dylan dancing together. Maybe it wouldn't be Dylan. Maybe it'd be some other guy. But eventually she'd find someone she couldn't live without, and he didn't want a front row seat.

"I'm ready to move on, you know? I need a change, and I'm looking forward to seeing what Georgia has to offer."

"Warmer winters, for starters."

"I could use some of that." He tried not to think about winter at the family farm. About the miles of rolling hills covered with evergreens, or the big red barn, all of it layered with a fresh blanket of snow.

"Well, I'm looking forward to it," Noah said. "Man, you gotta save me from all these numbers."

"So I'll see you in a few weeks or so. I'll text you when I have a day and time. I don't have a whole lot of stuff to move in, but an extra hand would be nice."

He wrapped up the call, turned off the phone, and shut off the water. A sound behind him made him turn around. Paige stood on the threshold of the kitchen, a dozen emotions fluttering over her pretty features.

❧

Paige rewound the conversation she'd just walked in on, trying to make it work any other way than the way it sounded.

Ready to move on . . . need a change . . . see what Georgia has to offer.

The terrible dread that had begun blooming inside her spread like a toxic gas. An awful and familiar feeling washed over her, making her sway a little.

"Hey." Riley turned back to the dishes. "Thought you were going to the store."

And that he'd sneak in his phone call while she was gone? His casual tone wasn't fooling her for one minute.

"I forgot my list." She snatched it off the table. "What was that about, Riley?"

He finished wiping the dish, ran it under the faucet, then turned the water off. Just when she thought he was going to ignore her, he dried his hands and turned around, meeting her eyes.

He gave her a strained smile. "I was meaning to talk to you."

"Were you?" She crossed her arms. Her mind charged back to the day she found out he'd enlisted. After the fact, and not even from him.

"Look, Paige. I appreciate everything you've done for me. This has been a big adjustment, and you've been there for me every step of the way. I'm grateful."

His words, his tone, were heavy with the weight of good-bye.

"I don't want your gratitude." She wanted his love. But she couldn't say that. Hadn't she done enough? It was probably the kiss that was driving him away. Had to be. The thought sent warmth flooding into her cheeks.

"I just feel like . . . I need a fresh start, you know? Everything has changed so much. It's too hard to be here in Summer Harbor with all the memories when I can't do what I love."

"I don't see why you can't. You're getting around really well."

"Walking and lobstering are two different things. It's hard work—tough enough for an able-bodied person."

"So you're just leaving. Again." Leaving his family. Leaving her. She should be used to it by now. But she supposed being abandoned never became old hat. Her eyes burned.

"Don't take it personally."

"How can I not take it personally? You're leaving me again, just like before."

"Paige—"

"You didn't even talk to me about enlisting! You just did it. And you know how I found out, Riley? Beau told me. You didn't even have the decency to tell me yourself."

He blinked. "You're mad at me for enlisting?"

"You left me! And you're leaving again. Everybody leaves me, so why should you be any different?"

"Come on, Paige . . ."

"You come on! You already left once, and by some miracle of God you survived that awful explosion. Do you have any idea what we went through, waiting to hear?"

"I'm sorry. It's not like I got wounded on purpose."

"No, but you're choosing to leave again. Now, when you need

us more than ever." When she needed *him* more than ever. "Maybe your body's healing, but you can't tell me your mind is keeping pace. I hear you at night. I've seen the nightmares. Watched you jump every time something falls."

His jaw muscles twitched, and his eyes snapped with fire. "Stop it."

"It's the truth. You need more counseling. You'll have to start over with a new counselor if you move, have you thought of that?"

"I'll be fine."

"You'll be back to square one."

"I'm not even seeing the flipping counselor!"

Paige's response died on her tongue. *Not seeing* . . . She searched his face.

He averted his eyes. The muscles of his jaw ticked.

"I take you every Tuesday."

He tossed the towel on the countertop. "Yeah, well, I haven't been going."

She waited until he made eye contact and saw the truth in those stubborn green eyes. He'd just been pretending? All those times she'd asked him how it had gone, he'd been lying to her?

She pressed her teeth together. "How long?"

His eyes shifted away again. "I went the first time."

"The first— That's it? One time?" She stared at him. No wonder the nightmares hadn't gotten any better. No wonder he was irritable and moody and distant. How could she help him if he wasn't willing to help himself?

"It didn't go well."

"Life isn't going well. And it's not going to until you get yourself some help. You think running away is going to make everything better?"

He glared at her. "I'm not running away."

"Oh yeah? Since when did you want to live in Georgia? All you've ever talked about was settling here in Summer Harbor."

"You don't understand."

"Then explain it!"

"I need a fresh start, different scenery, different people."

The thoughtless words prickled under her skin, and she winced.

Something like regret flickered in his eyes.

But it was too late. His words had already scorched her. Different people, huh? Maybe she should've been satisfied with best friend status. It sounded like even that was in jeopardy.

"Well. Thanks for the clarification." She stuffed the grocery list into her front pocket and hitched her purse higher on her shoulder as she turned to leave. "I'll be at the store."

"Paige . . . come on. I didn't mean it like that."

She kept going until she reached her car. Then she pulled from the drive as she tried to swallow back the painful lump in her throat. But it was lodged as firmly as the pain in her heart.

Chapter 26

The atmosphere in the community center was positively euphoric. The place had been decked out with balloons and streamers. Hors d'oeuvre trays were being passed around to a crowd of mostly single women, young and old. The volume of their collective chatter betrayed their level of excitement. Others had come just for the entertainment and, of course, to support the shelter.

Paige tried to get into the spirit of things as she settled a glitch with the microphone stand. She should be ecstatic. It was a terrific turnout. Standing room only. The entry fee alone would raise a lot of money, and if the bachelors went for the amount she suspected they would, the shelter would have more than enough to tide them over until the new donors' money came in.

Lucy approached from behind the makeshift stage. "The fellas are ready. All set to go?"

"I think so." Paige tested the mike stand, finding it stable. "Do you have the order of events and the bios?"

Lucy had agreed to emcee the event. She held up the sheet of paper. "Let's get this show on the road. You might want to turn up the air. I have a feeling it's about to get very warm in here." She waggled her eyebrows.

Paige notched up the air, then went to stand at the back of the hall by the door. After Lucy got the crowd quieted, she welcomed the guests and shared about the shelter and the important role it played in the community.

Adorable pictures of dogs and cats flashed on the screen behind her as she talked, and she reminded everyone that those very animals were looking for loving homes right this minute. Charlotte Dupree was stationed at the adoption table with a sweet little terrier, ready to take appointments.

Lucy went over the auction rules, then introduced the first bachelor, one of the local volunteer firemen. He scored a thunderous applause when he strutted out onstage in his turnout gear. He turned in a wide circle, arms out, clearly in his element. When Lucy finally got control of the crowd, the bidding was started at fifty dollars and quickly began rising.

Paige relaxed her hand on her paddle. Her main job tonight was to drive the bids up when necessary, but it looked like the firefighter wasn't going to need any help.

Some of the others might not be so fortunate. After encouragement from some of the middle-aged single women in town, they'd included a couple of seasoned bachelors: Eden's dad, who was a nice-looking man in his midfifties, and Sheriff Colton. After what happened between Miss Trudy and the sheriff at the reception, Paige had decided to win him tonight as a gift to Miss Trudy—whether the woman wanted him or not.

She glanced out the window toward the deck. It was dark out there tonight, no lights twinkling under the night sky. But her thoughts were drawn right back to the night of the reception. To the kiss she'd shared with Riley under that glowing moon.

Her stomach tightened at the memory. They'd reached a kind of truce the past few days. Paige regretted her outburst. He had every right to move away, just as he'd had every right to enlist. She shouldn't take it so personally.

The crowd was growing impatient, the noise level rising, and her stomach clamped down at the thought of what was coming tonight when Riley walked out onstage. He'd been so nervous getting ready. It showed in the way his hands trembled as he knotted his tie, in the unevenness of his gait, in the way he fidgeted with his lapels on the drive over. She'd tried to calm his nerves.

"You look amazing. You're going to have a dozen women competing for a date with you."

"Charlotte Dupree will start the bidding, right? What about Joe?"

Charlotte's husband was about as chill as a person could get. "Relax. It's all set up. If she ends up winning, she's gifting you to her niece."

He gave a wry laugh. "She'll probably be the first and only bidder."

The cheering crowd, mingled with a few boos, drew her attention back to the stage. The fireman had been auctioned off to Bridgette Gillespie for two hundred dollars. Paige allowed herself a moment's relief.

Maybe things with Riley were a mess, but at least the future of the shelter looked promising. Sometimes she got way too fixated on what was going wrong. She whispered a prayer of gratitude.

The next bachelor was Nick Donahue, a handsome pediatrician who'd briefly dated Lucy. A few minutes later Lucy closed the bidding on Nick, who'd scored two hundred eighty dollars for the shelter. Maybe she should've jumped in to nudge up the bidding if everyone was going to go this high. She was going to have to pay better attention.

She felt a moment's anxiety for Riley. As much as she dreaded seeing him auctioned off to some other woman, she wanted to see him humiliated even less.

Relax, Paige. That's not going to happen.

For the next seven bachelors, Paige had fun driving up the bids. There was a lot of whooping and hollering as the women made a friendly competition out of each bachelor. Paige had gotten some playful scowls from some of the women, and some not-so-playful ones from others. Oh well. It was for a good cause.

She skipped on bidding for Scott Lewis, not wanting to give him any ideas. A pretty young lady she recognized from the diner walked off with a date with him. Ellen Mays, a local photographer, won the bidding on Eden's dad. Paige thought they made a nice couple.

Dylan was up next, and the crowd went wild when he came out in his lobsterman gear. The bidding started off strong, then faltered at one ninety, so she lifted her paddle. He sent her a wink, as he'd done with several of the other ladies who'd bid. She hoped that did the trick, because two hundred was her cap.

"All right, ladies," Lucy called. "What's it going to be? Do I hear two ten?"

Millie Parker raised her paddle.

Dylan's smile faltered. Millie Parker wanted a husband more than she wanted her next meal, and every man in the county knew it.

"Two ten! Who's got two twenty? Come on, girls, look at those muscles!"

Dylan gave Paige a discreet look.

Fine. You owe me, pal. Paige raised her paddle.

"Two twenty!" Lucy called. "Come on, ladies! Two thirty's a small price to pay for a lovely evening with this handsome fella."

Paige scanned the crowd, mentally urging some of the women who'd been actively bidding to jump back in. Millie must've been tapped out because she seemed to be out of the bidding.

"Two twenty going once . . ."

Come on, come on.

"Two twenty going twice . . . Sold for two hundred and twenty dollars to Paige Callahan!"

Paige glued a smile to her face as the audience applauded and Dylan moved off the stage, no doubt relieved to have been spared from the clutches of Millie Parker.

Even worse than the damage to her wallet was the effect on the remainder of the auction. She knew the rules—she'd written them herself. A woman could only win one date. Now she couldn't bid on Sheriff Colton for Miss Trudy.

Maybe Charlotte could help. She'd happily provided some of the hors d'oeuvres and volunteered to man the adoption table. But no, that wouldn't work. If Charlotte wound up with Sheriff Colton, she wouldn't be able to start the bidding for Riley.

Drat!

Danny Colton stepped onto the stage in his uniform, earning a few piercing whistles. Color flooded into his face, and he tugged his hat lower.

On the other side of the room, Miss Trudy stood with Zac and Beau, her lips pinched. She hadn't even bothered to register for a paddle.

The bidding started at fifty and quickly rose. Paige made eye contact with Lucy and shrugged. There was nothing either of them could do. By the time the sheriff left the stage, his face was beet red, and Miss Trudy was white as a bedsheet, her shoulders stiff. The sheriff had himself a date with the owner of the Primrose Inn and head of the shelter's board, Margaret LeFebvre.

Paige felt a pinch of hurt on Miss Trudy's behalf, but she didn't have much time for regrets. Riley was coming out onstage, his gait perfectly even. He looked stoic and handsome in his dark suit. The crowd went wild. A jolt of pride washed over her. Paige was probably the only one who noticed the mottled pink rising into his neck.

They'd saved him for last, knowing there'd be plenty of single women left who'd be willing to fight over this last bachelor.

They were right. Or maybe it was just Riley's innate appeal, because the bidding, which started at fifty, quickly rose to three hundred and was still going strong. The paddles popped up and down so fast Paige lost track of who was bidding what. Lucy had all she could do to keep pace.

It finally slowed down at three eighty, and Lucy urged the crowd to bid higher. "Come on, ladies, he's our last bachelor of the night—your last chance for a date—and with a handsome marine, no less!"

A paddle went up, and Paige rose on her tiptoes to see whose it was. Roxy Franke, Riley's high school girlfriend. The girl had carried a crush for months afterward. Maybe years, judging by the hopeful smile on her face and the two casseroles she'd brought by.

Riley was wearing a poker face, but Paige's stomach bottomed out at the thought of a reunion between Riley and Roxy.

She tried to get Charlotte's attention, for bidding help. But the woman had backed out once the bidding had taken off, and now she was busy signing someone up for an adoption appointment.

Giving up on Charlotte, she sent Lucy a pleading look. A moment later Lucy caught her look of desperation.

"All right, we have three ninety. But ladies . . ." She walked forward on the stage and lowered her voice dramatically. "Did I mention he's the last single Callahan brother?"

Another paddle went up. Sara Porter. A pretty woman in her midtwenties, Sara worked part time at the shelter and typically liked her men with hefty bank accounts. Paige could live with that. Anyone was better than Roxy.

"All right!" Lucy said. "Four hundred's a nice round number. Going once, going twice—"

Roxy's paddle went up again.

Lucy's eyes flickered to Paige. "Four ten! All right. Now open up your wallets a little more, ladies, because I happen to be married to one of the Callahan men, and let me tell you . . . they're worth every penny!"

Sara Porter shook her head at Lucy, shrugging regretfully.

Shoot, she must be all tapped out. Paige looked toward Charlotte, but the woman was still busy with a customer at the table.

"Anyone else?" Lucy said. "Four twenty . . . and he's yours for the taking."

Riley shifted on the stage, clasped his hands in front of him, standing soldier straight.

"I'll bet he has a romantic evening all planned out for you. Four twenty . . . just four hundred and twenty dollars . . . and did I mention this is for an excellent cause?"

The crowd had quieted. If Lucy drew it out any more, this was going to get awkward.

"That's a hefty bid for our local hero," Lucy said. "Anyone else? Okay, we have four ten . . . go-ing once . . . go-ing twice . . ." She scanned the audience for a full three seconds. "And . . . Riley . . . is . . . sold! To Roxy Franke for four hundred and ten dollars!"

Chapter 27

*R*iley's stomach growled as he entered the Callahan house. He took a big whiff of the savory smells wafting from the kitchen. After greeting his brothers, he followed them into the dining room, where Eden and Lucy were setting the last of the side dishes on the table. Paige, he assumed, was still in the kitchen.

Micah, Eden's seven-year-old son, pulled him aside to show him a magic trick with a deck of cards. "Hey, that's pretty good," Riley said when Micah chose the right card. He tousled the kid's hair.

A knock sounded at the door as Aunt Trudy came from the kitchen with a huge pot of venison stew. Zac took it from her and set it on the table.

"I'll get it," Riley said.

He pulled the door open, and a fist tightened in his gut. Dylan Moore stood on the porch in a button-down shirt and pair of skinny khakis.

Riley tried for a smile. "Hey, how you doing?"

"Not bad, not bad. Uh . . . I was invited for dinner."

"Oh. Sure. Come on in." Riley opened the door wider, stepping aside. Seeing Paige bid so enthusiastically for him last night had been bad enough. Now he had to sit across his dinner table from the guy?

Great. Just great.

"Dylan!" Lucy said as they entered the dining room, where the family was seating themselves. "Glad you could make it."

"Hi, Dylan," Paige said, trading some indecipherable look with Lucy.

Riley didn't miss the way her cheeks flushed as Dylan crossed the room and seated himself beside her.

The hollow spot in his middle widened. She must like the guy a lot to have bid so much on him the night before. Probably couldn't bear the thought of him going out with someone else. He knew the feeling.

His stomach twisted as they settled around the table. Someone said grace, but he heard none of the prayer. When it was over, dishes were passed, and he heaped food onto his plate, though his appetite had gone the way of the Roman Empire.

"Last night was such a blast," Eden said. "Lucy, you did a terrific job up there."

Zac squeezed Lucy's hand. "Told you so."

"It surely was fun. I hope the proceeds are enough to get the shelter through."

Paige wiped her mouth. "More than I anticipated. I ran some numbers last night, and I think the shelter's going to be all right even if one of the grants doesn't come through. I owe you guys so much. Seriously, I couldn't have done it without all of you."

"That's what family's for," Beau said.

A pretty smile settled over Paige's features. She needed to hear that, and often. Riley was grateful for the way his family included her.

They relived some of their favorite moments from the auction, laughing often, and careful to avoid any mention of the sheriff's part in the escapades.

"That was a generous bid you made, Paige." Lucy's eyes toggled between Paige and Dylan. "Though I suspect you can have him for free anytime you want."

"Oh, it was a total rescue," Dylan said, chuckling. "She's my Princess Charming."

Paige's eyes flickered off Riley's. "I just wanted to do my part."

"So when's the big date?" Lucy asked.

Paige and Dylan shared a look, then Dylan said, "Next Saturday. We haven't decided on a place yet, though. I think I might surprise her."

Riley could hardly wait. He and Roxy had decided on the same night. At least he'd be gone when Dylan showed up to collect Paige. He'd make sure of it. If he managed to stay out late enough, he'd miss the good night kiss too.

Paige cleared her throat. "The whole community has really opened their wallets for the shelter. I'm grateful."

"Speaking of opening their wallets . . ." Lucy teased Riley with her eyes. "What about you, Mr. Callahan? Highest bid of the night. You were awfully popular with the ladies."

Warmth seeped into his neck. "Must be a lot of desperate women sitting around town is all I can say."

"Oh, please," Eden said. "You're quite the catch and you know it."

Beau rolled his eyes. "He's got a big enough head after last night. Don't add to it."

Riley smirked at him. "Jealous, big brother?"

"Please. I would've fetched twice the price you did." At Eden's pointed look he added, "Not that I would've cared. I've got all the woman I need right here."

He kissed a mollified Eden on the cheek.

Riley stabbed a chunk of venison. Sometimes it really blew being around so many happy couples. At least Aunt Trudy was still single.

He chided himself for the thought. For all her bluster, he knew she still harbored feelings for the sheriff. And Colton was soon going out with the attractive Margaret LeFebvre. It had to be eating her alive. Probably why she was so quiet today.

"Charlotte set fourteen appointments for this week," Paige said. "With any luck, we'll place a lot of our little cuties." She caught Riley's eye. "By the time this week's over, you're going to be chomping at the bit to get out of town."

Riley froze, his spoonful of broth halfway to his mouth. His look must've clued Paige in, because he saw the flash of confusion in her eyes, followed quickly by a cloud of regret. She bit her lip.

"Where you going?" Zac asked around a mouthful of stew.

Beau was a little quicker on the uptake, his eyes darting between Riley and Paige. "What's going on? There something we don't know?"

Paige winced, mouthing, *Sorry.*

Riley wiped his mouth, trying to come up with the right words. His family wasn't going to like this no matter how carefully he worded it.

"I was offered a job by a buddy of mine. His family runs a home improvement company, and his dad's wanting to retire. They could use my help in the office."

"You're not a secretary," Beau said. "You're a lobsterman."

Riley nailed him with a look. "*Was* a lobsterman."

"He's always been good with spreadsheets," Paige offered. "And he's done great at the shelter."

He wondered if she was suddenly in favor of his move. The thought was like a kick to the solar plexus.

Aunt Trudy finally joined the fray. "Where's this business even at?"

He traded looks with Paige. "Copper Creek, Georgia."

"Georgia!" Zac lowered his spoon.

Beau's jaw grew rigid. He sat back in his chair, and Riley could see his mind spinning from the other end of the table. He looked his fill, until Riley wanted to invite him to take a picture.

"And what about the farm, Riley?" Beau finally said. "The season's right around the corner."

Riley loved working the season at the Christmas tree farm almost as much as he enjoyed lobstering. The smell of fresh pine, the crunch of snow under his boots. Customers buzzing around the place, looking for the perfect tree, breath fogging in the air, hot chocolate braced in their mittened hands.

He pushed the images down beside all his other hopes and dreams. The ones that had been cut off right along with his leg.

He'd be slow and cumbersome in the fields now. Balance was tricky even on level ground. Add snow and ice, and he was probably the last person who should be wielding a saw.

"I'm sure you can find better help than me."

"This is a terrible time for you to leave," Beau said.

"What is it with you?" Riley tossed his napkin down. "You didn't approve of me joining up, and now—"

"And look what happened to you!"

"*Beau.*" Eden set her hand on his arm.

Riley's mouth snapped shut. He glared at his brother. How dare he. Riley would give anything to go back and make a different decision. But it wasn't enough that Beau had been right. He had to rub Riley's nose in it too. Never mind that he wouldn't have left at all had Beau kept his paws off Paige. Hot blood raced through his veins, the warmth pooling into his limbs, into his face.

The room had gone mortuary quiet. Every utensil still. The only movement the overhead fan, spinning in a lazy circle.

"Nice." Riley pushed out his chair.

"Don't leave, Riley." Zac cast a scowl Beau's way. "Let's talk about this."

But Riley used the chair's arms to push to his feet. "No thanks. I've lost my appetite."

❧

"He didn't mean it," Paige said as they pulled into the drive a few minutes later.

"Don't defend him." Riley shut off the engine and got out of the car.

"I'm not defending him. It was a stupid thing to say. You know he loves you."

Riley said nothing as she followed him to the door. Her heart ached for the both of them, but she couldn't help but be annoyed with Beau. What had he been thinking? It wasn't like him to spout off like that. To say something so hurtful.

"He's just reeling over the thought of you leaving." Guilt pinched her hard. "Speaking of which . . . I'm so sorry. It just slipped out."

"I guess they had to find out sooner or later."

"Yeah, but . . . not like that." Not that her introduction to the news had been any better.

Riley headed toward his room, his gait uneven.

"Where are you going?"

"I need a nap."

"Can't we talk about this?"

"Go back to the house, Paige. You shouldn't have left Dylan there to begin with." His door slammed in her face, the whoosh of air washing over her like a harsh breath.

Great. Now Riley wasn't talking to her. Dylan probably wasn't either, after she'd left him sitting in the Callahan house without her. She tried to feel bad about that, but she hadn't invited him to begin with. She was going to take that up with Lucy later.

Chapter 28

*P*aige approached the gleaming entryway of Hotel
Tourmaline. She'd only seen the place from a distance,
but up close it was even more impressive. The gray stone walls and
mullioned windows of the hotel faced the windswept shoreline of
Folly Shoals, competing in grandeur.

Once inside the lobby Dylan set a hand at the small of her
back, directing her toward the Sea Room, the hotel's fancy restaurant. Their shoes clacked on the pink marble tiles, the sound
echoing off the gilt-covered dome overhead.

"You did not have to do this," she said. "It's way too expensive."

"After you spent over two hundred bucks rescuing me, it's the
least I could do."

"I'm sure Millie Parker would've been a delightful date."

He sent her a wry look. "She would've been sizing me up for a
wedding band all night."

"Wedding band? Please. When Beau went out with her she was
naming their babies on the first date."

The look on Dylan's face was priceless.

They'd cleared the air about Sunday when he'd called to make arrangements for tonight. She'd apologized for deserting him, and he'd been very gracious.

"It's not like you were the one who invited me," he'd said. "Look, Paige, I know you and I aren't going anywhere, romantically speaking. So let's just go out Saturday and have a nice time."

His words had sent a flood of relief through her. She was afraid her bid had led him on, but clearly he'd seen through her somewhat mixed signals. Someday some woman would appreciate how kind and perceptive he was.

While they waited a moment at the host stand, Paige's mind drifted to Riley. Specifically to Riley and Roxy. He'd left while she was getting ready, calling good-bye up the stairs. She hadn't even put down her mascara wand to see what he was wearing. Or asked where they were going. The less she knew the better. She could already envision much more than she wanted to.

"Right this way," the well-dressed host said, pulling her mind back to the present.

They followed him into the main dining room where opulent chandeliers hung over intimate table settings. The atmosphere was romantic, candles flickering on the tables, the last of daylight filtering through the large windows. Delicious aromas wafted through the room, making her stomach growl.

Dylan pulled out her chair, and she sat at the table for two that was situated by an old brick wall. The place settings were like works of art, the china glistening, and the silverware lined up at the sides and tops of the plates. It looked so perfect she was afraid to mess it up.

A waiter poured ice water into their goblets as she picked up the menu and surveyed the tasty-sounding options. "How will I ever make up my mind?" she said when the server disappeared. "Everything looks so good."

"Well, the lobster bisque is to die for, and the seafood sampler is not to be missed. Maybe we can start with those."

"I'm allergic to shellfish, remember?"

"Oh, that's right. We'll try the mushroom caps or the escargot then. Save room for dessert though, because the cheesecake will make you cry."

"Ugh! I've gained five pounds just thinking about it."

He smiled. "I have to make sure you get your money's worth."

"By the time we're done, you might have spent more than I did."

"All for a good cause."

She couldn't deny that. Or the fact that she'd rather be here in this luxurious restaurant than at home obsessing over Riley and Roxy.

Riley and Roxy. Even their names sounded good together.

Shaking the thought, she settled on her main course, and when the server came, they ordered. As soon as they finished, another waiter came by and topped off their water glasses.

"It's a good thing I skipped lunch," she said. Dylan had ordered two appetizers besides their main courses.

"It's the Sea Room. We have to do it up right."

As they made small talk her eyes drifted over the opulent dining room, taking in all the details. The white linens, the red velvet chairs, the heavy draperies stretching from ceiling to floor and pulled back with tasseled ropes.

A family of five gathered around a large center table. The boys looked cute in their suits and carefully combed hair. Other families were present, too, but most of the patrons were couples. Her eyes followed the line of tables along the opposite wall. It was fun trying to guess whether the couples were on first dates, were newlyweds, or had been married for years.

Her eyes swept over an older pair and down the row before darting back. Her heart stuttered in her chest as she recognized Riley's familiar face.

Her chest tightened. Seriously? He'd brought her here, of all places?

Across the table from him, Roxy's bare shoulders shimmered under the chandelier, her wavy brown hair tumbling over them.

Paige's heart squeezed.

"Paige?"

Her eyes darted back to Dylan. "Sorry. I, uh, I missed that." She struggled to get her brain back into gear.

"I was just talking about the shelter. Greg, one of my work buddies, came in this week to look at the dogs."

"Oh, Greg." She straightened the salad fork she'd knocked askew. "Yes, he went home with a little terrier."

"His wife's in love with her. Last I saw the pup, she had a big pink bow on her head."

"Oh my. Well, I'm glad they're happy. She's a sweetie. Somebody dumped her, we think. We found her over by the Crofton Street Bridge, just as skinny as can be."

"It's hard to believe people do that."

"It's awful."

Dylan started talking about his childhood dog, a mutt his family had found on vacation, and she tried to listen as her eyes drifted to Riley. He was at least thirty feet away on the opposite side of the room. And very engaged in his conversation.

He looked so handsome, the candlelight shedding a golden light over his face. A white dress shirt stretched across the breadth of his shoulders, and a dark tie hung from his neck. His sleeves were rolled up, exposing his lower arms. He nodded at something

Roxy said. Smiled. The real kind. Not one of those strained things she'd been seeing so much of lately.

She found herself strangely relieved he'd be leaving town soon. *Nice, Paige. If you can't have him, no one else can either?*

Maybe it was selfish, but yes. That was exactly how she felt.

She curled her arms around herself. What was wrong with her? She should want Riley to be happy. He'd been through so much. No one deserved it more.

But as Roxy reached across the table and touched his arm, she wanted to smack the woman's hand away.

A few minutes later the server delivered their appetizers, and they dug in. The mushroom caps, which looked so succulent, went down her throat like sawdust. She oohed and aahed over the food even while her stomach tightened in rebellion.

She managed to hold up her end of the conversation through the remainder of dinner, but her heart wasn't in it. She couldn't seem to stop herself from glancing at Riley. Couldn't seem to stop tormenting herself with the way they seemed so absorbed in each other. With the way Roxy touched him, the way he leaned toward her, the way he laughed so often.

The server delivered their bill to the table with a flourish.

Dylan tucked cash into the leather folder and pocketed his wallet. "We're all set. Do you want to go say hi, or are you just going to pretend you didn't see them?"

Her eyes snapped back to Dylan. "What?"

He gave her a look that made heat wash into her cheeks. She was getting pretty good at pretending. Or maybe she wasn't, since Dylan had seen right through her.

"I'm so sorry. I've been terrible company. And after you've gone to all this expense."

"Not at all." He covered her clenched fist. "We could've gone somewhere else, you know."

"I didn't know he'd be here." Her love for Riley must be scrawled across her forehead. It was a wonder Riley hadn't noticed. Or maybe he had. Maybe that's why he was leaving town. Everyone she loved left. Why should he be any different?

Her chest tightened at the thought. Suddenly her eyes ached, and sitting up straight seemed like too much work. "I'm such an idiot."

"You're not an idiot. *He* is, if he finds Roxy Franke more appealing than you."

She gave him a thin smile. "You're very sweet." She didn't feel like explaining their long history as BFFs or Riley's history with Roxy. He couldn't help it that his feelings for Paige hadn't shifted any more than she could help that hers had.

Her eyes drifted once more to Riley's table, just in time to see Roxy glide her fingers down his forearm and tangle them with the hands Paige loved so much.

Those were *her* hands. She'd seen them first. Her stomach clenched into a hard knot as heat suffused her face.

She swallowed hard and pulled her eyes from the scene. "Can we just leave now?"

❧

Riley was reaching for his dessert fork when he saw her. Across the room, engaged in conversation with Dylan, looking like an angel in her white, shimmery top.

He'd been struggling already. He didn't want to be on this date with Roxy. He sure didn't want her hands on him or her eyes flirting with him. But after she'd paid four hundred bucks for the night, he felt obligated to at least pretend to enjoy it.

It was unsettling. And that was before he'd even seen Paige and Dylan across the room at the intimate table for two, looking totally absorbed in each other.

He continued eating his dessert. He wouldn't look over there again. Why fill his head with images that were only going to haunt him later?

A minute later he pushed back his plate, realizing he'd wolfed down dessert in an effort to rush the evening along. Roxy was only half finished with her crème brûlée. She paused between bites to draw her fingertip down his forearm. Again.

He managed to maintain eye contact with her, wondering why he couldn't feel something for his date. She was pretty enough, with her big brown eyes and dimples. She could keep a conversation going and expressed a polite interest in everything pertaining to him. She was positive and kindhearted and hadn't once mentioned his prosthesis. Her casseroles had been pretty tasty too.

Why couldn't *her* touch make his skin feel two sizes too small? Why did it have to be Paige? He yearned for her the way a castaway yearned for water. His spirit was dry and withering for want of her.

Wow, Callahan. Melodramatic much?

"Bite?" Roxy extended her spoon, filled with a quivering lump of the dessert.

As he opened his mouth to decline, she slid it in.

"Isn't it yummy? Crème brûlée's my favorite."

He let the bite slide down his throat, repelled by the pudding-like texture. "Delicious."

"We should go for a walk on the waterfront next."

"Whatever you'd like to do." It was her night.

But he was glad the ferry only ran till ten. He'd figured out early in the evening that she was after more than a single date. He'd made sure to work his move to Georgia into the conversation right away. He'd meant to ward her off, but she seemed to take it as some kind of challenge.

But then, Roxy always had been eager to escape Summer Harbor. His moving probably only made him seem more appealing.

"Another bite?" She extended the spoon.

He backed away before she could hit her target. "No thanks. I'm stuffed."

"Everything was really good. You do know how to spoil a girl."

She began telling him about a restaurant she'd eaten at during her visit to New York, but Riley's eyes were drawn again across the restaurant. Dylan's hand was now resting on Paige's.

Riley's jaw went tight even as the back of his neck prickled with heat.

He forced his eyes away, resolving to be better disciplined. What was the point in torturing himself?

He tried to tune in to Roxy's lengthy story, but like a traitor, his mind went back to his kiss with Paige. To the feel of her supple lips on his, the softness of her delicate skin, the heady weight of her hand gliding up his arm.

His eyes drifted back over to her and Dylan. Was she really able to just pretend the kiss had never happened? Apparently.

"Awww . . . ," Roxy whined, drawing his attention. She was staring over his shoulder out the window. "It's raining." She gave a little pout that was probably supposed to be cute. "There goes our walk on the waterfront."

Somehow Riley could only manage a deep sense of relief.

Chapter 29

*H*e didn't want to go home.

Riley pulled up to the overlook at Shadow Bay and shut off the engine, leaving the radio on. He'd borrowed Beau's old truck for the night. He had a feeling Roxy would've been glad to climb onboard his motorcycle, but given the way it was pouring now, the truck had been a wise decision.

His brother had taken the opportunity to apologize for his cruel words on Sunday. Riley knew he hadn't meant anything by it. He'd only been upset about Riley leaving again.

The bay was pitch black tonight, not even the moon or stars to light the sky. The kind of night he would've appreciated years ago when this was the local make-out spot. He'd even brought Roxy here a time or two and fogged up the windshields pretty good.

She would've been game for something similar tonight, but he'd put plenty of space between them on her doorstep and politely refused her offer of a nightcap.

He was going to have to move on at some point. But not tonight. Not with Roxy. Not when his heart still belonged to Paige.

He turned the station until he found the Red Sox game,

jacking it up so he could hear it over the rain pummeling the roof. It was in extra innings. He listened for a while, trying to give a flying fig, but really he just wanted the minutes to tick away so the night would be over.

He tried not to think about what Paige might be doing right now. Tried not to think about her inviting Dylan into the house, or about his lips on hers, or the current location of his hands.

He checked the time and snapped the radio off. Eleven thirty was late enough, wasn't it? The last ferry was at ten, and the Roadhouse was the only place open this late. If she wasn't home when he got there, he'd just tell himself they were at the restaurant.

Yeah.

He reached for the key and turned it. The engine tried to turn over, a weak effort. He shut it off and gave it another try. Nothing. Worse than nothing. A third time produced a familiar ticking sound, indicating a dead battery.

Great. Just great. He'd only listened to the radio for half an hour. The battery must've been weak.

He dialed Beau, waiting through five rings before his voicemail kicked on. He and Eden were probably in bed. Of course they were. Rather than leave a message his brother wouldn't get till morning, Riley hung up. This was the way his night had gone. The way his life was going.

Can't one little thing go right, God? Just one thing.

At least Zac would be awake. He dialed the number. When he got voicemail he phoned the Roadhouse's main line.

"Roadhouse. How can I help you?"

He recognized his sister-in-law's drawl. "Hey, Lucy, it's Riley. Is Zac around?"

"Um, he's kinda putting out a fire at the moment. And I mean that in a metaphorical way, thank the Lord. Is there something I can help you with?"

"Could you ask him to call me back when he gets a chance? No, scratch that. Just have him pick me up at Shadow Bay Ridge when he's got a minute. Beau's truck died."

"Shadow Bay Ridge . . . the overlook?"

"Yeah, he'll know where." Zac had spent an evening or two up here himself—not that Riley was telling Lucy that.

"Okay, will do. He shouldn't be long."

"All right. Thanks."

"Wait! Is Roxy still with you?"

"No, I already took her home."

Riley ended the call and leaned back against the headrest. Guess he was going to be getting home plenty late after all.

❧

Paige let her rain-splattered pants fall to the floor and slipped into her yoga pants and T-shirt. It was after eleven thirty, and Riley still wasn't home. Why would he be? He was a normal man, and he had a beautiful, super-eager date. She wasn't going to try to convince herself they were sitting at Roxy's kitchen table playing Scrabble.

Her heart gave a painful squeeze. Or maybe she would. A little denial never hurt anyone.

Unable to bear seeing her best pair of pants on the floor, she put them on a hanger and smoothed out the wrinkles. She was just hanging them in the closet when her phone buzzed. She checked the screen, wondering why Lucy was calling so late.

"Hey, girl. What's up?"

"How was your date?"

"Terrific. I had a front row seat to Riley's date, in fact."

"What?"

"Yeah. We were both at the Sea Room. But he didn't see me, so you don't know that."

"Aw, honey. I'm awful sorry. But hey, listen. You need to go pick him up at Shadow Bay Ridge. The truck won't start."

"What? Shadow Bay Ridge . . ." Her lips clamped down. Seriously? He was still taking women to make-out point? What was he, fifteen?

"He needs a ride."

"Oh no. I'm not crashing his date. Are you kidding me?"

"He already took Roxy home. He's alone."

Even so. "I'm already in my pajamas, and frankly, this whole night has just left me mentally exhausted. Have Zac pick him up."

"Um, Zac's busy with something. And I'm super busy too. Swamped. In the weeds."

Paige smirked. Sure she was. "There can't be that many people there. It's going on midnight."

"Did you say something, sugar? I'm afraid you're breaking up."

"Lucy . . . don't do this to me."

"I'm sorry, I can't hear a thing you're saying. So he's waiting . . . out at Shadow Bay. You should be getting along now." The phone went dead.

She pulled her phone away from her ear and glared at it. "Really?"

Paige punched her phone off. Nice. It was pouring down rain. What was he even doing out there all alone anyway? Giving a hard sigh, she slid on her shoes and grabbed her keys. It looked like her difficult evening wasn't quite over yet.

Chapter 30

*R*iley tried to take a little nap. Who knew how long it would be before Zac got freed up. Besides, sleep beat the heck out of dwelling on Paige and where she might be right now. What she might be doing.

He beat his head against the headrest. Once. Twice. The image of her at the Sea Room wouldn't dislodge. Of Dylan's hand on hers. Of the two of them leaning toward each other.

The rain grew louder, beating the truck for all it was worth. Lightning flashed over the bay, followed by a rumble of thunder. He closed his eyes again and resolutely kicked Dylan out of his head, replacing the image of them at the table with one of him and Paige. Out on the community center deck, a sultry country tune playing in the background. Her eyes, lost and lonely, searching his like he was her last hope.

Her small hand sliding up his arm as he kissed her, the sensation of her response. Yes, her response. She'd kissed him back. He couldn't let that little detail get lost in the mire of disillusionment. Maybe she'd been lonely. Maybe her desperation made her a little vulnerable, but she'd responded to him.

The thought warmed him from the inside out. Made his skin

tingle with awareness. Maybe it was hopeless, maybe he was only tormenting himself. But it was his memory. The only one he had, and he was going to cling to it as if it were a life preserver.

A pounding on the window made him jump. He hadn't even heard Zac pull up.

Riley flung open his door. But it wasn't Zac standing in the pouring rain. It was Paige.

"What are you doing here?" He pulled her in out of the rain, grabbing the door and pulling it shut as he scrambled toward the passenger seat. His leg failed to cooperate, and he landed on his elbow.

Paige fell against him, breathing hard, her wet hair dripping onto his chest and shoulder. "Lucy called."

"She was supposed to send Zac."

His upper body had made the journey to the passenger seat, his lower body, not so much. He grew aware of the way she was pressed up against the length of his side. Her slight weight, the delicious warmth of her.

Her sweet, flowery smell wove around him like a spell.

As if becoming aware of their intimate position, she stilled.

The rain drummed steadily on the roof, and a crash of thunder sounded nearby. He cursed the darkness, which left her thoughts a mystery. What he'd give to read those blue eyes right now. See if a frown puckered her brow or if her chin dimpled in thought.

"Well . . ." Her voice was soft and thready. "It's me."

She didn't seem in a big hurry to put space between them. Right then a shiver passed through her. The coolness?

He tried to tell himself it meant nothing. But he'd wanted her for so long, and here she was, like a Christmas morning wish. So close. So warm. So real. Her lips were mere inches from his. Their warm breaths fogged together, and he got lost in the want swirling inside of him.

"Yeah," he said softly. "It's you." *Always you.*

He leaned in until their lips touched. The briefest of kisses. A test. His heart sang when she responded. It kicked against his ribs, urging him on. He went back for another taste. Her lips were so soft. Pliant. Delicious. He palmed her face, still damp from the rain, and deepened the kiss.

Her hand slid to the back of his neck, cool against the heat pooling there. Her fingers brushed through the hair at his nape, awakening every cell. She turned into him, resting her weight more firmly against his side.

The feel of her against him kindled a fire inside. A feeling that sent a pleasant jolt of electricity to his brain.

She's kissing you. She wants you.

Was he really going to do this? What about all his noble reasons? What about her deserving someone better? Someone whole? Even now, his leg was trapped under her. Useless.

He was useless.

But the arguments seemed futile in the wake of her ready response. He was heady with it. The pull of want was like a riptide, towing, tugging at him, until he was helpless against it.

He got lost in her for a long, blissful minute. The rest of the world faded to black. Just the two of them in this cozy, perfect moment.

But this was Paige, his mind argued. What was he doing, rushing headlong into this like a fool? He couldn't do that. Not with Paige. There was too much at stake. Years of friendship. And then there was Dylan. She was with him only a while ago, looking pretty caught up. Maybe kissing him.

He had to think. He had to—

"Wait . . . ," he said against her lips. One more brush. And one more to go, just a little more . . .

Callahan.

He gathered the fortitude to break the kiss. "Wait." His breath was ragged. "Wait. Slow down. Let's slow down."

He fell back against the seat, taking her with him. Holding her head tight to his chest where his heart was setting new records for speed. Man, what she did to him. He took a deep breath, two. Felt her catching her breath as well. He threaded his fingers into her hair, cupping her head, unwilling to let her go. Did he mean that physically and literally? He couldn't think past the storm of emotions surging in him.

The rain had lessened in strength. The delicate pattering joined the seductive symphony of their breaths, their heartbeats. Beautiful, wonderful music. He could stay like this forever.

She wiggled, finding a more comfortable fit.

"You're killing me, woman," he grated out. He held her tight, his breaths gradually quieting. His heart rate slowing.

His good leg had fallen asleep. He was pretty sure he couldn't move even if he tried. And he had no interest in trying at the moment.

What was he going to do? They'd crossed a line. They'd taken a huge leap to the other side. And he liked it here. It was perfect. Like a dream. How could he give her up after having her in his arms? After she'd kissed him like that? He dug his fingers into her hair, tightening his hold on her. *Mine.*

"Riley?"

Her unsteady whisper awoke all his protective instincts. "Yeah, honey."

She paused for a long moment. Her fingers clenching and unclenching at the sides of his shirt. "Don't you dare say that was just a kiss."

The unexpectedness of her comment, the tenacity in her voice, caught him off guard. A chuckle rose in his chest before he could squash it.

She lifted her head, and he didn't have to see her to know she was glaring at him in the darkness. "It's not funny."

He found the curve of her cheek, hoping she couldn't see the smile he couldn't seem to extinguish. "I know it's not."

"So what . . . ?" She sat up more, an elbow digging into his ribs. "What are we going to do? What about Roxy?"

"What about her?"

"Do you like her?"

"I don't give a fig about Roxy Franke. But what about you? What about Dylan?"

"Dylan? We're just friends. I only bid on him to rescue him from Millie."

Her words flooded him with relief.

"So . . . what do you want to do?" she asked. "About this, about us?"

He heard a whisper of fear in the bold question. Was she afraid of moving forward? Or afraid they couldn't go back?

"I mean, we just *kissed*, Riley. *Really* kissed."

For some reason her tone, so sober, tickled him. "I'm aware."

She stiffened, edging away. "Well, I'm glad you find all this so amusing."

He tightened his hold, preventing her escape. "Hey . . . I'm not amused. I'm . . . ." There was only one word for it, and it came out on a contented sigh. "Happy."

A long moment passed. "You are?" she asked finally. "Really?"

What the heck. He'd gone this far, might as well go for broke. He slid his fingers along the curve of her cheek, relishing the softness of her skin.

"I haven't felt so happy in . . . I can't even remember."

She took a moment, as if digesting this bit of information. "So . . . this isn't weird for you?"

"Is it weird for you?"

"It should be, I guess. But it isn't. Not at all."

He smiled. "Same here."

"So . . . what do you want to do?"

He didn't even have to think about it. "Kiss you again."

There were no arguments as he leaned forward and captured her lips. He came up on his elbow, cradling her face with his other hand. He couldn't believe this was happening. It was surreal. Paige wanted him the way he wanted her. The way he'd dreamed about for years.

Her arms roped around his waist, her fingers moving up the planes of his back. Her mouth parted on a breath, and he took full advantage. He'd lost control of his heart rate again, and he was going to lose control of other things, too, if he wasn't careful. And he needed to be careful.

He needed to cool things off. Move slowly.

Reluctantly he eased from the deeper kiss with a few light, slow brushes on her delectable lips. Then he put a few inches of space between them.

"I have a confession to make," she whispered into the gap. "I-I've been wanting this for a while. Like, before the wedding. For weeks."

Weeks? Try years. Another chuckle caught in his chest.

"Are you laughing at me again?" She shifted.

Pain shot down his stump into a calf that wasn't even there. Stupid phantom pain. "Let's save that for later," he squeezed out.

"Your leg. I'm hurting you." She wiggled upright, scooching off him, against the door.

He used his arms to pull himself upright, gritting his teeth against the pain. It hurt, but it couldn't come close to dulling the joy in his heart. Paige wanted him. He wasn't going to second-guess himself this time or play the martyr. He couldn't bring himself to be that noble in the face of her confession.

"What's wrong? Are you okay?"

"Nothing. My calf's just hurting a little, that's all."

"Let me rub it."

"No, you can't—"

"Stop being so stubborn." She reached down and massaged the only calf he had. "Here? Is that the right spot?"

He gritted his teeth. "Wrong leg, Paige."

Her fingers stilled. He felt her eyes burning into his as the meaning settled over her. She settled slowly back against the door. "Oh."

The quiet tone of her voice, so solemn, struck his funny bone, and he chuckled. Didn't even bother to hold it back this time. He didn't know what was wrong with him tonight, but he didn't want to fix it.

"Stop laughing," she said, but this time he heard the smile in her voice.

"I can't help it. You sound so tragic." Saying it out loud only made him laugh harder. And it felt so good. *He* felt so good.

She elbowed him in the gut. "Riley Callahan, it's not funny." But she was laughing too.

He pulled her into a hug and let the laughter settle around them like a warm blanket. He buried his nose in the fragrant dampness of her hair. She smelled so good. So Paige.

And a wave of pure gratitude filled him. He closed his eyes and said a prayer that went *Thank You, Thank You, Thank You . . .*

"So . . . ," she said a while later. "What are we going to do?" Her words were muffled against his chest. "Are we going to do this? Are we going to see where it goes?"

Even though he heard the sweet longing in her voice, he hadn't forgotten all the reasons this was a bad idea. He'd been engraving them on his heart for three months. He knew he should say no. Knew it was the right thing to do. The right thing for Paige.

She looked up at him in the quiet, eyes searching. "Riley?" Her voice quavered.

And God help him, he couldn't do it. Not when she wanted him. Not when he'd dreamed of this moment for years. He wasn't that strong.

He kissed the top of her head, taking an extra moment to breathe her in. "Let's go home."

She leaned back but didn't release him. "What does that mean? You're supposed to leave in two weeks and—"

The patter of rain filled the silence. Lightning flashed in the sky, giving him a brief glimpse of her face, her eyes. A flicker of fear, a dash of hope. And then all was dark again as thunder rumbled in the distance.

"And what?" he asked.

"I don't want you to go," she whispered.

He cupped her face. He wasn't leaving her now. No way. Nohow.

He whispered into the dark, "I'm not going anywhere, Warren."

Chapter 31

$\mathcal{T}$he tantalizing smells of garlic and oregano floated through the Callahan kitchen, making Paige's mouth water. She'd skipped breakfast this morning. Had overslept, actually, after lying awake half the night with a giddy smile on her face.

The guys had driven out to Shadow Bay after church to jump the truck and bring it back. Micah had gone home from church with his grandpa. That left the girls in the kitchen, getting the food on the table.

There was a tug on her hand, and then she was being dragged from the kitchen by Lucy. Around the corner and into the deserted hallway they went.

"Okay, okay," Paige said, forcefully reclaiming her hand. "I think you dislocated my arm."

"Sorry." Lucy turned at the dead end by the bathroom. "All right now, talk."

"What do you mean?" She couldn't help but have a little fun. Lucy was too easy.

The woman gawked at her. "What do you mean, what do I

mean?" She lowered her voice to a whisper. "He was holding your hand in church."

Paige tried for innocence. "Who?"

Lucy gave her a look.

Paige gave up, her ever-present smile giving way. "All right. We talked last night when I went to pick him up."

Lucy gave a little golf clap. "It worked!"

"Don't get all smug," Paige conceded with a shrug. "But thank you."

"Tell me everything. What happened, what did he say, what did you say?"

She lifted a brow at Lucy's enthusiasm. "Hmm. There wasn't a whole lot of talking actually."

Lucy's eyes widened as she waited expectantly. "And . . ."

Paige let her hang a minute. "And . . . that's all I'm going to say about that."

Lucy made a face. "Cruel, cruel girl."

Twenty minutes later they were seated around the big table, Riley at her side. Their new relationship was the elephant in the room. As if by agreement nobody mentioned the bachelor dates of the night before, and surely no one brought up Sheriff Colton and his Friday night date with Margaret LeFebvre. Charlotte Dupree had spotted them at a window table at The Wharf. And there were rumors that the two had gone bird-watching—one of Margaret's hobbies—on Saturday at Otter Cove.

Paige tried to follow the small talk through dinner and afterward as everyone still sat around the table, full and content. The Roadhouse's new microphone system, the upcoming fall season for the farm, a grade school Thanksgiving program Eden had agreed to head up at church.

Riley set his arm around Paige's chair, and she lost track of the conversation altogether. His warm hand rested on her shoulder. And he began tracing little circles on her bare arm.

"So when's the big move?" Beau's question caught her attention.

Riley's eyes met hers, then he looked away. "Ah, looks like I'm not moving after all. I was going to let you know. I just . . . recently changed my mind."

There were murmurs of relief all around the table. Secret little smiles that told Paige they weren't fooling anyone. Not that they were trying to. There was something to be said for easing into this. They were already close. It seemed unnatural to make some kind of grand announcement.

Miss Trudy cleared her throat. "In that case, young man, I think it might be time you found a place of your own."

Riley's lips twitched. "Yes, ma'am."

A knock sounded at the door, and Lucy jumped up. "I'll get it."

Paige's eyes slid to Riley's, and they shared a private smile that warmed her skin. His eyes lingered on hers even as the conversation carried on.

A moment later there was a shuffling behind them.

Sheriff Colton stood on the threshold of the dining room, hat in his hands. "Trudy, might I have a word?"

Miss Trudy's spine lengthened a full two inches. "We're in the middle of dinner. I'm afraid it'll have to wait."

His eyes shifted over the table, filled with empty plates and wadded napkins. "All due respect, ma'am, looks like you might be finished."

She drilled him with a look. "All due respect, you were not invited over here, Danny Colton."

"Oh boy," Zac muttered.

The sheriff twisted the brim of his hat. "Well, you wouldn't talk to me at church, and you won't answer your phone."

"A man might take that as a hint."

The sheriff's face grew pink, and his poor hat was about crushed. "I aim to say my piece, Trudy. If you want me to say it in front of your family, that's what I'll do."

"An ultimatum? That's a fine way to treat a lady."

"You don't give me much choice."

They stared each other down for ten long, painful seconds.

Finally Miss Trudy's chair squawked as she pushed it back. "Fine. I'll give you three minutes."

"You'll give me as long as it takes to say what I've come to say." The sheriff pressed his lips together, making his red mustache twitch. The red flush suffused his face.

The table was midnight quiet as Miss Trudy rounded it, making a wide berth around the sheriff in the doorway. The front screen door squeaked open, and a moment later the front door closed.

Their voices could be heard, but they were too quiet to make out anything other than a word here and there.

The family sat around the table, their gazes flickering off one another's.

Eden drained the last of her lemonade. "We shouldn't eavesdrop."

"Definitely not," Lucy said.

But nobody got up to clear the table. Nobody started a conversation.

Paige listened discreetly as she wiped her mouth and shifted closer to Riley. She made out a few innocuous phrases, all spoken by Miss Trudy.

It doesn't matter.

Well, really.

Sure it was.

"She's pretty steamed about his date with Ms. LeFebvre," Eden said quietly. "Not that she'd ever admit it."

"She was steamed way before that," Riley said.

"With good reason," Paige added.

"What do you mean?" Eden asked.

Paige bit her lip. She'd forgotten for a second that the newlyweds didn't know what the rest of them had overheard at the reception. They'd been busy being bride and groom, then gone on their honeymoon.

"I guess we never told you guys," Zac said.

"Told us what?" Beau asked.

Riley filled them in on the argument between the sheriff and Miss Trudy. "And then she let the big one fly—turns out she was pregnant when Danny left her for the NBA."

Eden gaped.

"She was pregnant with Danny's baby when she married Uncle Tom?" Beau asked.

"Got married *because* she was pregnant," Zac said.

"And she never told Danny?" Eden asked.

"Apparently not," Lucy said. "I talked to her after she ran off at the reception. She didn't say why she never told him. Just that she lost the baby."

"How terribly sad," Eden said. "No wonder she's been so angry with him."

Beau shifted in his seat. "How do you think Danny feels about now, knowing she kept that from him?"

"That's a lot of water under the bridge," Eden said.

"I did not go bird-watching with that woman!" The sheriff's voice carried through the walls.

"Says you!"

"Well, *I'm* not the one keeping secrets, now, am I!"

A long moment of silence followed, into which Zac again muttered, "Oh boy."

Beau sat back in his chair. "Here we go again."

"It's like the Fourth of July with those two."

"Shhhh!" Eden and Lucy said.

Paige listened intently, but there was no more talking. A moment later the front door opened. Slammed shut. Miss Trudy's footsteps thudded across the living room and up the steps. Down the hall. Another door slammed.

Outside, the sheriff's car started up, and the hum of its engine faded as it went down the long drive.

"Well," Lucy said. "I guess that didn't go so well."

Riley and Paige spent a quiet Sunday afternoon at home. After the late dinner they weren't hungry enough for supper, so they headed to the ice cream shop instead. It was near closing time, and they had the patio all to themselves.

Paige was lured into a waffle cone by the sweet, delicious aroma that flooded the shop. She'd taken down half the cone by the time the sun had sunk over the hills.

They talked about Miss Trudy and the sheriff, about the church service this morning, and about Riley's upcoming appointment with his prosthetist. He needed another adjustment.

Riley shoved the last bit of his cone into his mouth and settled back in the wrought iron chair, his shoulder brushing hers. "I think my aunt's right about me moving out."

Hearing the serious tone of his voice, she met his gaze.

"I don't want to mess this up by moving too quickly. I want to date you properly, and I can't do that from under the same roof."

Something inside Paige went all warm and fuzzy. It wasn't like they needed to get to know each other. But they did need to find their footing in this new relationship. Ease into it.

"I agree. Let's do this right."

Riley had a lot to think about. A lot of decisions to make. He needed a place to stay and another job. She didn't want to press him on that subject though. His former occupation was a sore spot, and she didn't want to bring him down.

She took a little bite of her cone, chewing thoughtfully. "We should scour the paper when we get home. Find you an apartment close by."

"And a job. I heard there was an opening at the lobster co-op. I think I'll apply, since you won't need me at the shelter much longer."

"That's great."

"It might take a while to find an apartment, though. I think I might ask Beau about moving into the farmhouse temporarily." His eyes flickered to hers. "Like tomorrow."

"So soon?"

"Don't take it the wrong way. I just—" He gave her a long look that heated up with each passing second. "I'm only a man, Paige, and having you nearby is"—his Adam's apple bobbed as he swallowed—"difficult."

She followed the long stubbly column up to his sharp jaw-line and farther to his lowered eyes. His long lashes were a fringe against his skin. When he lifted them, the longing there made her insides melt. Not physical longing. At least, not *just* that.

"This is too important to rush," he said, his voice low and gravelly. "I don't want to do anything to ruin what we have."

"I get it. We shouldn't rush things. This is new."

His chest expanded on a long inhale, then he blew out his breath. "You said last night you've been feeling this way for weeks."

She was relieved to have it out on the table, but her cheeks still flushed. "I have. It seems like longer though. It's been hard. I was afraid you'd think I'd lost my marbles. Shoot, *I* was afraid I'd lost my marbles."

"The thing is, Paige . . . it's been longer than weeks for me." His eyes pierced hers. His look was intense. "Longer than months."

Paige's heart beat up into her throat. "How—how long? Like since you've been home?"

He smirked. "Remember that summer you came home from camp?"

"Which time?" she asked sarcastically.

"We were seventeen. We met out on the pier. You had your toenails painted."

Her heart gave a little tug. "You remember my toenails?"

"They were pink. I took one look at you, and everything was different somehow. I didn't see my best buddy anymore. I saw a beautiful young lady, and I wanted to kiss you."

Her skin tingled with awareness. "I never— You never— How can you have—" He'd never said a word. Never given a clue. Memories played out in her mind. Hours spent shooting hoops, walking the school halls, goofing off by the water's edge. She'd had boyfriends and crushes, and she'd told him about every one of them. The realization made her cringe.

And then her mind spun forward into adulthood, when she'd dated his brother. Her heart gave a little squeeze. "Beau."

His lips twisted, and his eyes hinted at the pain she'd caused. "Not my favorite period of time."

"Oh, Riley."

He put his arm around her, drawing her into his side. "It's okay."

But it wasn't. After watching him with Roxy, she had an inkling how it must've felt. All the Sunday dinners, the snowmobile treks, the Roadhouse gatherings. When Beau had broken up with her, Riley was the one who'd consoled her. He'd held her and kissed her forehead while she'd blubbered on and on about his brother.

How could she have been so clueless? Her heart ached for him. "Did Beau know?"

"Of course not. He still doesn't."

If it had been her, she wouldn't have been able to stand it. She would've . . . moved away or something. Gone somewhere, anywhere—

Her eyes darted to his as a terrible thought occurred. "That's why you left. Why you enlisted."

She saw the flare of admission in his eyes, and something inside her crumbled. It was why he'd traveled thousands of miles from home, why he'd gotten blasted by an IED.

Why he'd lost his leg.

The truth tore at her heart. Her chest tightened painfully. Her lungs malfunctioned. She covered her mouth, suddenly unable to breathe.

"Hey . . . don't."

"It's my fault," she said through her hand.

He grabbed her arm, pulled her hand away from her mouth, and held on to it. "*No.* No, Paige. It was my decision to enlist. You didn't even know what I was feeling. You can't take that on."

But it felt like hers. The weight of it was unbearable. "I'm so sorry. About Beau. About everything."

"You have nothing to be sorry about. Nothing. Understand? I didn't tell you to make you feel bad. I just need you to understand. I know you felt . . . abandoned when I left. You were angry."

"I shouldn't have said that. It wasn't fair."

"Perfectly understandable given what you've been through. I should've talked to you about enlisting. I'm sorry I didn't. The last thing I ever wanted was to hurt you."

"It's okay. I understand. Especially now."

"I just— Paige, I need you to know how important this is to me. I've wanted this—wanted you—a long time. This means a lot to me. I don't take it lightly."

"I get it," she said. "I do." Now more than ever.

He pressed a kiss to her knuckles, smiling around them. "Having you, like this . . ." He squeezed her hand as their eyes met and clung for a long, poignant moment. "It was worth it all."

Her eyes teared up, making Riley's face go blurry, even as she tried to blink them away. Her lower lip trembled.

He brushed his thumb across her cheek. "That's the second time I've made you cry."

"They're happy tears."

He brushed her lip with his thumb, and she tasted the saltiness of her own tears. Then he replaced his thumb with his lips, keeping it brief and sweet. And oh, so perfect.

When he drew away his green eyes melded with hers. "I like it better when you smile."

Chapter 32

*R*iley moved forward for a layup, testing his balance. He sank the ball, but his movements were less agile than he'd like. He caught the ball and tossed it to Paige.

"Go easy on me," she said. The ball smacked the pavement as she dribbled. "I haven't played in forever."

They both knew who was taking it easy here. He'd asked her to shoot hoops with him on the community center's outdoor court. He needed to challenge himself. He wanted to do more than walk with a steady gait and climb stairs. He wanted to move like he used to, fluid and fast. Or at least as close to that as he could get.

He'd almost called this off. He had a shooting, burning pain in his lower back recently that spread up to his shoulders. He needed to get in to see his prosthetist pronto.

The evening temperature was mild, the sun hiding behind clouds. There was a nice breeze coming in off the harbor, the air holding that familiar tang of salt and seaweed he loved so much.

Paige put up a shot. It bounced off the rim straight into his hands. "See, what'd I say?"

"You never were good at free throws."

She shot him a look, somewhat mollified when he winked at her.

"So how was work today?" He'd spent the past couple days training Paige's new assistant, Molly. She'd been able to start a week earlier than promised, and today was her first day flying solo.

"She did great. She has such a nice, sunny disposition."

"You saying I didn't?"

"Let's just say there've been a few thunderclouds."

He banked a shot. "Fair enough."

He'd moved back into the farmhouse on Monday. He'd found an affordable apartment near the library, but it wasn't available until next month.

"How's the job search going?" Paige asked.

That was a bit of good news. "I got the job at the co-op. I start Monday."

Paige held the ball. "That's great! Why didn't you tell me?"

"I just did. They only called a couple hours ago."

The co-op was a group of local fishermen who made fresh lobsters available direct to the consumer. They needed someone in the office full time.

"That's right up your alley."

He'd rather be out on a boat hauling in lobsters, but whatever. He pushed the thought away, determined to improve his outlook. And along those lines . . .

"I've been thinking about adopting that boxer at the shelter, Bishop. I kinda miss the little mutt."

Paige's face broke out in a smile. "I knew it! I knew the two of you were meant to be."

"Don't get all cocky on me."

"Let's go get him when we're done here. We can run to Ellsworth and get some supplies. It's okay with the family?"

"Yep."

"Yay!" Paige went for a three-pointer and gave him a saucy smile when she sank it, all net.

He retrieved the ball and dribbled toward her.

"Ready for a little one-on-one?"

"Sounds good."

The idea wasn't to win, but to help him find his footing—literally. Paige understood that and kept to his pace. It was depressing to realize she could so easily school him if she were trying. Even so, fifteen minutes later, he was sucking wind and dripping with sweat.

A few other guys had begun a game on the other end of the court, their calls and comments carrying downwind.

The game got more intense as he and Paige eased into it, found a level that was challenging yet still doable for him. His leg was hurting like a big dog, but he wasn't ready to quit just yet. He had to push himself if he was ever going to get better at this. And he was going to get better.

He dribbled toward the basket. Paige waited ahead, knees bent, arms out, looking way too pretty with her long blond ponytail and flushed cheeks.

"So when are you going to let me take you out on a date?" he said, making a slow approach.

"You trying to distract me, Callahan?"

"Is it working?"

"Nope." She swatted and missed.

"Ah-ah-ah. Working better than you thought."

Having the height advantage, he stopped and went for a jump shot, but it bounced off the rim.

Paige retrieved the ball and took it out. "You're doing great, Riley. I'm impressed."

"I wasn't kidding," he said, turning the subject back to them. "Let's do a real date."

"Okay." Paige dribbled toward him, her eyes smiling. Happy.

Man, he loved her. Those sparkling blue eyes, that little pointed chin, those kiss-me lips. He already missed living under the same roof. Seeing her sexy, tousled hair first thing in the morning, hearing her hum as the coffee brewed.

Something shifted in her eyes. She held the ball and took a few steps toward him.

"Travel," he said as she neared.

"Time-out." She pushed up on her toes and gave him a kiss. Soft and sweet. And over much too quick. But enough to jack his heart rate even more.

"What was that for?"

She shrugged, stepping back, dribbling, smiling. "Felt like it."

"By all means feel free whenever the mood strikes."

"I will." She dribbled forward, a flirty glint in her eyes.

He swatted and missed. Their eyes mingled, danced.

"Nice try." She faked left, then right.

He kept pace.

She spun away, but he was there when she returned.

"Impressive," she said. She was breathing hard, and he was glad to see he wasn't the only one winded.

She pivoted away, then toward the basket. He followed. His feet got tangled up in the move. She darted past him, putting up a shot.

But he was going down. He hit the pavement hard with his hip. A pain shot up his leg as he rolled, and his prosthetic came off, clattering a few feet away.

"Riley!"

"I'm fine," he said automatically. Stupid leg. His stump ached from overuse, his hip from the fall. But those injuries paled next to the bruise to his pride.

He sat up and brushed the grit from his hands. Heat flushed his face, and his breath hitched.

"Are you hurt?"

"I said I'm fine." His prosthesis was too far to reach, short of crawling over to it. He sat there, helpless as a baby.

Paige grabbed his prosthesis and walked it over. She towered over him.

He snatched it from her hands and went through the motions of donning it. He was breathing hard and aware of the stillness at the other end of the court. Great. An audience.

She squatted down, said nothing as he adjusted the sleeve.

"You're just overtired," she said when he was finished. "I shouldn't have been playing so hard."

"Stop blaming yourself for everything." It came out harsher than he intended.

He braced himself on the pavement and pushed to his feet, testing his body for pain. His stump was tender, his hip probably bruised, but nothing serious. He was going to hurt tomorrow though.

Paige had gone quiet, and his eyes flitted to hers. Emotion tightened the corners of her eyes. Those emotive blue eyes, filled with sadness and worry and all the things he'd never wanted to put there.

Guilt seeped in. It was just a stupid leg. What was wrong with him? He ran a hand over his face. "Man. I'm sorry. I didn't mean to snap at you."

Her chin dimpled. "It's okay."

"No, it's not." He reached for her, pulled her into his chest, and sighed hard. The guys on the other end of the court had resumed their game as if nothing had happened. As if he hadn't just lost his dignity right in front of his girl. But none of that mattered. Not really. It didn't change the way she felt about him. He knew it in his head. His heart was another matter.

He tightened his arms around her. "Less than a week, and I'm already a lousy boyfriend."

She gave a shaky laugh. "I'll be lousy sometimes, too, I promise. I'll forgive you if you forgive me."

He pressed a kiss to the top of her head. "Deal."

She leaned back, and their eyes aligned. He saw so much there. Things he'd longed for when he was thousands of miles away. When Paige was no more than a distant voice across the phone, a faded picture in his pocket, a wispy vision in his dreams.

"It's going to be okay, Riley. You'll see."

Sometimes it was hard to believe that might be true. But hearing it from Paige, seeing the promise in her eyes, made him want to believe it more than ever before.

"I'm sure you're right."

❧

"Alma Walker's here to see you," Molly said from the doorway of the kennel.

Paige gave the hound dog a final pat and stood. "Thanks, Molly."

She followed the girl down the hall and into the lobby.

Mrs. Walker waited. Her frail figure was always draped in

subdued fabrics, and her silver hair was carefully coiffed in what she'd once heard a teenager call a "granny fro." You'd never know it to look at her, but she was probably sitting on millions from her family's maple syrup business.

"Mrs. Walker, it's so nice to see you," Paige said, raising her voice a bit.

"I was out for a tea with my daughter and thought I'd swing by with that check I promised you."

Most of the shelter's donors used automatic withdrawals, but Mrs. Walker didn't trust electronic transactions.

Paige took the check she extended. "I can't tell you how much your support means."

"Well, you know my Winifred was a shelter pup. She's lost her sight in one eye and has hip dysplasia now. I'm afraid she's falling apart as fast as I am!"

"Oh, you're far younger than your age, Mrs. Walker. It's all that charity work you do."

"Well, I try, but age just creeps up on you. But what would you know about that, young thing like you are?"

"Have you met my new assistant, Molly?"

She introduced the two, and a few minutes later they said goodbye. Molly left early for a doctor appointment, and Paige went to clear her desk.

Riley had started his new position at the co-op three days ago. He'd seemed preoccupied when she'd gone over to the farmhouse the night before, though he said the job was going well. There was always a learning curve. He was probably just a little overwhelmed. Bishop seemed to have settled in well. The boxer never left Riley's side the whole time she was there, and there was a new sparkle in the dog's eyes.

She started clearing off her desk, stacking papers and replacing files. All the donors who had promised support had come through except for one. But at two hundred fifty a month, the ongoing donation was a substantial one. She was counting on it to pay her bills.

She wondered if she should give Mr. and Mrs. Gillespie a call and remind them she still needed their credit card number.

Before she could act on the thought, the phone rang. Paige reached for it, hoping it wasn't Mrs. Pritchard again. Paige had gone to her house that morning to capture a critter in her attic, but when she'd arrived there were no signs of wildlife. She had a feeling the elderly woman was only lonely. Paige determined to stop over one day next week with a plate of cookies.

"Perfect Paws Pet Shelter." She shouldered the phone as she shuffled some papers into a tidy pile.

"Is this Paige?"

"Yes it is."

"Hello, dear. This is Darleen."

Paige's hands stilled. She hadn't heard the woman's voice in years. She'd long since stopped calling her Mom. *Stepmother*, she supposed, was Darleen's official title.

"Paige? Are you still there?" Her voice sounded kinder than Paige remembered.

"Yes. I'm here. Sorry, I was just in the middle of something. How are you?"

"I'm doing fine. I was just thinking about you and realized how much time has gotten away from me."

"It's been a long time." Six years, to be exact, since Darleen had packed up her things and moved away, leaving Paige homeless at eighteen. "How'd you know how to reach me?"

"Oh, I still keep in touch with Ellen Mays. I hear you're doing quite well there at the shelter."

Paige ran a hand over her face, trying to gather her thoughts. "I love my work. We've had our struggles, but things are going well for the moment."

"You always did have a heart for animals."

Do you have to bring home every stray you find? Just look at this floor!

"It's very rewarding. How are you? Are you still in Augusta?"

"Yes, I'm helping my sister with the flower shop. It's grown quite a bit since I've been here. I hear you're with that Callahan boy you always liked so much."

Her tone was filled with approval. Strange, since she'd never seemed to like him much. "Riley. Yes, we're . . . we're a couple now."

"It must be difficult, what he's been through. Ellen told me he came home from Afghanistan a quadriplegic, poor thing."

"No, no, he's just—he's an amputee. He has a prosthesis, and he's doing very well. We just played basketball last week."

"Oh! How wonderful. I'm glad it wasn't as bad as Ellen made it out to be. He was always such a nice boy."

Paige frowned at the phone. Who was this woman? And why was she being so nice? Then she felt a twinge of guilt. People changed. They grew.

"Well . . . the reason I called . . . I know it's long overdue, but I wanted to apologize for my behavior after your father passed away. It's no excuse, but my grief was just overwhelming. I hope you'll forgive me for being so insensitive."

"Of course. I already have. Long ago."

"That's very kind of you, dear. Regardless of the circumstances, you know I always thought of you as my daughter."

Words choked in Paige's throat. In spite of the past, Darleen's proclamation made her chest squeeze tight. She was the only mom Paige remembered. She'd spent many years longing for such words. For a speck of kindness. Was it possible time and distance had softened the woman's heart?

"I was also hoping . . . if I made a trip to the coast, would you be willing to meet me for coffee or something, dear? I'd like to catch up."

Paige's emotions were jumbled up inside. She wasn't sure which way was up, so she said the only thing she could think of. "Sure, of course."

"I'm so happy to hear that, Paige. Would you be free this Saturday? Around two o'clock?"

This Saturday?

"Um, yes. I can do that." She imagined meeting at Wicked Good Brew, everyone in Summer Harbor bustling in and out. "Why don't you just come to my house?"

She gave Darleen her address, and a few minutes later Paige hung up, her mind whirling with disbelief and shock, and maybe just a little of something else. Hope.

Chapter 33

aige moved the centerpiece to the coffee table, then stood back and considered its new spot. No, it was too small for the table. She moved it back to the end table and frowned. The arrangement of artificial hydrangeas hadn't seemed so chintzy when she'd picked it up at a garage sale for two dollars. She shoved it under the table, out of sight.

Dasher swished against her legs, purring.

"Who's my baby, huh? You are, aren't you, little girl." She swept the cat into her arms, nuzzling the feline's fuzzy gray head as she walked toward her bedroom.

She set Dasher down on the bed, and the cat's back arched as she gave it a long stroke. "Sorry, sweetie, but Darleen isn't a fan. I'll have a treat for my girl later."

She returned to the living room, looking it over again. Everything was tidy, and the house smelled Pine-Sol clean. She walked into the kitchen, checking the time. The coffee beans were already ground, so she measured them out and poured them into the filter. The coffee had just begun to trickle out when a tap sounded at the door.

Paige drew in a steadying breath and blew it out. *Sheesh, Paige. Relax. It's only Darleen.* Except Darleen was also Mom. Or was she? She didn't even know what to call her anymore.

She straightened her blouse, and when she reached the living room she pulled open the door. The woman who stood on the porch looked much the same. Her hair was still the same shade of auburn, but it was shorter. The roots grown out a bit. She wore a pair of fitted jeans and a trendy top that was a bit frayed around the collar.

There were new shadows under her eyes, new crow's-feet at the corners. But she still had a dazzling smile, and it was laser focused on Paige. Her blue eyes—which Paige had once attributed her own color to—were soft and shiny and as warm as a June day.

"Mom." The word slipped out.

But before Paige could second-guess the attribution, Darleen pulled her into a hug. "Paige. Oh, honey, you look so good. Just beautiful."

Paige's arms settled around Darleen's sturdy shoulders. She'd put on a bit of weight. Surprising, since she'd always watched her diet so carefully. But Paige thought the extra weight softened her a bit. Made her look, and feel, less severe.

"Come in, come in," Paige said when they drew apart.

"What a lovely house. A friend from church used to live right across the street."

"Mrs. Farrell? She still does. Her husband passed away last year. A fishing accident."

"Oh, I'm so sorry to hear that. They were always such a nice couple."

"Have a seat. Do you still take your coffee with cream and sugar?"

"You remembered."

Most of what she remembered about Darleen she was trying to forget. Paige fetched the coffee. Her hands trembled as she pulled the carafe from the cubby. Why was she so nervous? For heaven's sake, it was only Darleen.

Mom.

Riley had been anxious about the meeting. He'd wanted to be here for it, but he worked Saturdays now, and he could hardly ask for time off already. Paige had assured him it wasn't necessary. But now that the moment had arrived, she wished he was there.

A moment later she carried the two mugs into the living room.

Darleen took a sip of her coffee, then set down the mug and pulled her sweater tighter. "I'd forgotten how chilly it is on the coast with the wind."

"Would you like a blanket?"

"The coffee will warm me right up."

Paige had worried about keeping the conversation rolling, but Darleen took care of that. She asked Paige about her work, and Paige told her about the shelter's financial difficulties and all the fundraisers and promoting she'd done over the summer.

They talked about Riley's return and recovery, Darleen tsking sympathetically over his injury. She patted Paige's leg, hanging on to every word. Paige caught her up on the Callahans. Mr. Callahan had passed away since she'd left town, and of course, Beau and Zac had each married.

Paige showed her pictures on her phone, and Darleen exclaimed over how handsome the Callahan brothers had grown up to be. She seemed eager for every detail of Paige's life, so Paige continued flipping through the pictures on her phone, expounding on some of them.

She found herself relaxing and enjoying the give-and-take of the conversation. She wasn't sure why she'd been so nervous.

When she'd exhausted her stories, Paige turned the subject to Darleen and listened patiently as the woman caught her up on life in Augusta. They carefully avoided the topic of Paige's father, and she wondered if Darleen was still grieving him. For all her faults, the woman had loved her dad.

Darleen's sister was seeing a handsome orthodontist, and Darleen regaled her with stories from his office. When she stopped for a sip of warmed-up coffee, Paige found the nerve to ask.

"What about you . . . are you seeing anyone special these days?"

"Me? Oh no. I've quite adjusted to the single life. I've gone out here and there, but there hasn't been anyone special. I'm quite content living with my sister."

"But won't she and her orthodontist get married eventually?"

Darleen's lips pressed into a line, and Paige immediately regretted her question.

But Darleen's face relaxed into a smile. "Deb will never remarry. She had a difficult first marriage, I'm afraid."

"I recall a little of that. She stayed with us for a while."

"Terrible man. The divorce about put her over the edge, he made it so hard on her. I say good riddance. She's doing so much better without him."

"I'm glad to hear that. She was always very good to me."

She reached over and took Paige's hand, squeezing it. "I'm so thankful you've made time for me today. I have such fond memories of you, dear. And of your father, of course."

Paige suppressed the surprise she felt. She gave a careful smile instead and searched for something to say. Something true. "We had some good times, didn't we?"

A few anyway.

"I miss him so. I fell so hard and quickly for him. It was love at first sight for me, you know."

Paige had heard the story many times, but listened anyway as Darleen reminisced about meeting her father at the skating rink. He'd been three years older and quite the ladies' man, apparently. And when he'd focused his attention on Darleen, she'd fairly swooned.

"I couldn't wait until I was eighteen and could marry him. People throw such a fit nowadays about getting married so young, but look at us. Happily married for thirty-one years."

She seemed to have forgotten that her husband had stepped out on her. Conceived a child out of wedlock. *Her.*

"He'd be so proud of you. Despite your troubles at the shelter, you seem to be doing quite well." Her eyes darted around the room. "You have a lovely house in a nice neighborhood, and a good job."

She hated to admit it was only a rental. "I'm very blessed." She toyed with the ring hanging around her neck.

Darleen sucked in a breath as her eyes caught on the ring, exhaling on one word. "Oh! Your father's ring. I thought it was gone forever." Her eyes teared up, and she blinked fast. She reached out and touched it as if it were a precious gemstone. "I was afraid I'd lost it in the move. I was just devastated at the time and not thinking straight. When I realized it was missing, I was just sick about it."

A prickle of guilt stabbed Paige at the longing in Darleen's face. She hadn't known the ring meant so much to her. But it meant a lot to Paige as well. She cradled the ring protectively and stuffed the guilt down deep inside as she leaned forward. "Can I get you more coffee, Mom?"

❧

Riley pushed out from his desk and stretched his legs. They were tight from sitting too long, and his stub ached. The co-op was hopping today. Orders coming in, going out. Paperwork and spreadsheets danced in his head.

RJ Rawlings, a retired lobsterman, was busy in the tank room, taking in lobsters fresh off the boats and packing up orders. The fishermen came into the lobby after dropping off their catches. They huddled around the coffee machine, swapping stories.

Riley remembered those days well, but he was too busy to join in. Wouldn't matter anyway. He didn't want to hear about the size of their catches or their pot malfunctions or this week's territory infringements.

The door opened, the bell jangling. Dylan stepped inside, looking windblown. He seemed taller than usual from Riley's seated position. His sleeveless shirt revealed tanned skin and rippling muscles.

His own muscles were going to wither away if he didn't find the time to lift weights soon. Just the upkeep on his legs took so much time he'd skimped lately on his upper body, and it was starting to show. The desk job wasn't helping.

"Hey, Riley," Dylan said. "How you doing?"

"Just getting ready to head out of here."

"Well, I won't keep you. Just dropped off my catch and stopped in for the coffee. It's noticeably better since you've been around." He filled a Styrofoam cup.

"I'd had enough of that sludge RJ called coffee. Good day?" Politeness demanded he ask.

"Excellent. We're off to a good month."

"That's what I hear."

Dylan headed for the door. "Well, I've got to run. See you later."

The clock had finally struck five, so Riley stood and sent Paige a text, asking how the meeting with Darleen had gone. He'd been worried about her all afternoon, dying to know how she was getting on with her stepmom. He hoped the woman had been kind. Paige had such a soft heart, and she'd always been desperate for the woman's approval. He hated that he couldn't be there to act as a shield.

His phone chimed with an incoming text.

It's going great. Mom's still here. Can you pick up food on the way over?

Mom?

His eyes faltered on the word. Call him cynical, but the woman had abandoned Paige six years ago, and now she was suddenly interested in her life?

He called in an order to Frumpy Joe's and went to pick it up, twiddling his thumbs as he sat at the counter waiting. He tried to make conversation with Charlotte Dupree, but his mind was on Paige. Now that he knew Darleen was still there, he couldn't get to the house fast enough. When Charlotte finally handed over the order, he was on his way.

Minutes later he pulled his motorcycle into Paige's driveway, parking beside an older model beige Cavalier. Its pinstriping had peeled in spots, and rust laced the panel behind the rear wheel well. It wasn't what he'd expected of Darleen Warren.

At the kitchen door he gave a quick tap and opened it up. "I'm here," he called, setting the bags on the counter and turning toward the living room doorway. He'd taken only two steps when he heard a raised voice.

"You always were a selfish girl. I should've known you hadn't changed."

He quickened his pace. "Hey," he said as he busted through the door. He found the pair facing off on the other side of the room. "What's going on?"

Before his words were out, Darleen leaped toward Paige. "It should've been mine!"

Riley sprang forward as the woman reached toward her. His prosthetic foot caught on the rug, and he fought for balance. His leg hit the coffee table, and his prosthesis clattered away as his body hit the ground.

Darleen darted for the door.

From the floor he reached out to stop her, but she skirted him. He scrambled toward her like a broken crab, but she beat him out the door.

He pounded the floor. "Stupid leg!" Sitting upright, his eyes flitted to Paige.

She was clutching her throat, staring after her stepmom, her face as white as death.

"What happened?" he asked.

She turned toward him, and her eyes sharpened on him as if she just realized he'd fallen. She dashed forward. "Are you okay?"

"I'm fine." He scuttled toward his prosthesis, his blood pumping so quickly his lungs could hardly keep up. "What did she do?"

"She—she took my necklace. But it's fine. I'm fine."

His eyes slid down to the empty spot where her fingers clutched at her chest. "Your dad's ring?" His teeth clenched, he donned his leg in record time and scrambled to his feet.

"Don't, Riley." She tried to grab his arm and missed. "It's okay."

But he was already out the door, heat flushing through his body, sweat prickling at the back of his neck.

He exited in time to see Darleen's car peeling out of the drive, gravel flying. The smell of exhaust filled the air.

He whipped his phone from his pocket.

"Who are you calling?" Paige stopped at his side.

"Sheriff Colton."

She grabbed his hand. "Don't. Please, Riley, don't."

His fingers froze on the panel, his eyes finding hers. Twin pools of vulnerability stared back. Frown lines puckered between her brows, and a muscle under her eye twitched. But he couldn't ignore the plea he saw in her eyes, the desperation in her tone.

He lowered his phone, a movement that went against every instinct he had. "Give me one reason I shouldn't go after her, or I swear I'll hunt her down right now and haul her back here." And God help him, he didn't know what he'd do to her once he had her.

She tugged at his arm. "Come inside. You're shaking."

"She ripped it right off your neck, Paige!"

"It's okay. I'm fine." But her voice was shaking, and her lip was quivering. Her face was still pasty white.

Riley wanted to turn back time and charge across the room

without falling on his face. He wanted to yank Darleen off Paige. He wanted to tell the woman to go away and stay away. He wanted to protect his girl the way she deserved to be protected.

But it was too late. He'd already failed at that.

So he just reached for her, pulled her into his arms.

She'd said he was shaking, but it was Paige who shook. The tremors went straight through him. He clenched his teeth together so hard his jaws were like knots. He tightened his arms around her as if the belated protection was enough.

"It doesn't matter." Her voice was a thready whisper.

She was talking about the ring—and it did matter. But what mattered even more was the betrayal she was feeling right now. In the space of a few hours she'd opened her heart back up to a woman who didn't deserve it. Given her a chance to stomp over it all over again.

He set his cheek on her head. "It does matter."

Paige deserved so much more. She'd been cheated when it came to family, for sure. That she'd turned out so loving, so giving, was truly a God-thing.

"She asked for a loan. I tried to tell her I didn't have any money, but she didn't believe me. She must be feeling pretty desperate."

His chest squeezed tight. He drew back, cupping her face. "It was the only thing you had of your dad's. It was yours. He would've wanted you to have it. Let me help you get it back."

She shook her head. "No. I just want to forget this." Her words wobbled like an uneven chair.

His eyes pierced hers. He wished he could take away the pain he saw there. Instead he had to make it worse by stating the truth. She already knew it, but she had to acknowledge it. He didn't want her having regrets later.

"Honey . . . ," he said gently. "She's just going to sell it. And then it'll be gone for good."

"I don't want to see her again. And I don't want people knowing what she did. I just want to forget it happened." Her eyes glazed over. "Please, Riley. It's just a ring."

He drew her back into his arms. It was all he could do to stand here. All he could do to keep from taking off after the woman or, at the very least, dialing the sheriff. They knew where she lived. Getting the ring back wouldn't be hard.

But it wasn't what Paige wanted.

Paige tightened her arms around him. "I thought she wanted me. I thought she missed me." There was anguish in the tightness of her voice. And then she broke loose. Her body shuddered in rhythmic jolts.

Her sobs tore at his heart. "Aw, honey. I'm so sorry."

"She was being so nice. She was asking about my job and about you, and it was like she was really interested. I'm so stupid!"

"No, you're not. This isn't about you. It's about her. She's just a rotten person."

"She's the only family I have, and she doesn't even want me!"

"That's not true. We're your family. God's your Father. There are lots of people who love you, Paige."

"It's not the same."

He tightened his arms around her. He'd never felt so useless. He hadn't protected her from Darleen, either physically or emotionally. He should've insisted on taking the day off, regardless of Paige's assurances. If he would've, this never would've happened. He wouldn't have let things escalate like that. He wanted to pound a wall.

What kind of man was he?

He was afraid he knew the answer to that question. He'd pushed it away since he'd been with Paige, let the joy of having her hold back the dark waters. But the truth had been slowly creeping back into his heart lately. And now it was as if the floodgates had opened.

He held Paige until her tears dried up. Dinner got cold on the kitchen counter while they talked, and they heated it up a while later. After supper they watched a chick flick, and when her eyes got tired, he tucked her in.

"Sweet dreams," he whispered as he pulled the covers to her chin. He planted a kiss on her forehead. "I'll lock up behind me."

"'Night," she said. But her eyes were already closed when he turned out the light.

He quietly tidied up the kitchen and locked the door as he left. The dark cloud gathered over him on the quiet drive home, seeming to enclose him. He tried to push his way out, but it was relentless. By the time he reached his room at the farmhouse, he had an ache in his gut the size of Anvil Boulder.

When Paige had needed him most, he'd been at work—at a job that now, in the dark of night, seemed pretty pathetic. He shuffled papers and lined up numbers. It was a job a high school student could do, and the pay wasn't much better than minimum wage.

Maybe he could make ends meet now, but how could he ever support a family with a job like that? He had no college degree. He was trained for only one thing. Had depended on that skill to get him through life, and now that was gone.

Feeling the heavy weight pressing his shoulders, he doffed his prosthesis and set it beside the nightstand. He hobbled to the bathroom with his crutch to wash his stump and sock. When he returned to his room he pulled off his belt and emptied his pockets.

His phone showed a voicemail from Noah, and he touched the arrow to play it.

"Hey there. Haven't heard from you, so I'm just checking in to make sure you're still coming next Saturday. I lined up some help to get you moved in. Plan on having dinner at my folks'. Give me a call and let me know what time you'll be getting in. Looking forward to having you here, buddy."

Riley stared at the screen until it went dark, his thoughts spinning, the darkness pressing on him like a lead cape. He finished readying for bed, turned off the lights, and settled under the covers. But sleep was a long time coming.

Chapter 34

S omething was wrong with Riley. Paige noticed it the next
  morning at church when he greeted her with a strained
smile. At first she thought he was only troubled about what had
happened the night before. But during the service he didn't reach
for her hand once.

She needed to get him alone, but she'd walked to church so
they rode with the family to the farmhouse after the service. Her
worry flared through the meal. There was enough going on at the
table to divert attention from Riley's withdrawn mood, but Paige
could focus on little else. She couldn't wait for the end of dinner to
get him alone on the ride home and press harder.

A terrible dread snaked its way up her spine as they walked
to Beau's truck. There was no hand at the small of her back, no
sideways smile.

The weather had chilled as September had eased in. The air
was still fresh with the smell of pine, but soon the deciduous
leaves would turn, and the smell of earth and decaying leaves
would suffuse the air.

Riley opened her truck door and walked around to the other
side. The corners of his eyes were tight, his lips in a straight line.

His broad shoulders seemed tense, and there was a slight hitch to his gait.

Paige's stomach twisted. Her hands trembled as she buckled her seat belt.

He got in and started the truck, then pulled around the loop and headed down the long drive. The silence was overwhelming. She could almost hear her heart thudding in her chest.

They had all afternoon to talk. They'd spent their recent Sundays cuddled up on the couch watching preseason football. But Paige couldn't foresee any cuddling today. Not when he could hardly look at her.

She steeled herself for the conversation and turned toward him as he pulled onto the main road. She had to get this over with.

"Riley . . . ? What's wrong? You've been quiet all morning."

His knuckles whitened on the steering wheel, erasing any hope that she'd been fretting needlessly. Something was coming, and by the strain on his face, she wasn't going to like it.

"Did I do something?" she asked. "Say something?"

His eyes squeezed in a wince. "No . . . no. You're—you didn't do anything wrong, Paige."

"Then what? Is it about last night? Are you upset about the ring? Because I'm okay. I was upset, but I'm over it. Darleen's gone, and I'm sure I won't be seeing her again."

"It's not that. It's just—"

Her eyes searched his face for a clue to what he was thinking. What he was feeling. She wanted him to say it already, whatever it was, but he was having trouble finding the words. She forced her tongue to lie still even as her stomach rolled with tension.

His fingers tightened on the steering wheel. "I don't think this is going to work."

His words opened a hollow spot in her chest, giving her heart plenty of room to implode. "What—what do you mean?"

His Adam's apple took a long, slow dip. "I think we should go back to being friends."

"Friends." The word grated past her dry throat. How could he even say that?

"You know I care about you," he said. "The last thing I'd ever want to do is hurt you, but—"

"Well you are. You are hurting me."

His jaw knotted. "I'm sorry."

She trembled from the inside out like his words had set off some earthquake. "What happened? What happened between yesterday and today, because I thought everything was fine between us."

He gave a long blink. "It's not you, it's—"

"*Me*. Yeah, I'm familiar with that one."

Beau had said the exact same words. But at least he'd looked her in the eye. Held her hands. Or tried. Riley hadn't taken his eyes off the road since he'd turned over the key.

"Look at me," she said.

His eyes flickered over to hers. She saw regret and plenty of steely resolve in those shadowed eyes. It was the resolve that worried her.

He looked back at the road in time to slow for a stop sign.

She let her thoughts spin for a moment. This didn't make sense. He wasn't telling her everything.

"What happened? What happened last night? After you left?"

"Nothing happened."

"You were fine. You tucked me in, kissed me good night. Something had to happen. Did someone say something?" A thought occurred to her. "Did you call the sheriff?" Her voice rose on the end.

"No. I said I wouldn't."

She was at a loss. She shook her head. "What then?"

He slowed down for a turn in the road, accelerated. He was quiet so long she thought he was never going to answer. And he owed her an explanation, daggonit.

"Come on, Riley."

He exhaled. "I don't know what to say, Paige. Maybe it's the timing. I have a lot going on right now. I'm dealing with a lot and—"

"I can help you with that if you'd just let me. I thought that's what I was doing."

"You were. You are. I just—" He gave another hard sigh. "Last night put some things into perspective for me, made me think, and then I got home, and there was a voicemail from Noah asking when I was coming, and I couldn't—"

"Wait." The word left with all the breath remaining in her body. "You never told him you weren't coming?"

"I meant to. I just . . . never got around to it, I guess."

"Never got around to it."

Riley had supposedly committed to her. Committed to an apartment, a job. Only he hadn't. He'd held on to Copper Creek as a backup plan. While she'd entered this relationship feet first, all in. Obviously that made only one of them.

She turned and looked out at the blur of passing homes. None of this made sense. Riley had said he'd cared about her for years. Had enlisted in the marines because of it. Those feelings couldn't have gone away overnight.

She turned and studied him. The corners of his eyes were tight, his jawline sharp with tension. She was missing something. And she wasn't going to let this go until he came clean.

"Tell me the truth," she said.

He stared forward, his jaw muscle ticking. He blinked three times in quick succession. "I don't know what else to say, Paige."

He turned into her drive. Gravel popped under the tires, then silence followed as the truck came to a halt. He turned off the ignition, avoiding her gaze.

"You love me." Her heart beat up into her throat at the bold proclamation. "I know you do."

His eyes shot to hers, locking in. She saw so much in those green depths. Pain. Longing. Truth. It gave her the courage to continue.

She grabbed his hand. His beautiful hand. "And I love you too, Riley. Whatever this is, we'll work through it. But you have to stay. You have to fight for it."

Don't leave me. Please don't leave me.

He pulled away, his hand slipping from hers. He stared out the front windshield. She saw the struggle on his face. In his pinched lips, his rapidly blinking eyes. She wanted to touch him. Wanted to pull him close and never let him go. But instead she waited, the silence almost unbearable.

His hands twisted on the steering wheel. "You don't understand." His voice was strained with emotion.

"Then tell me."

"There's nothing that can change this, Paige."

"Change what?"

He looked her way, his eyes snapping with fire. "Me! There's nothing that can change what I am. What I've become. I'm half a man, Paige! I can't even protect you. I'm flipping helpless."

Her heart squeezed tight. "That's not true," she whispered.

"Oh yeah? What about yesterday? I couldn't even protect you from Darleen. A *woman*. I fell flat on my face while she ripped that ring off your neck and ran for the hills."

"It was just a ring."

His eyes pierced hers. "What if it had been more? What if it had been a thief, or what if the house was on fire?"

"I can take care of myself."

"You shouldn't have to. You deserve more. You deserve better."

"I want *you*. I love *you*. I don't want anyone else!"

"Well you should."

Gah! She scrubbed her hand over her face. How could she rationalize with someone who was completely irrational? How could she convince him he was perfect for her just the way he was? She couldn't. He had to realize that for himself.

Paige's eyes found her lap. "You know what, Riley? The real problem here isn't down there." She gestured toward his leg, then waited an extra beat until his eyes met hers. Then she placed a finger to her temple. "It's up here."

He looked away. Peeled his fingers off the steering wheel and flattened them against his thighs. The air seemed to have been sucked from the cab, leaving a vacuum of tension.

Finally he placed his hand over hers. It was warm and gentle, the merest touch, but it gave birth to hope.

"I'm still your friend, Paige."

His friend. The word drove a spike into her heart.

Yeah, she was enough to fill that spot. She'd given him her heart, and he was handing it back on a platter. A dark space expanded inside, heavy and aching. Rejection.

The old doubts came flooding back, never mind that he was being completely ridiculous. She didn't belong. Didn't belong anywhere. He was leaving her. Again. It was what people did. And the fact that it was happening all over made her want to throw something.

She pulled her hand away. "Don't do me any favors." She felt the heat of his gaze, but she didn't look his way.

"Paige, don't."

She reached for the handle, noting, as if from afar, the tremble in her hand. But just before she opened the door, she turned back and drilled him with a look.

"Don't what, Riley? You've made yourself clear. You want to be friends, but you're moving fifteen hundred miles away? That sends a message loud and clear, don't you think?"

She opened the door. Needed to get inside. She could feel the panic bubbling up inside, about to spill over.

He caught her arm. "I care about you. I don't want to lose you."

She swallowed hard. Couldn't bring herself to meet his gaze. His eyes would be warm and worried. She'd fall right into them and break apart, right here, in front of him.

She swallowed hard. Sucked in a deep breath. Forced out the words he needed to hear. "I know. It's fine, Riley. I'll be fine. I hope you will be too."

And with that she slipped out of the car and into her empty house.

Chapter 35

*R*iley made his way through the maze of tables at the Roadhouse, heading toward the corner booth. He'd been dreading this all day. Bad enough he'd had to quit the co-op after only a week. Now he had to face his brothers. And they weren't going to go easy on him.

Well, that was tough. They couldn't know what it was like to go through what he'd been through. When he reached the empty corner booth, he slid into the seat. He hadn't heard from Paige since they'd parted the day before. Not that he'd expected to.

His mind kept flashing back to the hurt in her blue eyes, to the tremble in her voice. Just the memory of it made the walls of his chest close in. He felt the pinch of guilt along with the ache of loss, all of it overwhelming.

You're doing the right thing.

He had to think of her. Had to think of what was best in the long run. Maybe she was hurting now, but she'd be okay. She could do so much better. Deserved so much better. More than the emotional and physical wreck he'd become. He'd let himself forget for a while.

But losing her . . . it was worse than losing an appendage, and he could state with complete certainty. Now he had the memory of her kiss, the memory of holding her in his arms. He wasn't sure if the memories were a blessing or a curse.

He'd called Noah and moved up his plans by a few days. He had to get out of here before he slipped and begged Paige to give him another chance. Noah had seemed distracted and withdrawn during the conversation. Only after Riley twisted his arm did his friend come clean: His marriage was on the rocks. A divorce was likely forthcoming.

Riley tried to back out of coming. He didn't want to be in the way. But Noah insisted his help was needed more than ever. Maybe he could be a shoulder for Noah to lean on.

He didn't see Beau until he slid into the booth opposite him. Riley's strained smile died on his lips at the scowl on Beau's face.

"You broke up with her? And you're moving to Podunk, Georgia?"

He sighed. "Can't a guy break his own news around here?"

"What are you thinking?"

Zac approached, untying an apron stained with something brown. "Man, what a crazy day. No bread truck, an oven malfunction, and a prep guy with fresh stitches. Some days I should just stay in bed." He slid into the booth beside Beau, his gaze toggling between them. "What's going on?"

"Our brother's moving to Georgia."

Riley shot Beau a look. "Thanks."

Frown lines formed between Zac's brows. "What? What about Paige?"

"He broke up with her."

Riley glared at Beau.

"What the heck, Riley," Zac said.

Riley sat back in the booth, crossing his arms. Maybe he

should just let Beau handle all this, since he was so quick with the answers.

"You just got an apartment, a job . . . ," Zac said.

"And why'd you go and break up with her anyway?" Beau asked.

"Oh, do I get to talk now?"

Beau planted his elbows on the table. "Stop being such a tool and tell us what's going on."

"Yeah, you make it so easy."

Zac leaned forward. "Guys, come on. What happened, Riley? Why are you moving?"

"Nothing happened. I just—I need some space. I need to get away, and I've got that great offer from Noah. I can't pass it up."

"And what about Paige?" Beau asked. "You're going to just drop her like that?"

"You mean like *you* did?" Riley asked.

Beau's jaw ticked. "She's in love with you."

Heat pooled in the vicinity of his heart. Sweat broke out at the back of his neck. She'd said the words last night. The ones he'd longed to hear for years. Too bad he didn't deserve to hear them. But the look on her face . . . Guilt twisted inside, a feeling that was becoming more familiar than he liked.

"We're still friends."

Beau leaned back in his seat, huffing.

"You said you need space," Zac said. "Space from what, exactly?"

"He doesn't need space, he needs therapy."

Riley gave him a flinty look. "Shut up, Beau."

"Well, you do. I know you haven't been going. Maybe if you did you wouldn't be making such stupid decisions."

"All right, guys, come on."

"I don't need you to tell me how to live my life."

"Could've fooled me."

"Think what you want. This is going to happen, and there's nothing you can say to stop me."

"Just like when you enlisted, huh? You're going to take off with no warning."

Riley rolled his eyes. "And . . . we're back to that."

"That's what you do, Riley. You run. You ran then, and you're running now."

Riley gritted his teeth until his jaw ached. "You don't know what you're talking about."

"What are you running from this time?"

"This is nothing like that."

"This is exactly like that!"

His muscles tensed. "Oh yeah? 'Cause I'm pretty sure *I* have Paige now. I don't have to sit around watching you rub your relationship in my face."

Surprise flickered in Beau's eyes. He blinked. Sank back against the booth.

"Oh boy," Zac said.

Riley hadn't meant to say that. He tightened his fists under the table and fixed his gaze on the jukebox across the room. Stupid! Why'd he have to go and lose his temper?

"Wait." Beau's tone was tempered with dread. "What does that mean?"

"It doesn't mean anything." Riley's eyes bounced off Beau. "Bottom line is I'm moving on, and you need to come to grips with that. I have a good job, and I'll keep in touch."

"You had feelings for Paige back then? While I was with her?" Beau sounded torn between indignation and empathy.

Riley narrowed his eyes. "Let me help you out here, buddy.
I loved her way before you ever did." He let that register for a
long minute. Watched the emotions cycle across Beau's face.
Realization. Pity. Guilt.

For a moment Riley was back in time, watching the two of
them cuddling on the couch. Kissing hello and good-bye, mur-
muring quietly to each other. He'd been sick with jealousy over
his own brother.

Beau's eyes shadowed with guilt. Something like pain flashed
in their depths. "That's why you enlisted. You *were* running—from
me and Paige. And I was too big an idiot to see it."

"Stop taking credit for my decisions. I enlisted because I
wanted to."

"Because I was with the woman you loved."

"All right, all right," Zac said. "It's out on the table, but it's in
the past. Let's just move on, okay?"

"I don't understand," Beau said. "You've finally got her, and
now you're leaving again. What am I missing here?"

He just wouldn't quit. Riley's fingers twitched. "There's nothing to fix here, Beau. Just leave it alone."

"Not until you tell me what's really going on."

"It's none of your business. That's between me and Paige.
And you know what?" Riley moved from the booth. "I'm not really
hungry anymore."

"Riley," Zac said. "Come on."

But Riley was already walking away. He'd had about enough of
his brothers for one day.

Chapter 36

*R*iley was gone.

Paige picked up the basset pup, and he nuzzled her under the chin. Sometime between Sunday and today a wide hollow spot had opened up in place of her heart. She worked. She ate. She slept. Well, a little. Mostly she fretted and missed and cried.

She'd played his words back in her head a hundred times. And yet despite his claims that she deserved better, the old doubts crept back. She wasn't enough somehow. She'd known it all along, deep down. She hadn't been enough for her parents, hadn't been enough for Beau, and she wasn't enough for Riley. Maybe as a friend, but nothing more.

She set the pup back in the kennel and went through the motions of closing up shop. After the shelter was locked up, she walked to Wicked Good Brew, the folder filled with her carefully prepared financial statements tucked into her side. This was supposed to have been a happy day. She'd worked so hard. Her animals would be okay. Her sanctuary was saved.

At the coffee shop she ordered a latte and found an empty

table. Margaret arrived a few minutes later, looking elegant in a long tunic and trendy jeans. After the woman had collected her iced tea from the barista, Paige waved her over.

They exchanged small talk for a minute before settling into business. Paige went over the financials, detailing the new monthly sponsors she'd signed on.

"And," Paige said, injecting enthusiasm into her voice, "I just received word last week that the shelter is receiving a grant from a private foundation out of Boston. With the added funds we can host at least one spay and neuter clinic this year, maybe two."

Margaret sat back in her seat. "Well, you have certainly outdone yourself, Paige. The sponsors, the successful fundraiser, the grant. I don't know how you pulled it off, but I'm so happy you did. The shelter is a vital part of the community, and it would've broken my heart to see it close. You should be so proud of yourself."

For some reason the words made Paige's eyes sting. "That means a lot to me."

Margaret took the offered folder and drained the rest of her tea. "I have no doubt the board members will be most pleased. It's never been more obvious that we have the right woman at the helm."

"Thank you, Margaret."

A while later they parted ways in the parking lot and Paige walked home, wishing she could feel a glimmer of optimism through the haze of loneliness.

❧

"You still working?"

Riley's gaze shifted from the bright light of the computer screen to the doorway of his new office. Noah's fit form filled the space, and his hands rested on his narrow hips. He had jet-black hair and a pretty-boy face the ladies used to go crazy for. But his tired eyes spoke of sleepless nights and an aching heart.

"I was passing by and saw the lights on."

"Yeah, just getting familiar with this program. It's a little different from the one I used at the co-op."

"You know it's eleven o'clock on a Sunday night?" He'd invited Riley to go out for a late dinner with his friends, but Riley had begged off.

"I'd like to hit the ground running tomorrow."

"Right, well . . . We had fun tonight. Maybe you can come along next time." He doubted Noah had anything resembling fun in weeks. But they all had their own ways of coping.

"Sure," Riley said. But the last thing he felt like doing was meeting a bunch of new people.

Noah tapped the doorframe twice. "Okay, I'll see you in the morning."

After he left, Riley put in another half hour, then locked up and headed home. He'd brought Bishop to the office with him, and the boxer's claws ticked on the stairs to his apartment, located over Noah's garage.

"Home sweet home," he said as he opened the door for the dog.

A musty smell assaulted him as he entered. The streetlight filtered through the curtains, so he didn't bother with the light switch as he filled Bishop's water dish.

Riley doffed his prosthesis and washed up, then fell into bed, his body tired and aching. He should sleep well, if for no other reason than that he'd only had about ten cumulative hours over the past three days. The sofa bed was lumpy, and the window air conditioner didn't quite do the job.

He refused to admit the real reason he was losing sleep. A little denial went a long way.

Copper Creek was a pleasant enough place. About the same size as Summer Harbor, with plenty of small-town charm. The people were friendly and the scenery was nice. Maybe next summer he and Noah would go hiking in the Blue Ridge Mountains. He tried to dredge up some excitement about that and failed.

He settled into the pillow and closed his eyes. Within minutes Bishop was snoring.

The early evening sky lit with an explosion of light and sound. His body lifted, and he was flying like a rag doll. He hit the ground with a hard thud, knocking the wind from his lungs. Pain. Darkness sucked at him.

He couldn't pass out. His buddy.

He spit out a mouthful of dust and pushed up. Looked down at his leg, then wished he hadn't. Bile rose in his throat, but he swallowed it back. He looked around, assessing the situation through a fog of pain.

A body lay in the dust several yards away.

"Tex!" The name scraped across his throat.

His friend's abdomen moved up and down. Breathing. Moaning. Alive.

"It's okay! I got you." He crawled toward him, his elbows digging into the hard, dry ground of the goat path. His leg useless. "I got you, buddy!"

As he neared he saw the gaping wound. Bloody and big. Oh God, help him! *It was so big. And right where his heart was. Riley tried to stanch the flow of blood with his hand. It was all he had. Blood poured over him, staining his flesh red.*

"It's okay. It's okay, buddy." He looked up into Tex's face.

But it wasn't Tex's weathered face. Not Tex's eyes staring back at him.

It was Paige's. Her blue eyes, blank as death, fixed on him.

"Nooooo!"

Riley flew upright, his eyes opening to darkness. His heart was a jackhammer inside his chest. His breaths came quick and shallow, and he was shaking uncontrollably.

Paige!

But he wasn't in the sandpit. He was inside. In a bed. Bishop stirred at his feet.

Just a dream. Just a dream. *Oh God! Thank You!*

The image of her face haunted him. Her skin pale and lifeless. Her eyes like death. He tried to push the image away, but it wouldn't leave. He fell back in bed, catching his breath, a hand over his racing heart.

He lay there for hours, the bed shaking under the force of his beating heart. His mind filled with the terror of sleep.

He must've drifted off, because he wakened later to the buzzing of his phone.

He reached for it, answering, his voice nothing but a croak.

"Where are you, buddy?"

Noah. Riley ran a hand over his blurry eyes and checked the time. Ten o'clock! He must've turned off his alarm in his sleep.

He sat up, pushing the covers back. "I overslept. Sorry. I'll be there in twenty."

rumpy Joe's was filled with Saturday morning customers, some chatting animatedly, others still trying
to wake up with their steaming white mugs of coffee. The savory
smell of bacon hung in the air alongside the sweeter smell of
maple syrup.

Paige settled into the last booth. She was lucky to find an
empty one. She'd forgotten today was Open Lighthouse Day. The
one day a year the Coast Guard provided access to many of Maine's
lighthouses. Lighthouse Pointe drew its fair share of visitors.
Already the town was crawling with tourists.

Her empty stomach gave a hard twist. Had she forgotten to
eat supper last night? She'd worked until almost ten and yes, she
had fallen into bed exhausted. There might've been a vending
machine snack somewhere in there.

All her days were running together. It had only been two and a
half weeks since Riley had left. Was this what life without him was
going to be like? She had to find something else to do. She was all
caught up and then some at work. She'd already cleaned out and

rearranged all the files and scoured the place to death. She was probably driving Molly crazy.

Lucy bounced into the booth, all smiles. "Morning!"

Paige tried not to hate her. "Someone's already highly caffeinated."

Lucy made a face. "Guilty. Three cups. But let's get you some."

She signaled Charlotte, who was bustling around with a full carafe, her red hair coiffed in a low, messy bun.

Paige tipped her mug over as Charlotte approached. "Help."

"Is on the way," the owner said, pouring a steaming stream of the dark brew. When she finished she looked at Lucy. "Any for you, sweetie?"

Paige's hand fell to cover Lucy's upside-down mug. "Don't you dare."

Charlotte patted her shoulder before turning to the next table.

"What's Zac doing this morning?" Paige asked after she'd taken a long, slow sip of the java.

"Sleeping in. There was a band last night, so it was a late one. You should've come. It was fun. They played a lot of country classics."

"I had some work to get caught up on."

Lucy shrugged out of her jacket. "You've been working a lot lately."

"Just trying to stay busy."

Lucy gave her a sympathetic smile as the server came to take their orders. Paige ordered a Belgian waffle and added a side of bacon. She needed the protein. None of it sounded good.

A siren fired up in the distance, its wailing gaining steam as it neared and passed the café. Some crazy tourist had probably taken a dive off Lighthouse Pointe or something. She whispered a quick prayer for their safety, then felt a pang of guilt. One-liner prayers for help were becoming a habit. She couldn't even remember the last time she'd had a quality quiet time.

The bell over the door jingled, and Paige's eyes went to the entrance. Miss Trudy entered, and Paige caught her eye and waved her over.

"I can only stay for a minute." The woman slid into the booth next to Lucy. "I'm meeting friends. I'm just waiting for a table."

"Are you going through the lighthouse today?" Lucy asked.

"No, I'll be at the visitor center. It'll be a busy day." She looked at Paige. "And how are you doing?"

Paige tried for a smile and injected some enthusiasm into her voice. "I'm fine."

Miss Trudy scowled. "Don't you lie to me, missy. I can see the misery all over your face."

Paige settled back in the booth, her smile crumbling. So much for faking it. "Has anyone heard from him?"

"He called Zac," Lucy admitted after a brief pause. "He's settled into his apartment and his job, I suppose. Zac didn't think he sounded very happy."

Miss Trudy huffed. "Of course he's not happy."

A moment's consolation surged inside Paige, until guilt rose up in its place. Was that really what she wanted? For Riley to be as miserable as she was? After all he'd been through, he deserved better than her ill wishes.

"I hate seeing you all torn up like this," Lucy said.

"I'll be fine."

The server set down three ice waters, then scurried away.

Lucy pulled her straw from its wrapper and stuck it in the cup.

"I left Zac, too, remember? Last summer after I got my memory back? I just needed to go back home and get some things straight. But I came back."

Paige gave a wry grin. "I don't think it's the same thing."

"Maybe not . . . but you never know."

"I just feel so . . . adrift." Her mind shot forward to the long day ahead. To the long evenings in her near future. It seemed so empty. So lonely. The kind of loneliness that struck terror in her heart.

Lucy placed her hand over Paige's. "I know it's hard not to have any kinfolk, but you're not alone. You're one of us."

"Of course she is," Miss Trudy said. "She knows that."

"I do know, it's just . . ." Paige's face warmed. "I think about him all the stinking time."

"Riley made his decision," Miss Trudy said. "And there's nothing to be done about that. Maybe he'll come around, and maybe he won't. But if there's anything I've learned in all these years, it's that you can't control someone else. You can only control yourself—on a good day. You need to find something productive to keep your mind busy. Focus on you. On being the best *you* you can be."

"Why, Aunt Trudy," Lucy said. "That's wonderful advice."

"Don't know why you sound so surprised. I'm a virtual fount of wisdom."

"I have been staying busy," Paige said. "I've been working till bedtime, but I'm running out of things to do, and if I don't find something to occupy me, I'm going to go crazy."

"You could start jogging with me and Eden. We go three mornings a week."

Paige sighed. That would take care of three hours. It was something. "Maybe."

Miss Trudy's brows puckered in a thoughtful look. "What about volunteering somewhere?"

"Like where?"

"We could always use more help at the community center," Lucy said. "There are a few adults who help out on Saturdays and after school. The kids need mentors, and I have a few who need help with homework. Sometimes we get a little overwhelmed."

"That's a fine idea," Miss Trudy said.

A bit of hope bloomed inside Paige at the thought of helping kids who might be disconnected at home. She knew what that was like. She wished the center had been there when she was a kid. It would've been a place to go. A place where she might not have felt so . . . in the way.

"I could do that. I was good in school. Hey, maybe I could even bring an animal for the kids to play with—if it's okay with you."

Lucy's blue eyes sparkled. "I love that idea. I wish I'd have thought of it before. I have a couple kids who haven't really connected with anyone. A dog or a cat might be just the thing."

"Animals have a way of breaking through barriers." Paige thought of Bishop and Riley and immediately pushed the thought away. "Let's do it. I have a mixed breed adolescent that's very friendly. Calm but playful. I think he'd be perfect."

"Bring him on over. The kids will love it."

There was a lot of shuffling at the entrance of the café. A couple had just entered and were speaking with Charlotte. The owner put her hand over her mouth, her eyes going wide.

"What's going on?" Lucy turned to see what Paige was looking at.

Charlotte rang up an older gentleman with a cane, then picked up her carafe and came to their table. She turned over Miss Trudy's mug and filled it, her hand shaking.

"Everything okay, Charlotte?" Lucy asked.

"I don't think so. The Crawfords just told me there's been a terrible accident a couple blocks over." Her gaze went around the table, stopping at Miss Trudy. "I'm afraid it's Sheriff Colton."

Chapter 38

The columns on the computer blurred together. Man, he was dragging. Riley blinked hard a few times, rubbed his eyes. Even the coffee hadn't perked him up this morning. He propped his chin on his fist and continued scanning the columns.

The hum of a truck filtered into the office. Someone was loading windows or doors in preparation for their day. The air in the office was warm, almost stifling. Stupid Georgia weather. It was supposed to be fall. He thought wistfully of autumn in Summer Harbor. The temperatures would be cooler now, the trees shimmering with gold and red. Wood stoves churning out the homey smell of burning logs into the crisp fall air. He could almost smell it now.

"Riley."

His head popped up, his back straightening. He blinked.

Noah came into focus, standing just inside the office door, his lips pressed together. Dan, one of their roofers, was at his side.

"Dan needs his check."

"Oh, sure. Sorry." He rifled through the mess on his desk, heat climbing into his face. He couldn't believe he'd fallen asleep on the job. He finally found the envelope. "Here you go."

Dan approached the desk. It was his day off, so he wore a T-shirt and basketball shorts.

Riley's eyes trailed down to the man's prosthetic leg. He blinked in surprise.

Dan took the check. "Thanks. Have a good weekend, y'all." Then he strode from the office.

Riley stared at the empty doorway. The guy was a workhorse. He showed up at seven a.m. to load his truck, then spent all day climbing ladders and scrambling around on a hot roof. Hard labor. Physical.

"Didn't know he was an amputee?" Noah asked.

"Never seen him in shorts."

"Yeah, you'd never know. He's one of my best workers. I tend to forget it myself."

Riley wondered how long ago he'd lost his leg. And for just a second he wondered if he'd sold himself short. He thought about the conversation he'd had with Beau months ago. He'd been adamant that he'd never be able to do something as physical as lobstering. Had he been wrong?

Noah lowered himself into the chair across from the desk with a big sigh. "We need to talk, man."

Riley winced. Bad enough he'd overslept three times, now he was napping on the job. Heat climbed into his face again. "I'm sorry. I just drifted off for a second. It won't happen again."

"I'm not worried about the job. I'm worried about you. You got bags under your eyes, man."

"I'm just getting used to a new place, a new bed, that's all."

Noah stared back with knowing eyes. "I was outside your office the other day when that car backfired."

A tingling swept up the back of Riley's neck and into his face.

One minute he'd been clacking away on the keyboard, the next he'd been flat on the ground, his nose in the carpet. He hadn't thought anyone had seen.

"It's nothing to be ashamed of," Noah said. "A lot of guys hit the wall when they come back. Are you seeing someone about it?"

Riley's chair squeaked as he sat back. "No. I was back home."

Okay, one time. But the man hadn't understood. Didn't get it. How could he when he'd never been over there? Never seen the things Riley had?

"Look, I'm no expert, but everyone knows soldiers sometimes come back with PTSD. You got all the signs, man."

Shame crawled through him, making his stomach turn with nausea. A denial was on his lips, but he suppressed it. Suppressed the instant desire to cross his arms over his chest and get defensive. Noah was right. He did have all the symptoms. And they'd only gotten worse since he'd arrived in Copper Creek. Seeing his old buddy again probably hadn't helped. It just brought everything back.

"I care about you, man," Noah said. "I have a pastor friend. He's got a degree in psychology, but most importantly, he's very wise and a good listener. Believe me, I've been bending his ear plenty lately. I can text you his number if you want."

Riley exhaled. He was tired of fighting this. Tired of feeling this way. And just plain old tired. If he didn't do something, he was going to lose his job, and then where would he be?

"Sure. That'd be great."

"All right." Noah pushed to his feet. "Well, I got a job waiting. Forbes called in sick, and the Malloys say their windows can't wait till Monday."

The Malloys were a pain. "Have fun."

Noah strode from the room, and Riley watched him go, his heart beating up into his throat at the thought of dragging all his crap out into the open. But he had to do something. Lord knew, what he was doing now sure wasn't working.

Chapter 39

*P*aige took a sip of her coffee and nearly spit the cooled brew back out. Vending machine coffee was one thing. *Cold* vending machine coffee . . . blech.

She stood from the chain of waiting room seats, dumped the Styrofoam cup into the trash, and returned, sitting between Miss Trudy and Lucy.

As soon as they'd heard that the sheriff had been whisked away to the hospital in Ellsworth, she and Lucy had offered to escort Miss Trudy here. The older woman had been withdrawn the whole way, her eyes closed, no doubt storming heaven's gates for the man's life. Paige had been on the phone gathering facts.

The sheriff had been using the crosswalk in front of the Mangy Moose Gift Emporium this morning when a car struck him. The deputy said it was a tourist, an elderly lady, who hadn't seen him. Fortunately she hadn't been going very fast, but Danny had still taken a hard hit.

Now Miss Trudy's hands were wringing themselves to death. It had been almost two hours since they'd received word that he was headed into surgery. The hospital staff would tell them nothing, since they weren't family. He had no wife or children, and his parents had passed on, but his cousin had recently arrived from Penobscot, so they hoped for an update soon.

Paige set her hand over Miss Trudy's, stilling them. "The deputy said the car wasn't going very fast. I'm sure he's going to be fine."

"We don't know that." Her voice sounded strangled.

"We're praying, Aunt Trudy," Lucy said. "We're praying hard."

Paige closed her eyes and breathed another heartfelt prayer. Miss Trudy might be the most stubborn woman on the planet, but she loved the sheriff. There was no doubt in Paige's mind. She begged God to give the couple a chance to resolve their differences. If something happened to Danny with all this conflict between them, Miss Trudy would have so much regret.

Hearing the squeak of shoes on the sterile floor, Paige opened her eyes. The sheriff's cousin approached, running a hand through his thinning gray hair.

"Lloyd." Miss Trudy popped to her feet. "What'd they say?"

Lloyd lumbered to a stop. With his towering height and broad shoulders, he reminded Paige of an older Danny. "He got out of surgery a bit ago. He came through fine. His thighbone was broken, and he's pretty scuffed up and bruised. They said when they move him to recovery they'll let me go back."

Miss Trudy's legs seemed to buckle. Paige caught her elbow as she sank into her chair.

"See, he's going to be fine," Lucy said.

"He took a knock to the head too," Lloyd said. "He's got a concussion, so they're keeping an eye out for swelling, but he was lucid after the accident, so that's a good sign."

Half an hour later Lloyd was allowed into the room. Beau had arrived, and he sat on the other side of Miss Trudy. He'd brought her knitting bag, and the woman's hands hadn't stilled since he'd arrived.

Paige was grateful Miss Trudy had something to keep her busy—though her hands were uncharacteristically clumsy with the knitting needles. And she hadn't had a bite of the food Beau had brought.

"You should eat something, Miss Trudy," Paige said. "I can see about warming up the breakfast wrap."

"I couldn't eat a thing. My stomach's like a big ol' knot."

Lucy shifted forward in her seat. "You heard what Lloyd said. He's going to be fine."

"You heard what he said about the swelling. My friend's son took a knock to the head. Next thing they knew he was in a coma and brain-dead."

"Don't borrow trouble, Aunt Trudy," Lucy said. "You gotta have a little faith."

"He's on the prayer chain," Beau said. "Everyone's praying. I'll go get you some coffee." He got up and headed toward the nearest vending machine.

He'd no sooner disappeared around the corner than Lloyd reappeared, his tall frame lumbering toward them.

"How's he doing?" Paige asked.

"He was still asleep, but his color's good. It'll take a while for the anesthesia to wear off. One of you can go back now. Room 311. Just down that hall on the left."

"Aunt Trudy," Lucy said. "You go on now."

Miss Trudy set her knitting aside and stood, smoothing her shirt with trembling hands.

"I'll walk with you," Paige said. For all the woman's eagerness, she took her time getting to the room. Paige wondered what was going on in her mind.

Miss Trudy paused at the open doorway.

The sheriff lay still in the bed. His legs were propped up, his feet hanging off the end. There were wires and tubes and the steady beeping of the heart monitor.

"You okay?" Paige asked.

Miss Trudy pulled her spine straight, her shoulders rising. "I'm fine." Then she walked through the door, clutching her purse to her stomach.

Despite her bravado, Paige was worried about her. Her face was ghostly pale, and she'd been so quiet. And then there was the way her knees had buckled earlier. She didn't see a chair in the room, so she went to the desk to request one.

A minute later Paige returned with the chair. Upon nearing the doorway she heard Miss Trudy's voice and paused.

"When you left me, Danny," the woman was saying, "I was just heartbroken."

The sheriff's eyes were closed, his strawberry-blond eyelashes fanning across his ruddy cheeks. His stomach rose and fell steadily.

"I didn't know what to do about the baby. I know I should've told you. But I loved you so much, and I was afraid. I was stuck here taking care of Mama, and I was afraid you wouldn't give up your big chance in the NBA for me. And then I was afraid you *would*. And how could I let you do that? It was your dream.

"One day I was sitting on the porch weeping, trying to figure things out, and Tom came by. I spilled my guts. Told him everything, and he just listened. He came back the next day and told me he'd been pining after me for a long time, and would I do him the honor of marrying him?"

She wrung her hands. "Maybe I should've said no. I cared about him as a friend, but I didn't love him. I knew it wasn't fair to him. But he seemed to know how I felt. Told me he understood, and he could live with that. So we did it. And when I lost the baby he was so kind. He said there'd be others . . . but I guess that wasn't part of God's plan.

"He was a good man, Danny. And I did learn to love him. Just not the same way I loved you." She drew a deep breath and let it out. "I've been so busy being angry with you I never stopped to sort through that whole mess. Our past."

She looked down, her head bowed for a long moment before she looked up again. "I forgive you, Danny. And I hope you'll forgive me too." Her voice quivered with emotion. "I still love you, you old coot. I don't know why it took me so long to see it. I guess I'm just a stubborn old fool."

"Been telling you that for years," Colton said with a raspy voice.

Miss Trudy sucked in her breath. A long pause ensued, filled only by the steady beeping of the machines. "You're awake."

His eyelashes fluttered, and his hazel eyes locked onto Miss Trudy, softening. He wet his lips. "Couldn't have you talking to yourself like some crazy lady, now, could I?"

"How are you feeling?"

"Like I was hit by a car."

"That's not funny. You have a broken leg and a concussion."

"That explains a lot." He slid a hand up his torso, stopping on his chest. "But what about the pain right here?"

"Your heart?" Miss Trudy leaned forward. "You have chest pain?"

"I sure do."

Miss Trudy reached for the call button, but the sheriff grabbed her hand, holding it for a second before he spoke. "I've had a pain in my heart since I lost you. And I'm afraid it's gonna hurt till I let this out."

He paused to catch his breath, wet his lips. "I'm sorry I left you. And I understand why you did what you did. I forgive you." A long pause filled the air. "I love you, Trudy. Hasn't been a day that's passed I didn't."

His heart rate beeped faster on the monitor as his eyes pierced hers.

"Well." The word came out on a long breath.

His red mustache twitched. "That all you got to say?"

Her chin jutted out. "I think I already said my piece, Danny Colton." Her tone sounded more like the old Miss Trudy. With maybe a hint of something softer.

"I suppose you have." The bedsheets rustled as he shifted. "Now are you going to get me some water, woman? I'm dry as the Sahara."

Smiling, Paige set the chair down and backed away, blinking back tears. Tears of relief. Tears of joy. She loved a good happily-ever-after.

Even if she never seemed to get one of her own.

Chapter 40

The community center had come alive with the sounds of boisterous chatter and the slap of the basketball on the court outside the huge garage doors. An old fire station made an excellent hangout for kids. Lucy had done a terrific job making the place feel young and energetic, yet homey.

In the homework area Paige leaned closer to the table where twelve-year-old Brittany Conley sat hunched over her paper, pencil poised.

"Remember what to do next?" Paige asked.

Brittany began solving for the variable.

"Good job. You're really getting the hang of this."

Brittany never said much. But she was here every day after school. She liked to play basketball when she first arrived, as if decompressing from the school day.

Brittany finished the last problem, then tucked her paper inside her textbook.

"Do you have any more homework?"

"No." She looked up shyly, her big brown eyes meeting Paige's. "Did you bring Muffet?"

"Not today."

Brittany had bonded with the mixed breed Paige had brought the last few weeks. One of the kids had started calling him Muffet, and the name had stuck. The dog was becoming the community center mascot.

Paige checked her watch. "We have about fifteen minutes until your mom comes. Do you want to work a puzzle?"

When Brittany shrugged, Paige took that as a yes and grabbed the zoo puzzle from the nearby shelves.

She felt a bond with the girl. Though she'd never talked much with Brittany or her mom, the pair of them had attended Paige's church for years. Her dad had left last year, and Mrs. Conley was working long hours to make ends meet, which left Brittany here at the center until six each night.

They worked the hundred-piece puzzle, mostly in silence. Paige tried several times to start a conversation, but Brittany wasn't very responsive. She'd bring Muffet tomorrow. Maybe she'd even talk to the girl's mom about adopting the dog.

Brittany set a piece down and sat back in her chair. Paige's eyes glanced off her face only to dart right back. Brittany's eyes were filled with tears.

"Honey, what's wrong?"

The girl shook her head, but the tears spilled over and her lip quivered.

Paige dug in her purse for a tissue, then handed it to Brittany. "You can talk to me about anything. Whatever it is, things have a way of getting better with time. Is it anything I can help you with?"

When Brittany only continued crying, Paige went on. "When I was your age I lived with my mom and dad. My mom was never very nice to me, and I tried so hard to make her happy. It was my family, but I didn't feel like I really belonged."

Brittany sniffed. "Why wasn't she nice to you?"

"Well . . . that's kind of complicated. I found out later she wasn't my biological mom. Do you know what that means?"

"You were adopted?"

"Not exactly." Paige had gotten in a little deeper than she'd intended. "My dad had me with another woman, and the mom who raised me kind of held that against me."

"You can't help who your real mom is."

"I know, right? But that didn't seem to matter." Paige picked up an edge piece and placed it in the frame. It slid into place with a quiet snap.

"I miss my dad." The quietly spoken words broke Paige's heart.

Paige put her hand over the girl's. "Oh, honey. I'm sure you must."

Her lip quivered. "He used to work puzzles with me sometimes."

"I'm sorry. We can do something else. You want to play Jenga instead?"

"I like puzzles." She shrugged. "My dad didn't really work them with me anyway. He just sat there and typed on his phone."

"Oh."

"He just got married to some lady in Milbridge."

"Do you get to see him very often?"

She wiped her face with the tissue. "Every other weekend. She has two kids, but they're older than me. They just act like I'm not there, and I don't think my dad's wife likes me much."

"That's hard. I'm sorry."

She was definitely talking to Brittany's mom about Muffet. They needed each other. Maybe having a dog wouldn't solve the girl's problems, but having a loving pet would be a great outlet for her.

"I know what you mean about not belonging anywhere," Brittany said, one last tear slipping down her flushed cheeks. "My mom works all the time, and when she's home she's too tired to do anything with me. And when I'm with my dad . . . nothing's the same anymore."

Paige's chest squeezed tight. "You've got a mom who loves you very much. You belong with her. And you belong here. And you know what? You belong to God. I remember when you were baptized a few years ago. You gave your heart to Him, and that means you're one of His, and He'll never let you go. He'll never ignore you, He'll never be mean to you, and He'll never leave you."

It was only as she said the words that the impact of them hit Paige square in the heart. Her breath left on a quick rush as a shiver ran through her.

Maybe Paige's biological father hadn't been the kind of dad she'd needed. Maybe her stepmother had resented her and abandoned her.

But she did belong to a family. The best of families. She had a perfect Father who loved her more than any earthly father ever could. The creator of the universe loved her and wanted a relationship with her. That was enough to overcome all the rest.

She closed her eyes in a long blink as the wave of realization poured over her.

How long had God been waiting for her to remember her heavenly Father? To realize she still belonged to the most important family of all?

Thank You, God. I'm sorry I discounted You. I'm sorry I've been kind of going through the motions lately. Help this little girl to find the truth. Make Yourself real to her in her everyday life.

Paige leaned closer, setting her hand over Brittany's. "You can talk to God about anything, and He hears you. He loves you, more than you'll ever understand, and He has a plan for you."

"That's what my grandma says."

"Well, she's right."

Brittany's eyes shifted to the entrance and she began gathering her things. "My mom's here."

Paige stood with her, her eyes darting toward the door where a woman searched the room for her daughter. When her eyes fell on Brittany, her face broke out in a weary smile.

$\mathcal{R}$iley broke away from Dan and put up a layup. It bounced against the board and dropped through the net with a *swish*.

"Only six more baskets, and we'll finally be tied," Dan said.

Riley used the bottom of his shirt to wipe the sweat from his face. "I'm only getting warmed up, buddy."

"That's what you said last week."

He and Dan had been playing ball at a nearby park every Sunday evening for the past month. The guy's prosthetic didn't slow him down, and he sure didn't believe in taking it easy on a fellow amputee. Riley had yet to win against him.

They usually stopped at the Rusty Nail for a drink after Dan destroyed Riley's ego. He'd gotten to know the guy pretty well. He had an ex-wife who'd left him when he'd sunk into depression after losing his leg, and a seven-year-old daughter he doted on and saw every other weekend. He also had a very attractive girl-friend who was eager to set Riley up with one of her friends. Riley couldn't bring himself to agree.

Dan approached, dribbling. "I have to go home after I beat you."

"You're not going to beat me."

"Got to hand it to you, Callahan. You're one heck of an optimist." He dribbled the ball through his legs.

Show-off. Riley batted at the ball and missed.

Dan faked to the right, but Riley knew this move. He rebounded quickly and stole the ball, taking it all the way to the basket for another two.

"Worried yet?"

"Not bad, Callahan, not bad."

They played to twenty-one, Riley bringing the game to a tie before Dan shot the final basket, winning by the closest margin yet.

"Someday I'll turn around and you'll be beating me," Dan said, then gave him a cocky grin. "But not today."

Riley thumped him in the back of the head.

They were both out of breath as they walked off the court. They collected their belongings off the park bench, and Bishop came to his feet, tail wagging, eyes bright. He'd perked up a lot in the past couple months.

They started the short walk home, Bishop leading the way. The November sky was blue, the temperature in the midsixties. Riley didn't think he'd ever get used to the unseasonably warm weather. Thanksgiving was less than a week away, and he didn't even need a jacket.

A squirrel darted across the sidewalk and Bishop froze, eyes like lasers, until the critter disappeared up one of the maple trees that lined the street.

The neighborhood was quiet and modest, mostly two-story Cape Cods with small, well-kept lawns. There was a real sense of community here in Copper Creek. A closeness. Of course Riley knew what that meant. Everybody was up in each other's business.

Riley breathed in a deep breath of the fresh air and blew it out. Bishop wasn't the only one feeling better these days. Riley had started talking to Pastor Jack regularly. The minister had also recommended a psychiatrist who immediately put Riley on something that helped him sleep nightmare-free. That alone had been a lifesaver. He was functioning much better now.

He'd been meeting with Pastor Jack twice a week after work. He couldn't say he enjoyed his appointments. Sometimes they left him pretty raw. Sometimes he went home and went straight to bed, but he awoke refreshed. There was something about getting it all out there, something about hearing that what he was feeling was normal, that went a long way toward releasing the darkness that had built up inside.

When he was at work he could think more clearly. He was more productive and felt more social. When he went to church he actually heard the sermons, could feel the scriptures sinking in and bringing light inside. A heavy load had lifted from his shoulders, leaving him feeling as if he were filled with helium.

He still struggled with stuff. Still dealt with survivor's guilt sometimes and had the occasional flashback. After all he'd been through, he knew he'd never be the same Riley he'd been before—before war. Before the explosion.

But he was starting to like the Riley he was becoming.

Starting to see that a missing limb was really just a missing limb.

His phone vibrated in his pocket, and he looked at the screen. "It's my aunt."

"Go ahead," Dan said.

He tapped the screen, a little worry niggling in the back of his mind. Aunt Trudy wasn't much for the phone. He mostly kept in touch with her through Beau and Zac.

"Hey, Aunt Trudy." He could hear a football game on the TV in the background. He imagined his family gathered around in the living room and felt a pang of homesickness.

"You sound out of breath," she said. "Did I make you run for the phone?"

"I was just shooting hoops at the park with a friend. I'm on my way home now."

"Basketball. You do realize it's thirty-five degrees here in Maine."

"Well, I can't help it if you're too stubborn to move south."

Aunt Trudy humphed. "Wouldn't trade Summer Harbor for some landlocked city that doesn't even know what seasons are."

"Copper Creek has a population of eight thousand, Aunt Trudy. Hardly a thriving metropolis. But I'll admit I'm looking forward to a small taste of winter."

He was going home for Thanksgiving. It was all he'd thought about the last few weeks. His heart gave a tug at the thought of seeing Paige.

"You're probably due for some good home cooking."

"Got that right. It's been mostly mac 'n' cheese and frozen pizzas."

Aunt Trudy tsked, then started a lecture on a healthy, balanced diet, making him remember why he kept in touch with her through his brothers.

His thoughts drifted to home. To the Christmas tree farm. Back to Paige. He wondered if she was there at the farm right now.

Wondered how she was feeling about seeing him again. She must know he was coming home. She always spent Thanksgiving with the Callahans. As much as he wanted to talk to her, he was leaving the ball in her corner. It was only fair after what he'd done. He wondered how she was doing. How the shelter was doing. If she was over him.

Because he wasn't over her. Not even close. Just the thought of her made his heart rate accelerate.

"Are you even listening to me, young man?"

Riley smiled at his aunt's bluster. "Eat a protein-heavy breakfast and make sure I get six servings of fruits and veggies a day. Got it."

She muttered something about impertinent boys.

He chuckled, suddenly missing his aunt so much his chest tightened. "I'll work on it, Aunt Trudy. Did you call just to lecture me about my dietary needs, or is something else going on?"

"As a matter of fact, there is something else going on. I thought I'd better warn you to bring a suit when you come home next week. There's going to be a wedding."

His thoughts went straight to Paige, and a fist squeezed his heart. But that was crazy. He shook his head. Beau had told him about Danny Colton.

"Well, it's about time," he said.

"Is that your way of saying congratulations?"

Riley smiled. "I couldn't be happier for you, Aunt Trudy. The two of you belong together. So you're getting married Thanksgiving weekend?"

"On Saturday night. It's a small affair, just the family. We're going to Vegas the next week, then I'll move into that little ranch he lives in over on Crofton Street."

"Vegas?" Heaven help the city.

"Danny's always wanted to go. I'll be ready for a little warm weather by then."

"I'm sure you'll have a great time. How's he doing? Is he healing up from his accident?"

"He's still on crutches, but he's supposed to be walking on his own two feet by our wedding day. He's pretty anxious to lose those crutches, and I know just how he feels." Aunt Trudy had broken her leg a couple years ago.

"I'm happy for him. Happy for both of you." Then his curiosity got the best of him. "Can I ask you something, Aunt Trudy?"

"You can ask."

"When you found out you were pregnant . . . why didn't you just tell him? You were in love with him, right?"

"You always were the snoopy one."

He smiled at her crusty tone. "Sorry . . . you don't have to answer."

Her voice softened. "I did love him. But the fool man had just gotten drafted by the Celtics. It was his dream. And I was stuck here taking care of my mama. I couldn't ask him to sacrifice that. I thought I was doing what was best for him."

The words reverberated inside, sending aftershocks through his system. But before he could examine them, she went on.

"Shows what I knew. We spent a lifetime apart because I made his decision for him. That was wrong of me—I know that now."

Something squirmed inside his gut. "Thanks for sharing that with me."

Aunt Trudy cleared her throat. She'd always been uncomfortable with the touchy-feely stuff. "Well, Beau's reaching for the phone, so I'll just talk to you when you get here."

"All right, Aunt Trudy. See you then."

She handed off the phone and he talked to Beau awhile, mostly about the game, before he was passed to Zac. Just talking to his family made him miss them even more. He could hear them cheering in the background, and he suddenly wished he were there too.

He listened for Paige's voice, but he never heard her. He wondered if she was staying quiet because he was on the phone. The thought made his stomach twist.

A few minutes later he hung up and pocketed his phone. "Sorry about that," he said to Dan.

Dan shrugged. "You must miss them. You have two older brothers, right?"

"Yep. Beau and Zac. They're both married now."

"I just have a sister, but we're pretty close. So you're going home for Thanksgiving—I guess you won't be around for your weekly thrashing next week." He dribbled the ball between his legs and did a fancy spin move.

"Need I remind you that you only won by one basket today? You know what's next, right?"

"You keep thinking positive, buddy."

Riley shook his head. He didn't like losing, but the fact of the matter was, Dan had upped Riley's game considerably. He was going to smoke Paige when they played again.

When they played again.

He'd been thinking in those terms a lot lately. As if their next game was imminent. As if their next conversation was right around the corner. As if she were a regular part of his life.

Because she was. And moving twelve hundred miles away hadn't changed that.

I thought I was doing what was best for him.

Aunt Trudy's words played back in his mind, their familiarity pricking him hard. Wasn't that what he'd done? He'd been so depressed, so messed up in the head.

But he was thinking straighter now. The darkness had lifted enough that he could see more clearly. *I made his decision for him. That was wrong of me.* What right did he have to take Paige's decision into his own hands?

He thought of his trip home, and suddenly something shifted inside him, ever so subtly. His brain was finally catching up to what his heart had been telling him for weeks. What the Spirit had been whispering softly in the quiet of the night.

He wasn't going home for a visit. He was going home to stay. He was going to help his brother with the farm through the Christmas season. And in the spring he was going back to lobstering. If Dan could be a roofer, he could be a lobsterman. What was stopping him?

The thought settled into place as if it were the last piece of a long, complicated puzzle. It felt good. It felt right. It felt inevitable.

He'd needed Copper Creek. He'd needed Noah and Pastor Jack and Dan in this season of his life. He'd come and he'd done some important work that maybe he never could've done in Summer Harbor.

But it was time to go home.

Beside him, Dan gave the ball a couple dribbles, and Riley realized they'd reached the corner where they parted ways.

"Thanks for the game, buddy," Dan said. "I'll see you in a couple Sundays."

"Um . . . actually, I'm going home."

Dan gave him an odd look. "Yeah, I know. You just told me that."

"No." He stopped and turned toward Dan. "I mean, I'm going home—to stay."

Something shifted in Dan's eyes, and his head tipped back thoughtfully. "No kidding."

Saying it out loud only made it feel more right. Riley nodded slowly. "It's time."

Dan's mouth tilted in a smile. "Good for you, man. Good for you." He walked away, dribbling the ball as he went.

Riley stood there for a moment. He was finally ready to take his life back. And he was ready to win back the woman he loved. He'd never been so ready.

❧

Paige had lost track of the game about twenty minutes ago when Miss Trudy called Riley. By the pace and force of Paige's heart, a person would think she was talking to him herself.

She only became more frantic as the phone was passed to Beau. Did Riley know she was here? He must. She spent nearly every fall Sunday afternoon tucked into her favorite corner of the sofa, watching football.

Was he going to ask to speak with her? The question became even more relevant as the phone was passed to Zac on the other end of the sofa. Even with Lucy sitting between them, making comments on the game, she couldn't tear herself away from Zac's end of the conversation.

They talked about the restaurant and about Miss Trudy's upcoming wedding. Riley must've done his share of talking, because Zac was quiet a good bit of the conversation.

As their call wound down, Paige braced herself. They hadn't

spoken since he'd broken up with her over two months ago. Her heart did a little hitch kick.

But Zac told Riley he'd see him soon and hung up the phone, handing it back to Miss Trudy.

Paige's stomach seemed to sink all the way to the floor. So much for wanting to be her friend. She stared at the TV as if mesmerized by the game, but her eyes stung, and she had to recite the alphabet backward to keep the tears from gathering.

A commercial came on, and Beau lowered the volume. "Well, he was in good spirits."

"Yeah," Zac said. "He sounded good. I guess Georgia agrees with him."

The words should've made Paige glad. Instead they opened a wide, hollow place inside. It hurt to know he was happier without her. Because she wasn't happier without him. She missed him so badly she ached with it.

She lay in bed after a good, productive day and remembered the way his arms felt around her. She closed her eyes and recalled the feel of his lips on hers, soft and reverent. She reached for the pillow that had been his and breathed in his spicy, clean scent.

Life felt empty without Riley. And she wondered if that feeling would ever go away.

Chapter 42

*R*iley laced his hands behind his head and scowled at the airport departure monitor. The word *Canceled* flashed in red across the screen—right next to his flight number.

No.

He forked his hands into the hair at the base of his neck and squeezed until he felt a sting. The flight had been delayed for three hours. There was a storm system moving across New England, dumping lots of snow, but he'd been hoping to get out before the Bangor airport closed.

He'd booked this flight weeks ago, choosing to fly out on Thanksgiving morning because it was cheaper. Now he might not even make it home in time for dinner.

He got in the long line of disgruntled holiday travelers and waited his turn, going over his options. Driving his motorcycle wasn't among them. He couldn't drive it through a snowstorm, and even if he could, it was already crated up for shipment. If he rented a car it would take at least twenty hours to drive home—if he could even find a car, and that was doubtful.

Forty minutes later, when he finally reached the front of the line, he was told there was no way of getting him any closer than New York by plane. And they couldn't even get him there until late Friday. Better to wait for the storm to pass, she said.

She booked him on a Friday afternoon flight and told him to keep his fingers crossed. Of course that meant he'd be spending the night in Atlanta and going through security again tomorrow. That had been a treat with a prosthetic leg. Now he'd have to collect his luggage and Bishop, who'd been in his carrier and on his way to the grounded plane.

So he was going to miss Thanksgiving. He wasn't going to see Paige today. The thought sank like lead in his stomach. At this point he'd be lucky to make it to Summer Harbor in time for Aunt Trudy's wedding. He shouldered his duffel bag and pulled his phone from his pocket.

Paige pulled the bubbling pecan pie from the oven and set it on the wire rack beside the two cooling pumpkin pies. Her kitchen was filled with a sweet aroma and the buttery tang of homemade crust. She pulled off the oven mitts and frowned at the pecan pie.

Miss Trudy had only asked her to bring two pumpkin. But somehow whole pecans and corn syrup had found their way onto her grocery list, and next thing she knew she was standing in her kitchen, rolling out a crust for Riley's favorite pie.

He was her best friend, and he was coming home for the holiday. It was only natural she'd want him to have his favorite.

You keep telling yourself that, Paige.

Ever since she'd found out he was coming home for Thanksgiving, she'd been a mess. How was she supposed to act? Like a friend? Like nothing had changed? It seemed impossible when everything in her cried out for him. When her pillow was still damp with tears on the occasional bad night. When that hollow spot inside seemed to have only grown wider in the weeks since his departure.

You're going to have to get me through this, God.

It was going to be painful. Seeing him again was only going to tear off the scab that was just beginning to form. She wondered what he was feeling. Was he dreading seeing her? Would it be as awkward as she feared?

She hadn't heard from the family since Sunday. She assumed they'd been as busy as she with the shortened workweek and getting the Christmas tree farm ready to open. She'd never even asked when Riley was arriving, but she assumed it had been sometime yesterday. She tried not to feel hurt that she hadn't heard from him.

She looked out her kitchen window at the swirling snow. She should just be grateful he wasn't flying in this mess.

Time to get ready while the pies cooled.

Dasher crept over to her, looking up at her with those big green eyes, and let out a soft *meow*. Paige scooped her up. "What's wrong, baby?"

Dasher always seemed to sense when she was anxious. It made the feline unsettled. The cat nuzzled her neck, her body vibrating with a low hum.

"I'll be okay. Just as soon as I get this weekend over with."

An hour later she was still trying to reassure herself as she pulled into the long, snowy driveway that led past the Christmas tree farm and to the house. Her windshield wipers squawked with each pass as they swiped away the huge snowflakes pelting the glass.

She squeezed the steering wheel with her gloved hands, her pulse kicking into double time as she rounded the curve, bringing the farmhouse into view. She drew in a steadying breath, then two, but it did nothing to calm her nerves. There was nothing she could do to prepare herself for seeing Riley again.

Part of her wanted to go right around the circle drive and head back to town. She looked at the house, huddled under a grove of mature white pines. Smoke curled from the chimney, the wispy trail disappearing into a frenzy of flakes. The sight was as inviting as a welcome sign.

But the familiar feelings arose as quickly as the thought. Did she really belong here? Aunt Trudy wasn't really her aunt, nor were Beau and Zac her brothers. Riley sure wasn't. Her presence would only make him uncomfortable. Make them all uncomfortable. The old insecurities rose to the surface, swirling around as frantically as the snowflakes outside.

Help me, God.

She'd come so far the past two months. She'd thought this was settled. But she supposed the feelings she had nurtured for so long weren't going away overnight.

She closed her eyes for a brief moment as the car coasted down the incline, letting her new favorite scripture play over in her mind. *See what great love the Father has lavished on us, that we should be called children of God! And that is what we are!*

She'd found the verse for Brittany, and they memorized it together. The frequent reminder brought her comfort. She hoped it did the same for Brittany, especially this holiday weekend, which she was spending with her dad and his new family.

Her heart gave a thud as she pulled alongside the house and turned off the engine. She gathered the pie carriers and got out of the car, dashing through the cold. When she reached the door she gave a quick tap, then entered.

A football game was on the TV, but the living room was empty. Even though it was hours from supper, the house was already filled with savory aromas. A fire crackled in the fireplace and voices drifted from the kitchen.

"Hello!" she called as she kicked off her snowy boots on the rug.

"In the kitchen!" someone called. Eden, she thought.

You can do this. Just walk right in there and hug him hello like you would've done five months ago. Act like nothing's changed. Like he's still your best friend. Like your heart is still whole. Like seeing him again isn't going to tear you up.

Lucy burst through the dining room door. "Hey, girl."

"Happy Thanksgiving."

"You too." Lucy gave her a quick hug and then took the pie carriers, allowing Paige to shrug out of her coat.

"It's freezing out there."

"Beau just shoveled the walk, and it's already covered again."

"I hear we're supposed to get eight more inches."

"That's what I heard. Are the roads a mess?"

"Pretty much."

"Did you get my text?"

"No . . ." Paige hung her coat on the coatrack and checked her phone. "Oh, there it is. I didn't hear it come in." She scanned the message, her heart sinking as her eyes darted back to Lucy. "He's not here?"

"He was supposed to fly in this morning, but with the storm . . ."

The hollow place inside filled with something dark and heavy. "He's not going to make it for Thanksgiving."

Lucy set her hand on Paige's arm. "No, but he's rescheduled on a flight that's supposed to arrive tomorrow late afternoon."

"But the forecast says the storm won't let up until Saturday." Paige searched Lucy's eyes, hoping she was missing something. But judging by the look on her friend's face, she wasn't missing a thing. If Riley's flight tomorrow was canceled, he wasn't going to fly in on Saturday only to turn right back around the next day.

"He's not even going to make Miss Trudy's wedding," Paige said.

Lucy gave her a sympathetic look. Paige knew she wasn't fooling anyone. She wasn't worried about Thanksgiving supper or Miss Trudy's wedding. Despite her reservations, her foolish heart had counted on seeing him again.

"We'll just have to wait and see." Lucy patted her shoulder, her lips lifting in a smile. "Come on in the kitchen. Zac's trying to trick Aunt Trudy into getting under the mistletoe with the sheriff, but she's always a step ahead of him. It's quite entertaining."

Paige tried for a smile. "I'll be there in a minute."

As Lucy carried the pies into the kitchen, Paige pulled off her gloves, stuffing them into her coat pockets. She tried to tell herself that the heavy feeling weighting her stomach was hunger and not profound disappointment.

Chapter 43

*R*iley glared at the airport monitor. "You've got to be kidding me."

It was only an hour before his scheduled flight on Friday, and yet again the red *Canceled* sign flashed.

Why's everything have to be so hard, God?

He let loose a big sigh. It was time to reclaim Bishop and his bag—again—and come up with plan B. Or was it C?

Improvise. Adapt. Overcome.

So he wasn't going to fly. He'd see, if by some miracle, there was a car he could rent. If he got on the road by six tonight he could make it to the wedding, allowing time for gassing up, traffic, and snowy roads.

He started the long walk through the airport, hitching his duffel bag higher. He was tired of waiting around. He wanted to see Paige. It had been all he could do not to call her yesterday just to hear her voice. He wondered how she'd felt about his absence. Had she been relieved she didn't have to face him across the Thanksgiving table? Indifferent?

The thought was a punch in the gut. He wanted nothing more

than to see her, tell her how he felt, and gather her into his arms. But would she welcome him after the way he'd left?

He reclaimed Bishop and his suitcase and went to the rental terminal, where all the kiosks were filled with snaking lines. He had to get home. He just had to.

A little help here, God?

While he waited in line he reassured Bishop, sticking his fingers through the carrier's holes to be licked. The poor dog was probably hoping this airport thing wasn't some awful new routine Riley was going to subject him to every day.

When Bishop lay down with a sigh, Riley stood and sent Beau a text to let him know his flight was canceled again. He scrolled through the Facebook pictures posted yesterday. His index finger stopped the scrolling and paged back up to the photo that had caught his eye. Eden had posted a picture of the family gathered around the table last night. His eyes homed right in on Paige. On her long blond hair, her gorgeous wide smile, her sparkling eyes.

She sure seemed happy. Happy Riley hadn't made it home? Happy she wouldn't have to face him?

His lips pressed together as he pocketed his phone and inched forward in line, scooting the carrier along. He wondered if she'd starting seeing Dylan again. Or someone else. Maybe she even had a date for the wedding. He knew how she felt about going to weddings alone, and a lot could happen in eleven weeks. Look how far he'd come.

Twenty minutes later he reached the front of the line.

An older woman with cocoa-colored skin smiled at him. "How can I help you, hon?"

"I need to rent a car, please. I'll take whatever you have."

"Give me a minute here." She clicked and clacked on the

keyboard while he fiddled with the frayed strap of his duffel bag. "We've been super busy today. Did you have a nice Thanksgiving?"

"Not really. I got stuck here by the snowstorm. I'm hoping to make the drive."

"You must be determined to get home, young man."

"Oh, I am. The sooner the better."

She gave one more series of clacks, then stopped. "Well, good news and bad news. We just had a cancellation, but I'm afraid it's a transit van."

His breath left his body in one long stream. He was going home to Paige. "I don't care. I'll take it."

Chapter 44

$\mathcal{P}$aige put the finishing touches on her makeup and stood back from the mirror. She'd curled her long hair, and it hung in shiny waves over her shoulders. The mascara made her eyes look wide, but even makeup couldn't disguise the sadness there.

Her eyes fell over her T-shirt and yoga pants. She'd lost a little weight in the last couple months. She hoped the dress she'd worn for Beau and Eden's wedding still fit. It was the only one she had. It made her think of Riley—of when she'd walked down the stairs at the Roadhouse, of the look of awe on his face. Of the kiss they'd shared on the moonlit deck later.

Enough of that, Paige.

Zac and Lucy were picking her up on the way to the chapel so she wouldn't have to navigate the snowy roads. She checked her watch. She still had twenty minutes until they arrived. She put another curl in her hair and tousled it, wondering why she was bothering.

She couldn't believe Riley hadn't made it home. As much as she'd had mixed feelings about seeing him again, there was nothing like keen disappointment to expose her true feelings.

She longed with all her heart to look into his deep green eyes, listen to the steady tone of his voice, and know he was okay. If he was, she could live with it; she'd finally decided that late last night when sleep was long in coming. She could be separate from him and still have peace. It wasn't the same as being together—not even close. But after hours of conversation with God, she'd finally come to the point where she could accept it, if that's what Riley needed to be whole and happy.

The doorbell rang, and Paige set down the brush. Shoot. They were early. Way early. "Come in!" she called.

She darted from the master bathroom and whipped her dress from the closet.

She heard the front door open and a shuffle in the living room.

"You're early," she called. "I just have to change into my dress and I'll be ready." Dasher scurried out of the bedroom to investigate as she closed her door. She changed into her teal wrap dress, smoothing it over her hips. Its fabric was stretchy, making the lost pounds barely noticeable. She put on a gold necklace and fluffed her hair one more time before leaving her bedroom.

"Sorry to keep you. It's probably good you're early, with the roads—" Her bare feet stopped on the threshold of the living room. Her lips parted.

Riley stood just inside the door.

"Riley." His name escaped on a breath. Adrenaline flooded her body, leaving her legs weak and wobbly, her heartbeat erratic.

He was an imposing figure, with that broad chest of his. Those muscular arms. So handsome in his suit. His cheeks were flushed, his hair windblown. He looked the same. But there was something different in his eyes. A clarity she hadn't seen in a long time.

Those eyes fastened on her as he straightened from the wall.

Dasher meowed from the cradle of his arms. "I guess you were expecting someone else."

She'd forgotten the wonderful rough texture of his voice. "I thought you—" She cleared the wobble from her voice. "Your flight was canceled."

"I rented a car."

"You drove all night? And all day? Through the snow?"

"I had to get here."

Her eyes flickered to the picture window, where a white monstrosity huddled in her drive. "What in the world are you driving?"

And why was she worried about trivial details when Riley was standing ten feet away, looking at her like that?

"Basically a kidnapper-mobile, but it was all they had." He took a step forward, then another. Tension pulled the air tight between them.

His eyes pierced hers. She couldn't have looked away if she tried. His eyes were saying so many things. If she were quiet enough, maybe she could hear them all. He stopped an arm's length away. Her heart was thudding so hard she thought it might burst right from her chest.

His gaze sharpened on her. "I made a mistake, Paige."

She swallowed hard. "You—you did?"

"A lot's happened since I've been gone. I've had a lot of time to think and a lot of time to sort things out." He looked down and set his jaw.

He paused so long she wondered if he was going to go on. Then he cleared his throat and continued.

"When I came back from my tour, it was like I had this dark cloud hanging over me. No, not just over me—*inside* me. I tried to be my old self, but I just didn't feel like the old me anymore."

She longed to reach out and touch him, but instead she curled her hands at her sides. "You'd been through so much."

"It took a toll on my mental health." He gave Dasher one last stroke and set her down, his eyes returning to Paige's as he straightened. "I've been talking with someone back in Georgia, a pastor. He's helped a lot. You were right. I needed counseling, and I was too stubborn, too scared, to get help. I'm sleeping better now and thinking more clearly. So much more clearly."

He looked at her with such intensity that her knees wobbled. Her heart gave a slow roll.

"I'm coming home, Paige. For good. I missed my family and—" His voice was as thick as honey. "I missed you."

Her chest gave a hard squeeze. The look in his eyes made her insides melt. She couldn't believe this was happening. That he was here, looking at her this way, saying these things. She clutched at the neckline of her dress.

He stepped closer, touched her face tentatively. "I missed you so much. I'm sorry I left you. Sorry I hurt you. I thought it was for the best—but I was wrong."

Just the memory of his rejection made her eyes sting. It seemed like a bad dream now.

His thumb grazed slowly along her cheek. "I know you're probably seeing someone else now, but . . . I couldn't live with myself if I didn't ask for another chance. If you'll just take me back, Paige, I'll never leave you again."

She couldn't hold back any longer. She reached for him. Her hands framed his face, the rough feel of his stubble achingly familiar against her palms. She looked up into his eyes and let hers fill with everything she was feeling. "Oh, Riley. You never lost me at all."

Something flared in his eyes before the line of his mouth softened. He closed the distance between them. His breath fell against her lips, a prelude to the reverent touch that followed. Her fingers found the soft hair of his nape as he began a slow exploration that nearly buckled her knees.

She must be dreaming, because she'd never seen this coming. But it was real. Riley was here. He was whole again. And he wanted her.

The realization spread through her like the most pleasant euphoria, invading her senses. He pulled her close, erasing the space between them. The strength of his arms seduced her. The heat of his body warmed her. The spicy smell of him intoxicated her.

He broke the kiss only to pull her tighter against him, his arms enclosing her as if he, too, could hardly believe they were here, like this. Together. As if he was never letting go of her again.

He'd better not. The memory of his last departure made her go all tense inside. She shoved the heel of her hand into his shoulder. "Don't you ever leave me again."

His fingers threaded into her hair. "Never," he whispered into her ear. He buried his nose in her hair just as a car door slammed shut outside. She hadn't even heard the vehicle's approach. A moment later a knock sounded at the door.

Riley pulled away, his forehead against hers, and gave her a long look. "Am I going to have to kick someone's butt?"

She gave a little laugh, feeling almost giddy with his nearness. She couldn't resist a little impish remark. "Oh, I don't know, Riley. I'm not sure you can take him."

His lips tightened at the corners as he turned and resolutely strode toward the door, flinging it open.

Paige wished she could've seen the look on Riley's face, because the look on Zac's was priceless.

"Riley!"

After a stunned moment the brothers embraced, doing that shoulder bump/back pat thing guys did.

"What are you doing here?" Zac asked. "I thought you couldn't make it."

"Long story. I'll tell you on the way to the church. Can you give us a minute? We'll be right out."

"Sure thing." Zac dashed back out into the cold.

Riley shut the door and turned to give Paige a look, the corner of his mouth turning up in a familiar smirk.

She opened her eyes wide and gave a slow blink. "What?"

"You don't think I can kick my brother's butt?"

"*That's* what you're upset about?"

He strutted toward her, and she marveled that a man with a prosthetic leg managed to strut. "We're brothers. We're competitive. I've been able to take him since I was fifteen and you know it."

When he'd closed the distance between them, she patted his cheek. "I'm sure you're right."

Humor flickered in his eyes. "You're patronizing me."

"Not at all." She went up on her toes to give him a peck on the lips.

But he grabbed her elbows, holding on. The peck turned into a long, slow kiss, and soon she forgot all about Zac and Lucy waiting in the truck. Forgot all about the wedding. Forgot her own name.

A long moment later she drew away, feeling a little dazed. "What were we talking about?"

He nuzzled her nose. "I don't remember."

She loved the low scrape of his voice. He swooped in for another kiss, but a horn sounded outside just before his lips touched hers.

"Stupid brothers," he whispered.

She drew away with a smile, patting his chest, and went to grab her purse. When she returned he helped her on with her coat. Her legs were wobbly, and if he noticed the way her hands trembled as she slid them into the sleeves, he didn't say anything. She still couldn't believe this was happening.

But the hand he set on her back as he ushered her out the door felt real. The adoring gaze he gave her as he helped her into the truck looked real. And the way he gathered her close in the backseat felt real too. The conversation began, the questions and explanations flowing, and Paige had to admit that not only did all of it feel real . . . it felt just right.

Chapter 45

It was a small group that gathered on the padded pews of Harbor Community Church, only family and a few close friends. The lights had been dimmed, and a few white candles flickered on the altar table, their sweet fragrance scenting the air.

Paige turned as Sheriff Colton and his cousin Lloyd walked in from the side door, joining Pastor Daniels at the front. The sheriff barely had a hitch in his step.

He looked out of his element in a black suit, and Paige wondered where they'd found one to accommodate his tall frame. His bald head gleamed under the altar lights, and his face was flushed. The man had sure waited long enough to make Miss Trudy his.

Word had spread through the family that Riley had made it in time for the ceremony. Not wanting to steal any of Miss Trudy's thunder, they hadn't yet told anyone that he was staying for good. There'd be time enough for that later.

Riley reached for Paige's hand, clasping it against the firmness of his thigh.

Her eyes flickered to his. She couldn't get enough of the love shining there. She couldn't wait to get him alone again. They had a lot of catching up to do.

She squeezed his hand, her thoughts going back to the last wedding they'd attended. To the changing feelings she'd been harboring. To the anxiety roiling through her. To the moment on the deck that had started all this.

She leaned closer and whispered into his ear, "The last wedding we attended we shared our first kiss."

She drew away until their eyes connected.

Something flared in his eyes, and his lips gave a little twitch. "Oh, that wasn't our first kiss, sweetheart."

She gave him a questioning look as she breathed a laugh. "What do you mean?"

The first notes of "Spring" began on the piano, and there was a rustle as heads turned to the back doorway, still empty.

She looked back at Riley, not willing to let him off the hook so easily.

He was still looking at her, the mischievous expression in his eyes teasing her. "Remind me to tell you about that later."

Paige scowled at him and squeezed his hand threateningly. But before she could verbalize her complaint, movement at the back caught her eye.

Miss Trudy appeared on Beau's arm. The sight of her made Paige gasp.

She wore an ivory dress that enhanced her slim figure. Her short silver hair had been straightened and tousled around her face, softening her features. Someone had done a stellar job on her makeup, and the earrings dangling alongside her cheeks caught the light, sparkling. But it wasn't the trappings that transformed her appearance so much as the joy that glowed in her eyes.

The small group rose to their feet as the music swelled.

Paige turned to the front where Danny Colton stood, shoulders straight. He released the hands that were clasped behind his back and they fell to his sides, almost stretching forward as if wanting to reach for his bride. His eyes were fixed on her as if he were mesmerized by the sight. He blinked away tears as his Adam's apple bobbed.

Paige fought tears herself at the raw emotion on his face. He'd waited a lifetime for his bride, and she had no doubt he'd do it all over again if that's what it took.

Riley squeezed her hand and gave her a soft smile. The look in his eyes told her he knew everything she was feeling.

When Beau and Miss Trudy reached the front, Beau gave the sheriff a hearty pat on the shoulder and took his seat in the pew beside Eden and Micah.

The ceremony was short but tender and sweet, with just the traditional vows and exchange of rings. It was as if the brevity of the service claimed they'd waited too long already and they weren't wasting another moment.

The presentation of the couple as Mr. and Mrs. Danny Colton culminated in a standing ovation and much whooping and hollering. The happy couple strode down the aisle toward the back as an inspired rendition of "Spring" picked back up, affirming the celebratory atmosphere.

They filed from their pews, and Riley's hand came to rest on the curve of Paige's waist. She felt the warmth of him as he closed the distance behind her, and she was treated to the delicious, spicy smell that was all Riley.

He leaned down until his lips were near her ear. His breath stirred the hair at her temple, sending a shiver down her arms. "We're next, Warren," he whispered.

Her breath caught in her throat, and she fought to keep her

composure. She angled a look his way. "You have to ask me first, Callahan."

The corner of his lips lifted. "Oh, I will, sweetheart. Don't you worry about that."

She wished she could bottle up the look in his eyes so she could see it over and over again. It was a look of hope. A look of love. A look of promise. And she couldn't think of anything better than that.

Discussion Questions

DISCUSSION QUESTIONS

1. Which character did you most relate to? Why?
2. Did you have a favorite scene in the book? Which one, and what made it your favorite?
3. Riley came home from war bitter about his circumstances and toward God. Have you ever experienced similar feelings?
4. Paige never felt as if she belonged in her family. Have you ever felt like that?
5. The Callahans made Paige one of their own. Are you mindful of others who may not have family connections? Share a time when you welcomed someone into your own family. What was the result?
6. Have you ever fallen in love with a friend or known someone who did? Share what happened and how it worked out. Do you think being friends first is an advantage or disadvantage in a romantic relationship?
7. After losing his leg Riley no longer felt capable of returning to his life as a lobsterman, and he no longer felt worthy of Paige. She told him, "The real problem

isn't down there; it's up here." Have you ever let yourself believe a lie? What happened?

8. Despite Paige's bad history with Darleen (her stepmom), she opened up her heart again only to have her trust betrayed. Share a time this has happened to you. How do you decide if someone is worthy of a second chance?

9. How is God like a father to you? How is the church like a family? What does it mean to be a "child of God"?

10. If you read the complete Summer Harbor series, which one was your favorite story and why? *Falling Like Snowflakes*, *The Goodbye Bride*, or *Just a Kiss*?

Acknowledgments

Writing a book is a team effort, and I'm so grateful for the fabulous fiction team at HarperCollins Christian led by publisher Daisy Hutton: Amanda Bostic, Becky Philpott, Becky Monds, Jodi Hughes, Karli Jackson, Kristen Ingebretson, Kristen Golden, Samantha Buck, and Paul Fisher.

Thanks especially to my editors, Karli Jackson and Becky Philpott, for their insight and inspiration. Thanks also to editor LB Norton, who saves me (and you!) from overexplanations, redundancy, and all manner of literary sins.

Author Colleen Coble is my first reader. Thank you, friend! Writing wouldn't be nearly as much fun without you!

I'm grateful to my agent, Karen Solem, who's able to somehow make sense of the legal garble of contracts and, even more amazing, help me understand it.

Kevin, my husband of twenty-seven years, has been a wonderful support. Thank you, honey! To my kiddos, Justin and his wife, Hannah; Chad; and Trevor: I am so blessed to be your mom. Love you all!

Lastly, thank you, friend, for letting me share this story with you. I wouldn't be doing this without you! I enjoy connecting with friends on my Facebook page, authordenisehunter. Please pop over and say hello. Visit my website at www.DeniseHunterBooks. com or just drop me a note at Denise@DeniseHunterBooks.com. I'd love to hear from you!

Chapter One

adison McKinley scanned the crowded town hall, wondering how many of her friends and neighbors she'd have to fight to get what she came for. Half of Chapel Springs had turned out to support the fire department. The faint scent of popcorn and coffee from last night's Rotary club meeting still lingered in the air, and the buzz of excitement was almost palpable.

When she reached the front of the line, she registered for her paddle, then looked for her mom. She spotted Joann McKinley seated on the left, near the old brick wall.

Before Madison could move, Dottie Meyers appeared in the busy aisle. "Madison, hello, dear. I was wondering if I could bother you about Ginger. I found a little knot behind her leg. I'm worried it might be something serious."

Last time it had only been a burr. Still, Madison set a hand on the woman's arm. "I'm sure it's fine, but I'll have Cassidy call you tomorrow and squeeze you in, okay?"

"All right, everyone," the emcee was saying into the mike. "It's about that time."

"Thank you so much, dear," Dottie was saying. "I'm so excited about this year's play. It's called 'Love on the Line.' You are planning on coming out again, aren't you? You'll be fabulous as Eleanor."

Auditions were still two months away. "Looking forward to it. See you tomorrow." Madison participated in the town's production every year. She enjoyed the theater, and the proceeds supported the local animal shelter, a cause she was committed to.

She turned toward her mom and ran straight into a wall. "Ooomph."

Or a chest. A hard chest.

She looked up into the face of the one man she least wanted to see, much less slam into. She jumped back, looking square into his unfathomable coal-colored eyes.

She nodded once. "Beckett."

He returned the nod. "Madison."

His black hair was tousled. He wore a Dewitt's Marina work shirt and at least two days' stubble. His jaw twitched. She hadn't spoken to him since she'd confronted him two weeks ago—for all the good it had done.

"Please take your seats," the emcee said.

Gladly.

She stepped to the left at the same time as Beckett. He was wide as Boulder Creek and twice as dangerous. She'd always thought so. The incident with her little sister had only confirmed it.

"Excuse me," she said.

He slid right and swept his arm out as if to say, *After you, princess.*

She shot him a look, then hurried down the aisle and slid into a metal chair beside her mom.

"Hi, sweetie. Good day?" Mom's short blond hair and blue eyes sparkled under the fluorescent lights, but it was her smile that lit the room.

"Twelve dogs, seven cats, two bunnies, and a partridge in a pear tree."

Beckett passed her row and slid into a seat up front by his sister. Layla had long brown hair and a model-pretty face. Their mom must've been beautiful, though Madison didn't remember her. Beckett leaned over and whispered something to his sister.

Madison tore her eyes away and loosened her death grip on the auction paddle. She refused to think about Beckett O'Reilly tonight.

The emcee took the podium and spoke about the importance of the fire station and their financial needs, then she introduced the auctioneer—hardly necessary since he also ran the local gas station. Moments later the bidding was under way.

Madison's eyes swung to Beckett's dark head. She could swear he was stalking her lately. He seemed to be everywhere she turned. If anything, the man should be avoiding her. Should feel ashamed of . . . well, whatever he did to Jade.

Madison tracked the auction items, ticking off each one as they sold to the highest bidder. A handmade quilt, piano lessons, pie of the month, a cabin rental at Patoka Lake, and dozens of other things generously donated by the community.

Someone had made a miniature replica of the town's sign. Welcome to Chapel Springs, Indiana, it said. Prettiest River Town in America. A writer from *Midwest Living* had used the phrase twelve years ago, and the town had squeezed every last drop from it.

Evangeline Simmons, eighty-five if she was a day, amused all by driving up the bids. It was no secret that the fire department had saved her beloved Persian from a tree last month. So far her generosity had left her with two items she probably had no need for. But money was no object for Evangeline.

People trickled out as the auction wore on. Beckett left after losing a tool kit. Over an hour later, Madison grew tense as her item came up. The auctioneer read from the sheet.

"All right, ladies and gentlemen, this next one's a winner. Dewitt Marina has kindly donated a sailing/regatta package. Lessons taught by sailing enthusiast Evan Higgins. Learn how to race on the beautiful Ohio River, just in time for our 45th Annual River Sail Regatta, and sail with Evan Higgins, winner of the regatta for two years running! Now, who'll give me five hundred?"

Madison's grip tightened on the handle, waiting for the auctioneer to lower the bid. Her breath caught in her lungs. *Patience, girl.*

"All right, a hundred, who'll give me a hundred? A hundred-dollar bid . . . ?"

Casually, Madison lifted her paddle.

"A hundred-dollar bid, now a hundred fifty, who'll give me one and a half . . . ?"

In her peripheral vision she could see her mom's head swing toward her just as Evangeline raised her paddle—and the bid.

"A hundred fifty, who'll give me two, now two . . . ?"

Madison lifted her paddle, keeping her eyes straight ahead.

"Two hundred, now who'll give me two fifty, fifty, fifty . . . ? Got it! Now three, three hundred, who'll give me three . . . ?"

Madison sighed, waited a moment before nodding.

"Three, now who'll give me three and a half, three fifty, fifty, fifty . . . ?"

Evangeline turned toward Madison, her eyes twinkling. She raised her paddle.

Evangeline. Madison hadn't counted on spending so much. Would serve the lady right if she dropped out. Just imagining the spry old woman on the bow of a boat, trying to manage the ropes and sails and whatnot, all four foot eleven of her . . . It was tempting.

Madison could, after all, just go down to the marina and buy the lessons, but then she wouldn't be virtually assured of a win, would she? She needed Evan Higgins for that.

"Three fifty, do I hear four . . . ? Got it! Now four fifty, who'll give me four and a half . . . ?"

A murmur had started in the crowd that remained, a few chuckling at Evangeline's antics.

The woman lifted her paddle.

"And now we're at four and a half, four and a half, who'll give me five, five, five . . . ?"

Madison clenched her jaw. She glared at Evangeline's silver head. *It's a good cause. It's a good cause.*

"And we have five, five, who'll give me five fifty, five fifty, five and a half . . . ?"

The rumbling had grown louder, though half the crowd was gone now that the auction was nearly over. The remaining people were being rewarded for their patience with a good show.

"Five fifty, fifty, fifty . . . ?"

Evangeline turned, and their eyes met. Her thin lips widened into a grin, then she folded her hands on top of her paddle.

"I've got five, now, five fifty, five fifty . . . anyone, five fifty . . . ? And . . . sold at five hundred to Madison McKinley."

Madison expelled a heavy breath. She was five hundred dollars poorer, but she had her lessons. She was going to learn to sail, and she was going to win the regatta. For Michael's sake.

Chapter Two

"You want to do what?" Dad stopped the basketball mid-dribble, straightening from his crouch. His short gray hair was tousled and damp with sweat.

Ryan gave up the guard and faced Madison, hands on slim hips, frowning at the interruption. The firstborn of the McKinleys and steady as an oak, he was the sibling they turned to in a crisis.

Madison hadn't planned to tell her family just yet, what with the stress over Jade, but they were going to find out eventually.

"She said she wants Michael's boat." PJ, the baby of the family, flipped her long brown ponytail over her shoulder. She'd inherited her dad's brown eyes and her mom's winning smile—though it was missing at the moment.

"So that's what the sailing lessons are all about," Ryan said.

"You know they actually put the boats on water," PJ said.

Madison swatted her sister's arm.

"Jo," Dad called, his eyes on Madison. "Know what your daughter's planning?"

Joanne set a container of potato salad on the cloth-covered picnic table. "You mean the regatta? I was at the auction, remember? You know the burgers are getting cold, right? Daniel, honey, could you grab the silverware?"

"Sure thing, Momma Jo." Daniel Dawson had been an honorary member of the McKinley family since Ryan brought him home in junior high. His wealthy grandma had raised him while his parents were off doing more important things. Daniel had recently won the mayoral election in Chapel Springs, following in his grandfather's footsteps.

At the mention of burgers, Dad dropped the ball. It patted the concrete as they walked off the court.

PJ kicked Ryan in the backside for no apparent reason, and he threw her over his broad shoulders just because he could. She squealed and pounded his back, but he didn't set her down until they reached the table.

"Brute," PJ said, giving him a playful shove.

"Brat."

Ryan saved lives, and PJ could feed an army, but when they got together it was like they were twelve. She was home for the weekend from culinary school.

They took their seats at the picnic table. Twilight had swooped across her parents' backyard, but the white lights strung over the patio and along the landscaping twinkled brightly. The mild spring temperature had beckoned them outside for the weekly family meal. Somewhere nearby, a cricket chirped from the flower garden, which was already burgeoning with new life.

Across the yard, the white farmhouse sprawled over the oak-shaded knoll like a plump aunt, arms spread wide for a comforting embrace. Beyond the house, corn grew about half the year on two hundred forty acres of gently rolling farmland. Her dad, proud to be one of Indiana's sixty-one thousand farmers, had never pressured the McKinley kids into filling his shoes, freeing them to find their own way. They were still working on that part.

Once they were seated, Dad said grace and they dug in. Grilled burgers, potato salad, green beans from last year's garden, and of course corn. There was always corn at the McKinley house.

"How's the planting going, Dad?" Ryan swatted a fly. "I can help next week if you want."

"Sounds good. I could use the help." Dad dished out a heaping spoonful of potato salad. "She wants to sail that old broken-down barnacle, Jo."

Madison placed her napkin in her lap, her eyes glancing off Mom. Despite her mother's perpetual smile, sadness had lingered in her blue eyes since Jade's sudden departure.

"Is that so?" Mom's look said more than her words. She knew Madison better than anyone. Knew the turmoil losing Michael still caused, even though Madison hadn't shed a tear, even though she rarely spoke of it. A girl didn't lose her twin brother without repercussions.

"For Michael." Her family stilled, even PJ, and that didn't happen often. "It's important to me."

Michael had been a capable sailor, though he hadn't lived long enough to sail in the regatta. It had been his dream to be the youngest winner ever—the current record holder being twenty-seven. And with their twenty-seventh birthday around the corner, time was running out.

"And you think you can actually win in that thing?" Dad asked.

She hadn't meant to blindside him. "I'm sorry, Dad. I didn't mean to upset you."

"It's a hunk of rotten wood."

He was making it sound far worse than it was. "I'm going to restore it."

Her dad breathed a laugh.

Okay, so it was in rough shape, but Michael had saved for it for two summers. On the doorstep of seventeen, he'd bought a boat instead of a car. She still remembered the look of pride on his face when he'd shown it to her.

"She's all mine, Madders," he'd said, running his hand along the flaking white paint at the bow. "I'm going to be the youngest winner ever, you'll see."

"In that thing?" she'd asked.

"It's just cosmetic stuff. Her bones are good."

"It's still in the barn, honey," Mom said now, setting her hand over Dad's clenched fist.

"Thanks, Mom. It won't be the fastest boat out there, but the race is handicapped, so I have a good shot."

"She can't swim, Jo."

"That's what life vests are for, Daddy," PJ said gently.

Dad's lips thinned. He was torn, Madison knew. Between wanting to support her and being afraid for her.

"I'll be fine. I'll take every precaution. I'm getting lessons, aren't I?"

"Let me know if I can help," Ryan said. "I can, you know, crew or whatever."

PJ nudged him with her shoulder. "You wouldn't know a sail from a bath sheet."

"Oh, and you would?"

"Children. Eat your supper."

A few minutes later PJ launched into a story about a soufflé disaster, lifting the mood. By the time Mom set the apple pie on the table, Dad's expression had lightened, though Madison noticed that Daniel was quiet tonight. She caught him casting a look at the empty seat next to her. She understood. It seemed strange without Jade there.

After supper, Madison helped her mother with the dishes while the others played HORSE. She scrubbed the burger platter while Mom loaded the old brown dishwasher.

Madison loved the little house she rented—which until two weeks ago Jade had shared—but there was something comforting about her parents' home. Something about the predictable squeaks in the old wood floor, the hourly chime from the grandfather clock, and the familiar scents of lemon and spray starch. She rinsed the platter. Even the ancient spray hose, which was more trickle than spray.

After the dishwasher had whirred into action, Mom leaned against the sink ledge. The pendant lights illuminated her face, settled into the laugh lines around her eyes.

"Are you sleeping okay, honey? You look tired lately."

"I'm fine." Madison had never told Mom about the nightmares, and she wasn't about to worry her with them now.

Her mom gave her a long, knowing look. The kind that made Madison realize that she could shutter off her heart to the outside world, but Mom would still see right through.

"You know, Madison . . . if it's peace you're looking for, you won't find it on the regatta course."

Madison put the platter away, the old cupboard giving a familiar creak. Was that what she was after? Peace? Did a person ever find such a thing after losing someone they loved so much? Someone so innocent and undeserving of death?

Mom took her hands, which had begun wringing the towel. "I wish I could help. I can't, but I know Someone who can."

"I know, Mom." She'd heard it often enough. From her parents, Pastor Adams, even Ryan. If showing up at church could fix what ailed her, she'd have been healed long ago. She was as regular as the pianist. All the McKinleys were.

Mom's eyes turned down at the corners and glimmered with sadness.

"Don't worry about me. I'm fine. Really. Learning to sail will be . . ." She squeezed the word past her lips. "Fun."

"I don't know how you'll have time with the play and all. You know how busy you get every summer with all the rehearsals."

"It'll be a lot, but I can handle it." It wasn't like she had a husband and kids. Or even a boyfriend.

Madison hung the towel on the oven door, and they meandered outside and sat on the concrete stoop. Mom grabbed a handful of sunflower seeds from the bag she kept there and tossed them onto the dirt path near the birdbath.

"I should've gotten you a birdfeeder for Mother's Day."

Mom tossed another handful. "This is just as easy."

"It's a wonder you don't have a sunflower forest out there for all the seed you've thrown over the years."

"The ground's too hard. Besides, the birds snatch it up as quickly as I scatter it."

A sparrow fluttered to the ground, picked up a seed, and made off with it.

"See what I mean?"

On the court, PJ whooped. "That's an R. So that's H-O-R for all of you." She might be small, but the girl could shoot. The men groaned as she sank another shot.

"I finally heard from Jade today," her mom said.

Madison turned. "Why didn't you say something?"

Joanne shrugged. "I told the others before you arrived. She only left a message. Didn't say where she was. I don't think she's coming home anytime soon."

Madison's lips pressed together. Beckett. What did he do to her? "She didn't say what happened?"

"No. It's been a long time coming, I think. Jade's always been restless, and I've had a feeling she'd leave sooner or later. I just wish I'd said something. I hate the thought of her out there all alone."

Madison put her arm around her mom. "She's an adult, Mom. She can take care of herself."

Neither of them said what they were both thinking. Jade might be an adult—she wasn't even the youngest sibling—but she was the most vulnerable of all the McKinleys.

Chapter Three

*B*eckett guided the twenty-foot Bayliner *Caroline* into the narrow slip. The river was fast and high today from the late spring rain, but now the sky was clear, the setting sun bright as it dropped behind the hills.

His boss met him on the dock as he tied off the boat. Carl Dewitt was short and thick with a paunch that strained his shirt buttons. "Hey, you fixed it?" he asked.

"Yep."

Carl nodded, his bushy gray brows lifting toward his receding hairline. "Good, good. Our customer will be thrilled. His mechanic in Tampa couldn't figure it out."

Beckett shrugged, handed over the keys. "Been at this awhile." He'd been fixing motors long before he was legally employable, more from necessity than anything else.

They parted ways at the shop entrance, Carl going inside to shut down for the night, Beckett heading for his truck. He turned over the engine, and it purred smoothly. Friday night, thank God. A nice quiet evening with Rigsby and ESPN, a short day tomorrow, and then a day off.

Several minutes later he turned into his gravel drive on the other side of town. The front yard was hardly big enough to host a flea, and the house wasn't much bigger, but it was home. Had been since he was a boy. The backyard was more generous. After saving for years, he'd put up an outbuilding last year. It took up most of the yard, but that only meant less mowing. The building was spacious, heated, and well lit. The perfect place to build boats.

His landline was ringing as he unlocked the door. Rigsby, his black Labrador mix, barreled him over on the threshold. "Hey, big guy." Beckett gave him a quick scratch behind the ears before reaching for the phone.

He shrugged from his work shirt as he answered. "Yeah?"

"Hey, Beckett. It's Evan Higgins." His old friend sounded winded.

He greeted Evan as he flipped on ESPN.

"I'm in a fix," Evan said. "Wondered if you could help."

"Name it." Evan ran a crew for Exterior Solutions. He had helped Beckett put up his outbuilding.

"I donated sailing lessons for that auction last week, but I just found out I'm going to be working a lot of Saturdays. The crew on an apartment complex in Louisville quit, and they were way behind. Left it in kind of a mess, and the owner's ticked. I'm headed there now to straighten it out. Long story short, can you fill in for me tomorrow . . . and maybe a few other Saturdays? Your boss donated rental of a sloop."

Rigsby barked, facing the back door, his black tail nearly knocking over the wastebasket as it swished around. Beckett let him out, turned on the porch light.

"Sure, I don't see a problem, as long as Dewitt doesn't mind me taking time off. I can fill in as much as you need."

"I ran it by him first. He was happy to donate to the cause."

"All right then. What time tomorrow?"

"One o'clock at the marina. Listen, I appreciate this. The package was for lessons with a racing pro, so my options were pretty limited. I think she's a beginner, so you'll have to start with the basics. We're crewing together for the regatta, so teach her well."

Evan, saddled with a beginner. That only upped his own chances at the regatta cup. Beckett chuckled at the thought.

Evan caught on. "Hey. No giving her bad instruction."

Beckett opened the door and let Rigsby back in. "No worries. I like to win fair and square. So one o'clock at the marina. Who am I meeting?"

"One of the McKinley girls—the vet. She's eager to learn and bright, so she should pick it up quickly."

His hand froze on the door. "Madison?" Her accusations from two weeks ago returned with enough force to sting. Last thing he wanted was hours alone on a boat with Madison.

She wouldn't be any happier about the change of plans than he was. But he'd already agreed. Why hadn't he asked more questions first?

"Does she know?" Beckett asked.

"I left her a voice mail. I'm sure it'll be fine. I mean, you're almost as good as me."

Beckett ground his teeth. Well, things just went from bad to worse where she was concerned, didn't they? First the supposed date with her sister, now this.

"Just kidding," Evan was saying.

"Yeah, right, I know, I was just . . . thinking about something else." He squeezed his eyes closed, pinched the bridge of his nose.

He couldn't believe this was happening. How many lessons had he agreed to?

"Well, I'm almost there. Let me know how it goes, and thanks again."

"No problem."

After they said good-bye, Beckett set the phone on the counter and beat his forehead against the tight mesh of the screen door.

Lessons with Madison. Great. Just great. How could he be alone with her, out on the water where he could see her, smell her, touch her?

Why is this happening, God? I promised to stay away from her, and now look.

For the thousandth time he chided himself for his impetuous decision two weeks ago. What kind of fool was he, showing up at Madison's house, flowers in hand, on the night of the Spring Sowers Banquet? What had he been thinking?

He'd had his speech all prepared, but instead of Madison, Jade had answered the door. She took one look at the cluster of pink roses, and a shy smile bloomed on her face. Half a dozen silver rings glimmered in the waning daylight as she brought her hand over her heart.

"It was you?" she said.

He didn't understand, didn't know what to say.

She took in his collared shirt and dark jeans, then smiled, her green eyes sparkling. "The banquet . . . ?"

He felt like a heel. "Jade, I—"

But suddenly she was gone from the doorway. "I haven't been to the Sowers Banquet in forever. I'll be back. I have to change."

She was down the hall when she seemed to remember she'd left him on the porch.

She returned, letting him in. "Sorry, sorry! Come in. Let me just . . . You think you could find a vase in the kitchen? They're so pretty, thank you!" Her cheeks bloomed with color.

"Jade, listen, I don't think—"

"Don't worry, it won't take me a minute." And then she was gone again.

Madison's kitchen was meticulously clean and smelled of pine and lemon. He rummaged for a vase inside the maple cabinets. What now? He didn't have the heart to tell Jade the truth. Not after seeing her face light up. Not after she'd scurried to her room to change like she'd waited all her life for this date. Not when she was finally coming alive again after losing Seth.

Stupid. Why didn't you just call Madison and ask like a normal person? Better yet, why didn't you just keep your feelings stuffed deep inside where they belong?

He reviewed Jade's behavior. It was like she'd been expecting him. Well, it couldn't be helped now. He was going out with Madison's sister, like it or not.

He shut a cupboard hard. Opened another.

He'd been reminding himself for years that Madison was beyond his reach. What kind of a future did the son of Wayne O'Reilly have with the daughter of Chapel Springs' most respected family? It just didn't happen. He'd always known that.

What didn't make sense were the moments of insanity today, when he'd convinced himself it was worth the risk. And now here he was, in Madison's kitchen readying for a date with her sister— what was she anyway, twenty-one, twenty-two? He may as well kiss his chances with Madison good-bye.

Not that you had one anyway, O'Reilly.

Could things get any worse?

"Can I help you?"

He pulled his head from a low cupboard to find the object of his thoughts entering the kitchen.

The sight of her stole the moisture from his mouth. She was all dark flowy hair and big brown eyes. One finely arched brow lifted.

He found his tongue. "Looking for a vase."

Her eyes flickered to the cluster of roses on the counter, then back to him as he rose to his feet.

Her jaw set, she passed him, going to the high cupboard above the stainless steel fridge. She wore a pair of fitted jeans and a white T-shirt—an outfit that promised a comfy evening home on the couch. His source had been right. She wasn't going to the banquet. Especially not with him.

She stood on tiptoe, pulled down a clear glass vase, and handed it to him.

"I'm ready." Jade fairly skidded into the room, having pulled off what must have been the fastest wardrobe change ever. She wore a black gauzy skirt, leggings, and a funky off-the-shoulder top.

"Good, you found a vase. He brought me flowers," she told Madison.

Madison crossed her arms. "I see that."

Beckett squirmed under Madison's stare. He suddenly wanted out of there more than he could say. He ran water in the vase, willing it to flow faster. He could hear Jade whispering to Madison over the rush of water, but couldn't make out the words. Was pretty sure he didn't want to.

He stuffed the flowers into the vase and set them on the counter. "We should get going."

Rigsby gave a sharp bark, and Beckett ran fresh water into his dish, his heart still thudding hard at the memory. He'd tried to salvage Jade's feelings, but in the end he'd done just the opposite. And he was sure, lessons or no, Madison wasn't about to let him forget it.

The story continues in *Barefoot Summer* by Denise Hunter—available wherever books are sold!

THE CHAPEL SPRINGS ROMANCE NOVELS

"... skillfully combines elements of romance, family stories, and kitchen disasters. Fans of Colleen Coble and Robin Lee Hatcher will enjoy this winter-themed novel."

—*LIBRARY JOURNAL* ON
THE WISHING SEASON

THOMAS NELSON
Since 1798

About the Author

*D*enise Hunter is the internationally published bestselling author of more than twenty-five books, including *Falling Like Snowflakes* and *The Convenient Groom*. She has won the Holt Medallion Award, the Reader's Choice Award, and the Foreword Book of the Year Award and is a RITA finalist. When Denise isn't orchestrating love lives on the written page, she enjoys traveling with her family, drinking green tea, and playing drums. Denise makes her home in Indiana where she and her husband are rapidly approaching an empty nest.

❧

Learn more about Denise online!
DeniseHunterBooks.com
Facebook: authordenisehunter
Twitter: @DeniseAHunter